Time to Save a Cowboy

Western Time Travel Romance—Book 1

Niki Mitchell

ISBN: 978-0-9992600-8-1

DEDICATION

This book has been a long time coming. I'd like to dedicate
TIME TO SAVE A COWBOY to my friends and family who
have supported me throughout the years.

Anyone who has ever considered writing a book, keep at it.
Never give up on your dream.

.

Romance Novels by Niki J. Mitchell

COWBOY'S CUPID
TIME TO SAVE THE COWBOY

Coming in 2019
REBEL'S CUPID
FIREBRAND'S CUPID
TIME TO SAVE THE SHERRIF

Romantic Short Stories Included in Anthologies by Niki Mitchell
SUMMERS SWEET EMBRACE, "Love's High Tide"
LARIATS, LETTERS, AND LACE, "Chantilly's Choice"

Children's Books by Niki Mitchell
KURIOUS KATZ
KURIOUS KATZ AND THE BIG MOVE
KURIOUS KATZ AND THE PLAY DAY
KURIOUS KATZ AND THE NEW FRIEND
KURIOUS KATZ AND THE BIRTHDAY PARTY
KURIOUS KATZ AND THE HALLOWEEN COSTUMES
KURIOUS KATZ AND THE CHRISTMAS TREE
KURIOUS KATZ AND THE BEST CHRISTMAS EVER

Coming in 2019
FOSTER CATS: ARTEMIS AND HER SNEAKY BROTHER
KURIOUS KATZ AND THE FOURTH OF JULY

Chapter One

Present Day, Old Town Rialto, California

The sepia photograph of a cowboy in the antique shop's window drew Amelia Kellogg closer. For the moment, she shut out the clamor of people and the bustling noise and stared at the man in the dark Stetson. His bronze complexion. His square chin shadowed with dark stubble gave him a handsome rugged quality. His lips pinched together as if he tried to stay serious. And failed.

Her cousin's floor-length skirt swished as she stepped next to Mia. "What are you looking at?" Birdie tilted her head. The pink ostrich feather in her old-fashioned knob-shaped hat quivered.

"This guy's gorgeous." Mia did a Vanna sweep of her hands to the picture. His direct gaze mixed with playfulness and confidence "It seems like he's staring right at me."

"You do realize it's only a picture."

"Way to ruin my fantasy." Mia let out an exaggerated sigh. Underneath her long taffeta dress, her corset pinched her waist. Her cousin had cinched her strings so tightly Mia could hardly breathe, while insisting their costumes looked authentic for their trip on a turn-of-the-century steam locomotive.

"You need to get out more."

Birdie had a point. For the past few years, Mia's career came first, ruining her last few relationships. She didn't need a man to be happy, but she definitely needed this mini-vacation on a nineteenth century steam locomotive.

Her focus drifted back to the photo. What kind of life had this cowboy led? She imagined a hint of longing or heartache in his expression. *Crazy. Now I'm making up a life story for this guy.*

Antique bottles and glassware were placed on shelves below the picture in the window. It made her wonder about other treasures the shop might have inside.

"Let's go in. I wann check it out." Birdie pushed open the door and bells chimed.

"We'll miss our train."

Birdie glanced at the time on her phone. "It's only quarter to one. We have forty-five minutes before the train even arrives."

"All right, ten minutes." Mia strolled inside the cluttered room, fingered a hand-blown glass vase, then picked up a porcelain cat figurine. "Too bad the paw broke off. It's cute."

"I suppose." Birdie scrunched her nose. "This room smells like dirty socks and moth balls." The scent didn't stop her cousin from wandering toward a pile of children's books, grabbing one, blowing off the dust and leafing through the pages. "Look, an original *Dick and Jane.*"

"Nice." A text-message beeped. Mia grabbed her phone.

Congrats. You're in charge of the Cashmere Kitty website.

The account came with an ultra-demanding client. She stifled a groan.

"What's the matter?"

"A work thing." Mia shook her head. "But we're in partying mode. No stress for the next forty-eight hours." She clicked off her cell.

Birdie rested her hand on Mia's shoulder. "It's about time you relax and have fun."

"Fun?" Mia's upper lip twitched.

"You know, being amused, happy, entertained."

"Sounds kinda familiar." Mia giggled. "I'm gonna see if there's any jewelry."

"Go ahead. I'll meet up with you." Birdie waved her on.

As Mia strolled into a long musty room, a current of mystery stirred the air. On the wall, a variety of coiled ropes hung on horseshoe nails. She passed a saddle on a stand and headed for a glass display case. Incandescent light gleamed off shiny trinkets. A rusted pistol, knives sheathed in leather, spurs, a silver belt buckle, gold-hooped earrings, a cracked cameo. Nothing of interest.

An older gentleman popped up from behind the counter. "May I help you?"

She jumped, and her pulse warped to fast lane speed.

"Sorry to have startled you." He twisted the silver ends of his mustache. "I was busy cleaning out a bottom drawer over there. Thought I heard footsteps."

Still a bit spooked, she fidgeted with her purse.

"May I help you find anything in particular?"

"You have something to go with my ruby earrings?"

"I may have just the thing for you. This ring came in yesterday." He reached behind on a shelf and produced a small black box with a fancy golden latch. His long fingers carefully opened the container, as he moved it over for her to see. "The previous owner said the ring has been in the family for several centuries. Supposed to fire up the heart for love," he said in a quiet voice.

"I don't believe in superstitious things." Although she liked watching paranormal movies.

"It makes a fun story. We get all kinds. A man brought in that rusted gun; said it was cursed. People say just about anything to try to get a better price."

"I can imagine." She couldn't blame the seller. When money's tight, you do what you can to survive.

"Would you like to try the ring on?"

"Yes, please." She slipped the thin gold band shimmering with inlaid rubies on her finger—it fit perfectly. Then she turned the case over and saw the price. Hmm ... two-hundred dollars was a steal but only if the stones were real. "Do you have a certificate of authenticity to prove it's ruby?"

"No. I'm going by what I was told. Our appraiser won't be in 'till next week."

She held it up to the light and noted the deep red color. "It's garnet, not ruby." Taking the ring off, she placed it back in the case. She didn't need the ring, but wanted it, and asked, "Would you take a hundred?"

"One twenty-five's the lowest I can go."

She'd consider it a souvenir from this trip. "Okay, I'll take it."

"Excellent choice."

The superstition behind the ring would make a great tale to tell her friends.

The man carried the box to the front and rung up the sale. On the counter, a frayed scrapbook lay open to a newspaper clipping with an etching of a cowboy. She edged in close enough to recognize the same man from the window photo.

The clerk handed her the purchase, and she slipped her ring inside her purse.

"Interesting article. The same person with your ring brought in this scrapbook and the photo in the window."

Hesperia Weekly Press, July 6th, 1890
Local Foreman, Dusty Mann, Hanged as Horse Thief.

Her heart saddened at the caption.

~*~

Cedar Springs, California

Thanks to a couple of hours attempting to break a cantankerous stallion, Rhett Holloway needed a good stiff drink. His back spasmed, his shoulders throbbed, and nearly every muscle in his twenty-nine-year-old body ached.

He limped into the rundown Last Call Saloon. A scratchy song drifted from the jukebox as old as the building. "Can't Help Falling in Love" crooned, sung by Elvis. A love song. Ugh! How could someone pay to hear this miserable drivel?

Three or four yards across the room, he spotted his friend's blond hair at the bar and walked toward Ace. Something pink lay on the scuffed floor, and he picked up a woman's Stetson. Pink. His ex wore a pink hat similar to this one that painful Valentine's night two years ago.

He threw the lame hat on top of the long mahogany bar and slid into the barstool next to his high school buddy.

"Trying to change your image?" Ace taunted as he motioned to the hat.

"Actually, I brought it for you."

The Stetson's heart-shaped centerpiece sparkled with rhinestones. Hearts reminded him that his family's Valentine's Day party would be in two weeks. To avoid dealing with well-intended meddling, he'd hang out with the cute brunette working at his neighbor's ranch.

The bearded bartender wiped down the counter. "Want a draft?"

"You bet. Make it lager." From a side room, pool balls clacked. Somebody groaned, another person broke out in laughter.

Handed a mug, Rhett took a swig of the dark brew. He overheard a lady's distressed voice at a table behind him. "You can't work on Valentine's Day."

"I have no choice," a man answered.

Rhett considered Valentine's Day another way for florists and jewelry stores to make a buck.

"Rough day?" Ace said. "You get that horse broke yet?"

"Not sure who's breaking who." Rhett laughed. "Think it might be time to change professions. Must be nice to stay home and get paid to play video games."

"Hey, I'm a programmer." His stocky friend punched Rhett's sore shoulder.

Rhett winced and held back a moan. Asshole stallion.

"You okay?"

"I'll live."

Ace motioned the bartender for another beer. "Want one? I'm buying."

"Sure." Rhett removed his hat, set it next to the ridiculous pink one, and asked the bartender, "Any idea who might've lost this?"

"My guess it's one of the out-of-towners playing pool."

"I noticed those chicks when I walked in. They're hot." Ace put on his white Stetson. "You up for a game of pool?"

Rhett shifted so he could watch a leggy redhead. She leaned over the pool table, her long hair fell forward as she positioned the shot. She must've sensed his eyes on her because she glanced over her shoulder and smiled in his direction. He raised his glass. The motion made his shoulder twinge.

"You comin'?"

"Not this time." Rhett took another drink.

Ace shrugged. "Mind if I try 'n' find the owner?" He snatched the pink hat and twirled it on his finger.

"Go right ahead." He watched his friend chat with the ladies. Usually, Rhett would have joined him, flirted with the women, and let the night develop, but his aching muscles kept him rooted to his seat.

The redhead donned the pink hat, reminding him of that fateful Valentine's Day, and ruined any attraction he had for her.

~ * ~

Los Flores Ranch, Hesperia, California, 1890

The horse's long shadow against the flat desert landscape signaled the last speck of day. Dusty's gut gurgled, telling him to hurry back to the ranch's dining hall or there'd be nothing left.

Fifty yards away a calf struggled, his leg caught in a barbed wire fence. Dusty dismounted, untangled the wounded calf, and slipped a noose around the frightened animal's neck. It kicked, nicking Dusty's shin. "Ouch."

The calf's eyes rounded, and it let out a bleat.

Ignoring the creak in his knees and the twinge in his back, he bent down. Today, he'd only chased maybe fifty cows, yet his twenty-eight-year-old bones crackled as if he were sixty. Every weary muscle on his six-foot frame ached, but the poor critter needed tending, and he wouldn't sleep without helping it.

"Gotta clean this. If you cooperate, we'll both get sleep tonight." He tied the rope around a Joshua tree and used his bandana to wipe off the worst of the blood.

Walking to his saddlebag, he grabbed supplies. His canteen clicked against his belt buckle embedded with a quarter-sized garnet. The silver heirloom once symbolized a future filled with happiness. He ran his fingertips over the inlaid stone. Today, the blood-red garnet symbolized the loss of his family ranch.

Ten yards away to the east, a blonde woman gathered wildflowers. Where'd she come from? A lone woman didn't belong in the middle of the desert.

He stepped toward her and waved his hat. "Howdy, miss."

The young lady didn't see him. Her colors faded as her shape became transparent, and she vanished.

"Where'd you go?" He rubbed his eyes. Sagebrush, plenty of sagebrush and nothing else. *Must be seeing things.*

The calf bawled, bringing him back to his task.

"Quit complaining." Holding the dang animal between his legs, he cleaned the cut while thinking about the bonus from tomorrow's roundup. With what he'd saved, it might be enough money to buy a ranch. He applied a generous amount of smelly salve to the calf's leg. "Easy there, we're 'bout done."

By the time he finished, the sun had set. A full moon led him along the trail. Certain dinner would be gone, he snatched jerky from his saddlebag, and took a bite and pretended he was biting into a juicy steak. Pulled out hardtack and pretended he was eating fried potatoes. Pretending never worked.

Thirty minutes later inside his cabin, he stretched out on a goose-feathered mattress and drew his ragged patchwork quilt to his chin. His shin throbbed. Damn calf.

Exhausted, he needed sleep, but his mind whirled. *Check the creek for strays. Remind Ace to ride lead. See if the holding pens are sound. Stop fretting and get some shut-eye.*

He counted. "One cow, two cows, three cows—a whole dang herd."

Quit being a fool and go to sleep. He eyeballed the ceiling and counted one million cows.

His eyes closed, and he envisioned the blonde. Why'd she keep popping up, making him question his sanity? Maybe a dozen times in his life, he'd see a vision of a blonde. She was always in the distance, never close enough to see her face. It usually happened when he was overly tired.

He'd obviously been too long without a woman.

It couldn't have been more than an hour, and the old red rooster crowed his greeting. He yanked back the covers, stumbled out of bed, and dressed. What happened to his other boot? It took getting down on his knees to locate the object under the bed.

Slamming the door, he stomped over to the main house in a sleep deprived, cantankerous mood. The already warm morning meant the day would be a scorcher.

"Howdy." From under the eaves by the dining hall entrance, the cook flipped flapjacks on a cast iron stove.

Dusty gave a cordial don't-bother-jawin'-to-me-nod and went inside. A dozen cowboys sat in mismatched chairs and ate at long wooden tables. They jabbered, forking food in their mouths. Full mouths didn't cease their conversing. The men were noisier than a wagon on a frozen road.

He headed for the sideboard, filling his dish with scrambled eggs, crisp bacon, flapjacks, and fried taters. Holding a cup of thick Arbuckle coffee, he slunk into a vacant chair on the end of a table.

Reynolds and Slick sat in the corner. Their loud voices jangled Dusty's nerves. Reynolds' chuckling turned to snorting. Slick's chortle could pass for an enraged bull.

The ranch owner's nephew on his wife's side, Reynolds, touched the brim of his hat, and called, "Mornin' boss," to Dusty.

Dusty would bet his boots and saddle Reynolds brewed trouble. His sly glares kept Dusty wary. Yesterday, Dusty had found his cinch snipped, making him wonder if the incident had been intentional.

Dusty's friend, Trevor, took the chair next to him. The skinny wrangler had to be pushing forty; still, he could ride and rope like a man in his twenties. "You okay?"

"Yep." His problems were none of the cowboy's concern.

Trevor wore a goofy grin. "Hard to reckon, freedom comes tomorrow afternoon."

Dusty smiled. "No cow punching or chores for three days. Can't wait for that room at the Hesperia Hotel." He planned a hot bath, a stiff drink, perhaps the company of a woman.

~ * ~

"Can't stop thinking about the cowboy, Dusty Mann," Mia said, standing next to Birdie at the depot's wide-open platform. Dusty didn't look like a criminal. His eyes seemed bright, not dull like the men on internet mugshots.

"Dusty Mann?" Birdie laughed. "What kind of name is that?"

"Be nice. The poor guy hanged." Mia held her hand against her throat.

Birdie made a pretend noose motion. "Hanged, as in from the highest tree death?"

"Now you're making fun of him."

"If you're interested in cowboys, I'll set you up with one of my brother's friends."

Mia rolled her eyes. "No more blind dates."

"We'll see." Her cousin's smirk meant she'd be persistent. She reached in her purse and handed her a delicate floral tapestry coin purse. "Found this in grandma's attic last week and added three silver dollars to commemorate our trip."

Mia hugged her cousin. "You're so sweet." She tucked the items inside her purse, deciding to check out the coins when they were seated on the train.

Directly in front of her, a barbershop quartet harmonized an old love song. Their red striped vests, straw hats, and handlebar mustaches added to the ambiance.

No surprise, Birdie knew the lyrics.

Auntie Mickie walked up and pulled Mia inside a lavender-scented hug. "I'm glad you moved back."

"Me too." Mia didn't mind housesitting for her grandparents, especially since she didn't have to pay rent for a year. She didn't mind her relatives—but would miss hanging out with her friends in the city.

"Something bugging you?" Auntie Mickie asked.

Darn intuitive aunt.

"Nope." Mia had to fight to keep from clenching her teeth.

"Uncle Al's old west cookout sounded fun," Birdie said. "Why didn't you go with him?"

"Riding horses for hours and sleeping on the hard ground has absolutely no appeal for me." Her aunt fidgeted with the netting on her Knobby hat.

"I'm with Auntie." Mia tugged a capped-sleeve down. "Last time I camped, I stepped in a gopher hole and twisted my ankle. Now I'm more into resorts."

"Well, I'd do it. Must've been quite a trip." Her cousin made a wanna-be-a-cowgirl lasso in the air.

Auntie Mickie tapped her pointy black-and-white boots and laughed.

The train's horn blasted from a distance. Voices buzzed. Everyone crowded the gate as Mia edged forward. The steam locomotive chugged, hissing and billowing steam clouds as it stopped.

Birdie posed by one of the car's wheels. "The rims are taller than I am."

Mia grabbed her phone and took a picture. "That's not saying a lot."

Birdie stuck out her tongue.

The conductor flipped open his pocket watch. "Welcome to the California Southern Railroad. You'll find traveling on this fifty-thousand-pound wonder a step back into the year eighteen-ninety."

Dusty may have ridden on a train like this. Birdie was right; Mia had to stop thinking about the darn cowboy.

Auntie Mickie led them up grated metal steps and into the gaming car. Half-a-dozen men in period black duster-coats, tooled leather boots, and dark Stetsons leaned against a mahogany bar, drinking beer out of glass mugs. To her left, gamblers played cards at a felt-covered table. A redheaded man winked at her.

She flashed him a smile, rushed behind her aunt, out the vintage train door, and into the passenger car. A lady held a young girl on her lap; both wore matching periwinkle dresses and bonnets.

Auntie Mickie pointed two rows ahead to a middle-aged woman with tangerine glasses. "Let's sit over by my friend."

Mia took the window seat next to Birdie, facing her aunt.

Birdie crossed her right leg and leaned over to Mia. "Can't wait for the Daggett Western Shindig tomorrow night."

"Remember those crepe-papered high school dances in the gym?" The high school gym where Mia initially danced with her cowboy crush, Craig.

"Sure. They were a blast."

The server handed Mia champagne. She sipped. Bubbles tickled down her throat. A giddiness filled her for the first time in months.

Her cousin lifted her glass and toasted, "To adventures."

After far too many hours staring at her computer screen, Mia was more than ready for an adventure. The whistle blared, and the train jerked forward. She lazed back into the plush seat. A gentle breeze drifted in from the open windows as the car rolled along the tracks. Its wheels clickety-clacked.

"You double-crossing son of a polecat," a raspy voice came from a bearded man, less than a foot from Birdie, blocking the middle of the aisle. He wore a dirty red-checkered shirt, a weathered cowboy hat, and his lip twisted into a glower.

At the opposite end of the train car, a man, resembling Wild Bill Hickok, fingered the handle of his gun and kept his eyes on his opponent. "It's a mistake to draw first."

The other man pulled out his six-shooter and squeezed the trigger.

Fake gunfire boomed. Wild Bill's opponent fell to the carpet.

Even knowing they were actors, Mia flinched and told her heart to chill. She glanced at Birdie. Her eyes fixed on the still body as her fingernails dug into the seat's padded arm.

The conductor squatted beside the body. "The man's dead!" he shouted to Wild Bill.

"If you don't want to die with your boots on, let that gun lie!" Wild Bill's voice projected the famous line to the audience.

"Bravo." Her cousin whistled, her face shone, and her eyes sparkled. "Wild Bill's hot."

"Probably married," Mia whispered.

The actors stood, bowed, and headed into the next car.

Mia stared out the window. The train rolled past a stand of eucalyptus trees as they wound through the foothills and ascended to a plateau. Creosote bushes and Joshua trees scattered along the dry ground. She found the desert's simplistic beauty calming.

Auntie Mickie pushed her head out her window. "We're climbing the Cajon Pass." The train meandered east and crossed under the freeway. "Summit Valley's over that hill."

Birdie nudged her. "You got any gum?"

Mia moved her valise onto her lap and took out her purse. "In here somewhere." She pulled out a small black box. "I forgot about this." Flipping the lid open, she put the ring on and admired the gemstones. "Got it at the antique shop."

"Let me see." Birdie's green eyes glittered.

Mia lifted her hand up so her cousin could get a look at her purchase.

"Nice."

"The Hesperia Airport's around the bend. Ellen and Sally said they'd be waiting by the tracks." Auntie Mickie pointed. "There they are, right by the bridge."

The metal band felt hot against Mia's finger. She twisted and pulled on the ring, but the thing didn't budge. Her heart raced. "Birdie, do you have lotion ... anything to get this ring off? It's burning my finger."

"I'll check."

Mia's vision blurred. Vibrant colors rotated like a hyper kaleidoscope. Dizzy, she shut her eyes.

A whistle shrilled, the train stopped, and her valise thunked to the floor.

She opened her eyes and turned to Birdie. "Hey—" An unknown woman slept in her cousin's place. "What the heck?"

In her aunt's spot, an older man smoked a hand-rolled cigar. An icy wave shivered up her spine. This couldn't be right. The combination of her tight corset and lack of oxygen must've caused her to hallucinate.

The man puffed smoke in her direction. A gray haze curled around her face. Her eyes watered, fumes went up her nostrils, and she coughed.

Fresh air, she needed fresh air. She hurried along the center aisle to an open doorway and stopped, catching her breath.

Chapter Two

Mia's view from the passenger car's doorway fit with the old-fashioned theme of the trip. Actually, the scene could pass for a western movie set. On the walkway next to the train, women wore floor-length dresses, men in suits or jeans and cotton shirts with vests.

Since Victorville was their first scheduled stop, she should see the bus terminal to the left. Instead, a young boy in knickers and knee-highs ran up to a man. A tin star pinned to his black vest sparkled. They entered a building, not much bigger than a shed, with JAIL painted on the side. It reminded her of a squared building she'd seen in the ghost town of Bodie.

Where could she be? Once she found Birdie or her aunt, she'd figure out where the train stopped. Fifty yards from the jail, workers lifted pallets from a boxcar and stacked them on the deck. A few yards further, three men in overalls herded squealing pigs onto a ramp and into metal holding pens.

Wooden storefronts lined both sides of the main street. This wasn't Goffs' Ghost Town. Goffs is at least a hundred miles northeast of the Cajon Summit. And it wasn't Calico. Calico is in a hillier location, while this area appeared flat, dead flat. Her heart sped up like the train's pistons at full bore. What's going on?

The glaring sun made it tough to see the brick building across the street. She reached for her sunglasses. *Oh shit, I lost my purse.*

"Excuse me, miss. I believe you left this behind." A porter squeezed between passengers and held up her bag.

"Thank god." She took her luggage and let out a soft sigh.

"There's no reason to use the Lord's name in vain," a woman behind her huffed.

"Sorry," Mia said.

"I hate to ask you to keep moving, dear, but my husband's waiting for me."

"Sorry." Mia turned to go back to her seat. People crowded the aisle, forcing her to pivot and go down the grated steps to the walkway.

Maybe her aunt and cousin went outside. She got on her tiptoes to search. A full passenger car length ahead, she recognized her aunt's dark-cocoa-colored bun and hurried next to her. But the lady with a large bulbous nose was not her aunt.

Mia paused near the engine. A blast of steam shot out. Startled, she lost her footing, fell toward the monstrous wheel of the train, and screamed, "Noooooo!" She landed on the ground inches from the tracks. "Whew! That was close."

Two hands gripped her arms from the back and pulled her to her feet. Swiveling, she stared at a disheveled guy who grinned, missing a front tooth. He wore tattered overalls held together with colorful patches. "Are you all right?"

"Other than being annoyed at my clumsiness, I'm good." She dusted off her dress' skirt. Her knees smarted.

"Then I'd best be going." He hurried away.

Now her scraped palms stung.

"Excuse me." A teenage boy stepped around her balancing a cage full of chickens.

Chickens? Not something she expected to see. She expected to see a familiar face or a notable costume or someone using a cell phone. A dull ache throbbed in her temples.

Above the window at the ticket booth, the word, *Hesperia,* was carved into a wooden sign. The guy inside tipped his derby hat, showing off a full head of dark wavy hair. Kinda cute.

Light reflected off his gold band.

Married.

Off to the side, two men, one white-haired and the other a taller redhead, read pages. Might be a script. One of them could be a producer and the other a director. If she acted like a sophisticated nineteenth-century lady, she might get noticed, maybe get to be an extra. She straightened her skirt and sauntered by with a lady-like decorum. Neither man looked up.

It didn't matter. She needed to find her aunt or cousin.

The train whistle sounded.

"All aboard!" a porter shouted.

About to get on, her cousin's long feather bobbed down the stairs. "Birdie, wait!" Mia caught up with her near the bottom step. "Didn't you hear me?"

A teenage girl about Birdie's height halted. "Are you addressing me?"

"I thought you were my cousin. She has a hat like yours."

"Haven't seen her."

"Gertrude, please stop dilly-dallying and come along," an older man told the girl.

She gave an I've-gotta-go shrug and headed across the street.

Mia stared at a three-story building. The Hesperia Hotel. The hotel she'd seen in old photos. The hotel was torn down in the nineteen-seventies, well before she was born.

Assuming she must be seeing things, she blinked a couple of times and looked at the hotel again. It had to be a replica.

Another whistle blared, the train's wheels huff-clacked forward. She took three steps and spotted the tail end of the caboose.

"Stop the train!" she screamed and ran up to the platform. Her lungs felt like a collapsed airbag. Panic pinged through her like a pinball machine. The train rolled out of sight.

Stay cool. Think. Quit freaking. Talk to the guy at the ticket booth. Like he could put the train in reverse. Wait, he could radio the train and relay a message to her cousin.

Message? Of course, she would text Birdie.

She dug into her purse, found her makeup case, Kleenex, a hairbrush, an apple, a romance novel, more crap. Her phone must be at the bottom. The bench across the street would work to dump out her bag.

Humongous horses pulled a wagonload of hay on the dirt road. She waited to cross.

21

In front of her, a gentleman in a dark suit and top hat assisted a lady into her carriage seat. The driver positioned himself to her left and picked up the reins. His horse neighed.

Mia shifted back a few steps, giving the horse plenty of room as she leaned her elbows against a railing behind her. The buggy took off leaving thin ruts in the powdery dirt.

Hot air raced down her neck. Something hit the back of her head, jerking her forward, pushing her, making her stumble into the street. She gained her footing. Spun around. Her arms pinwheeled. "Stop tha—"

Her words clogged her throat, cut off her breath.

A horse, oh shit, a horse.

She stared at its large, triangular brown head inches from her face. No, not large. Gigantic. Her heart tripped in her chest; her legs became immovable.

Its nostrils flared, its obsidian-colored eyes widened.

She tried to move, but her limbs became rigid, her feet cemented in place. The horse stomped one hoof against the ground and swished its tail against its flank. A thousand pounds of imposing beast sniffed the air.

She stood frozen, watching its nostrils flair and flatten, flare and flatten. "Get, get back."

The horse's mouth opened, and it bared teeth the size of playing cards.

Move, she told herself. Move, before it stomps on you.

The horse let out a high-pitched snort and threw its head up.

She was gone, racing down the street, sprinting up the hotel's wide wooden staircase, straight through an open door, running fast. Fear propelled her like a slingshot.

She charged inside and plowed into a solid object with an umph.

"Slow down." Large hands steadied her and released its hold. The man stepped away.

At only five-foot-two, she stared straight at his massive shoulders. This guy must spend hours at the gym. Okay, she had to quit gawking at his chest. She gazed up as he took off his worn-leather Stetson.

He gave her a lopsided grin. "Somethin' troublin' you?"

"No." Not wanting to seem like an idiot, she stoned her expression, while her knees wobbled.

"You're kinda pale. Best you sit a spell." He placed his hands on her shoulders and guided her to an overstuffed couch near a brick fireplace. Heat sizzled through her gown's fabric, and her insides tingled.

"Excuse me." The cowboy flagged a waitress in a long black dress and white apron. "I'd be obliged if you brought this lady some water." He relaxed in an adjacent armchair and flashed her a brazen smile. "Never had a beautiful gal barrel into me. What's the hurry, miss?"

"Um, you see, this horse, it scared me. The horse, um, was huge, enormous." Sounding stupid, she concentrated on a multicolored glass-blown vase on the side table and rearranged the orange poppies to be in front of the violets and lupines.

"Must've been one of Ben's Belgian draft horses," he said, and she noticed his russet brown hair touched the top of his shirt collar.

The server handed her a glass of water. She took a sip. "It's warm."

"No surprise. This is the desert." The cowboy's drawl didn't seem practiced.

"I'm not as freaked as—" She looked at him, really looked at him, and recognized those wide-set gray eyes from somewhere. "You look familiar."

"I'd remember meeting a pretty gal like you." His smile lit up his handsome face, and her heart fluttered.

She focused on the people at the front desk. A clerk slid a key to a man, and he left with a lady in a long chiffon dress. Most likely people from the train.

A heavy-set woman approached her. "I'm Jenny Hayes. My husband, Bob, and I manage the hotel."

"Mia Kellogg." She held out her hand.

Jenny gave her a sideways glance.

Why wouldn't she shake her hand? Must be a germaphob.

"Saw Dusty walk you in. Did the heat get to you?"

"Maybe a little. I'm fine now." Mia examined the man's features. His tan complexion set off his wolf gray eyes. He was a ringer to the cowboy from the picture in the antique shop. "You're name's Dusty?"

He straightened and rewarded her with a mischievous grin. "Yep."

"His given name's Harold Mann, but folks have been calling him Dusty since he was knee high to a grasshopper." Jenny butted in. She must be related to him somehow. "What brings you to our town?" Jenny asked.

"A short vacation."

"Well, you certainly chose an ideal time for your stay. Tomorrow's our monthly ball." Jenny's cheeks reddened.

Now Mia was confused. She and Birdie had tickets for the Daggett dance. Maybe she got the name of the town wrong. Still, if her relatives were here, she should have seen them by now. "Could I borrow your phone and call my cousin?" Mia asked, anxious to talk with someone she knew.

"Golly, we don't have a telephone here. Our general store is the only business in town that has one. The shop's closed 'till morning," Jenny said.

Mia's throat got tight. Only one phone in town. This took the turn-of-the-last-century thing a bit far.

"I imagine you're famished, miss. May I find you a table in the dining room?"

"Please." Starved, at least her stomach didn't rumble.

Jenny turned to Dusty. "Will you be joining Miss Kellogg?"

Mia expected him to refuse politely. Not say, "I'd be honored." He stood and offered his arm. His scent of leather and masculinity made her lean closer. Wrong response for a guy she'd just met.

Jenny led the two of them through the spacious ballroom. Mia's right foot hit a slick, polished spot on the hardwood flooring. "Oh no."

Dusty tightened his grasp on her arm. "Careful, darlin'."

Was her lightheadedness from lack of food or ... was it him? She took small mindful steps to their linen covered table. Mindful of the waxed floor. Mindful of clutching his muscular biceps.

25

"Here you go." He pulled out her chair. His gray eyes darkened when he looked at her. He appeared well-mannered, but she wondered if his kisses would hold a bad boy edge. She couldn't believe she thought about kissing him. Not exactly appropriate for a guy she barely knew—but he was cute.

Her eyes drifted to the five-o'clock shadow on his chin. Certain she'd been caught staring, she unfolded her napkin and placed it on her lap.

"Enjoy your meal," Jenny said and scurried off.

Mia should be looking for her phone, but hunger won out. She knifed jelly on a roll and bit into the warm orange-flavored dough. Wickedly scrumptious. She drank from a crystal glass. "The lemonade's sour." A pound of sugar wouldn't take away the tartness.

He held up a crystal bowl. "Want some sugar?"

"Please." She should use Sweet'N Low, but being on vacation why not splurge a little? She added three generous teaspoons, deciding she'd make up for her indulgences at spin class on Monday. "What do you do?"

"Do?" His brow rose, and he looked at her like she asked him to explain the theory of relativity.

"Your job."

"Me? I'm just an old cowhand." His drawl came out a bit over exaggerated.

Her dad regularly watched old westerns. This guy had a casual Gary Cooper presence. She focused on the jagged scar on his chin. She liked the flaw, showed he wasn't plastic-perfect. "Where's your ranch?"

"It's not mine." He winced for a flash. "I'm the foreman of Los Flores Ranch."

The hot cowboy sitting across from her lived in the next town over. Moving back to her hometown suddenly had a big advantage, namely him. She could see him working on the ranch on the outskirts of Hesperia. Lifting bales of hay would explain his beefy arms.

She'd have to give him her number before she left.

~ * ~

By now, Mia's cousin and aunt should've noticed her absence on the train and at least texted her. Maybe they did. She fished through her jam-packed valise for her phone as she waited at the counter. Where was her cell? "Did my cousin check in? Her name's Birdie Kellogg." She knew it was a long-shot but had to ask.

Jenny scanned the ledger. "No Kellogg's signed in."

A tremor chilled down her arms.

Her lipstick rolled on the counter toward the proprietress. She picked up the case and held it up to the light. "What a bizarre bullet. Never seen one with flowered etchings."

"It's just lipstick." Mia took off the lid and glided the light color on her lips.

"No paintbrush? How marvelous. The color looks natural. Walter should order some for his shop. I'd never buy mouth rouge myself, but it might interest the younger women."

Mia didn't comment. Given the setting of this hotel, part of the woman's job must be to act like she's from the Wild West era.

"Put you in a corner room on the second floor."

"How much?" Mia reached for her wallet. She'd paid for a room in Daggett when she booked this trip. Darn it. She'd have to pay for another.

"One fifty. We raised our rates this weekend because of the ball."

"One-hundred-fifty is pretty steep." She hated stacking more debt on her credit card after already paying for her costume and the ring, but she pulled out her wallet.

"Dearie, it's a dollar fifty."

"A dollar fifty?"

"Yes, miss."

You can't stay in a dump for at least forty. Something's off. Too tired to question why it's ridiculously cheap, she looked inside her billfold.

No cash.

Earlier today, Birdie gave her a coin purse with three silver dollars because three was her lucky number. She rummaged through her bag, found it, and gave the matron two coins. Another odd coincidence today, unless ... Birdie was playing a joke on her.

Jenny pushed the change into her drawer and gave Mia two quarter-sized coins. "Follow me, and I'll take you to your room." Jenny brought her to the stairwell and went up the steps at a brisk pace.

Mia rushed to keep up, careful of the kerosene wall sconces lighting their way. The management should know this much kerosene is a fire hazard. It'd be her luck to knock one over and start a fire. It's much safer using electric lighting.

The woman unlocked the door, walked to the dresser, removed the globe from a kerosene lamp, struck a match and held the flame to the wick until it lit, before returning the glass covering.

"Doesn't this place have electricity?" She didn't care for the burning oil scent.

Jenny tilted her head. "I've read about electricity in the newspaper. A bolt shot straight through some poor fellow's heart like lightning hit him." She took her role as a turn-of-the-century woman seriously, but this was way over the top. "I mentioned earlier about the ball tomorrow night. Suspect every eligible bachelor will be eager to dance with you."

What an odd comment from a hotel manager.

"Anyway, we have running water on both floors. Feel free to use the bathhouse," Jenny said quickly. "Left you shampoo and soap on the bureau. The room's down the hall on the left. Towels are on the shelves."

Of course, there weren't private bathrooms. What did she expect? She only paid one dollar and fifty cents. Still, why was it so cheap?

"Breakfast is served from seven to nine. See you in the morning." Finally, Jenny left.

Mia spotted an entertainment center. Ready for a mindless comedy show, she opened the boxy cabinet. No TV, no remote. One robe and plenty of wooden hangers on a rod. Typical no-frills bed and breakfast.

She poured her purse's contents on the bed. *There's my phone.* She pushed the side button—it didn't turn on. Needing her charger, she found it near the top of her luggage and searched for an electrical outlet. She checked the walls, crawled on her knees under the desk by the window, and failed to find anything. The woman wasn't kidding about not having electricity.

Tomorrow morning, she'd borrow someone's cell.

This stuffy room lacked air-conditioning. At the window, she struggled with the latch. It took three tries to get the pane to slide. It stuck halfway.

She dipped a white embroidered cloth into a blue and white pitcher. Using the thin material, she wiped it along her face and neck to cool herself down.

The moon shone brightly, and she gazed out the window. A man draped his arm around a saloon girl. Two riders on the street kicked up dirt. The particles floated up through her unscreened window, and she sneezed.

This didn't make sense. If Hesperia had decided to restore this section to its original township, thousands of pictures would've been posted on social media. Besides, it'd be crazy to dig up an asphalt road and replace it with dirt.

Her ring dug into her finger. She twisted and pulled on it, but it wouldn't move over her knuckle. Closing her eyes, she fantasized about Dusty galloping along the endless desert terrain. His russet hair flying. His shirt molded to his toned chest, muscular thighs gripped his horse, calloused hands controlled the reins.

She blamed the illusion on a silly cowboy infatuation.

Tired of all the drama, she flopped on her bed. Her corset pinched. Removing her dress, she stretched to undo the string on the back of her corset and couldn't reach it. The mirror reflected a row of small buttons on the left side, allowing her to take off the torturous device and breathe.

She put on a silky nightgown from her bag and collapsed into the mattress. A feather poked her elbow. Too wide awake to sleep, she might as well take a bath. Snatching her robe from the wardrobe, she headed down the hall and opened the bathroom door to a claw-footed bathtub. She turned on the water, added a few drops of rose oil left on the ledge, and sank into the pleasant warmth.

Tomorrow, she'd go back to her normal life.

Chapter Three

Dusty found dining in the hotel a smidgen too refined for his tastes. He didn't need to eat breakfast at linen covered tables or use fine silver or stare at flowers in a vase. Used to six-shooter strong coffee, he downed the hotel's weak version. "Coffee's plain awful," he said to Trevor.

Sitting to his right, Trevor sipped from his cup and sighed. "Beats choking down burnt grounds, egg shells, dirt and rocks."

"Sure have odd notions 'bout cowboy brew."

"Just being honest." Trevor chuckled.

Dusty polished off a strip of bacon and started on his stack of flapjacks.

Trevor motioned to the door. "Who's the lady?"

Mia stood at the entrance; uncertainty showed in her wide eyes. Eyes Dusty recalled were the color of clovers. "Miss Kellogg. Met her yesterday."

"Pretty girl."

Jenny escorted her to their table, the only table left with empty seats. "Trevor, this is Miss Amelia Kellogg. If it's not too much trouble, may she join you two for breakfast?"

"I'd be honored." Dusty tipped his hat, got up, and pulled out her chair.

Her eyes became slivers as she squinted at Trevor. "You're one of my uncle's friends, right?"

"Who's your uncle?"

"Al Kellogg." Her eyes turned pine needle sharp. "Or maybe you know my cousin, Birdie?"

"Bertha?" Trevor looked like a rabbit stuck in a snare.

A server filled her cup. She added cream and stirred fast. "It's Birdie, like a bird."

"Miss, I've never met anyone named Birdie." Trevor used a soft, steady tone that worked to calm horses.

"Oh." She bit her bottom lip. "Do either of you have a cell I could borrow?"

"A cell?" The only cell Dusty knew of was at the jailhouse.

"Telephone," she said matter of factly.

"Walter's got one at the general store, but his doors don't open for another hour." Dusty had no idea why she kept fiddling with her napkin. The server brought out her breakfast, and she politely thanked him.

Dusty concentrated on his meal, figuring he'd leave her to her own thoughts.

"What brings you to Hesperia?" Trevor never could keep his trap shut for long.

"I'm on vacation," she said without smiling.

"You come here for the ball."

She gazed at Trevor like he was one shy of a full deck.

"You'll like it. Plenty of food. Band's lively. The caller's a real hoot," Trevor blathered.

"Sounds like paradise," her tone said otherwise. It was like she was afraid, apprehensive. Might be shy.

Dusty could relate. He wasn't comfortable around strangers.

"You from San Bernardino or somewhere else?"

"Until recently, I lived in L.A. county, near the beach." Her green eyes shimmered as if she might tear up.

He finished eating, took his last swig of coffee. "Think you could save me a dance tonight?" He stood.

"I'll think about it."

"I'll take that as a yes." He couldn't resist whistling as he walked away.

~ * ~

As Mia left the dining room, an idea popped into her head. What if Dusty and Trevor were Birdie's actor friends?

She envisioned her cousin's plan. Days, weeks, maybe even months before the trip, Dusty showed Birdie his latest sepia toned headshot, one with him wearing a Stetson. Knowing Mia had a weakness for cowboys, her cousin borrowed the picture and asked the antique shop's owner to display it in the window. She photoshopped Dusty's image to look like an etching, embedded it into an old article about the hanging, added the printed page to a scrapbook, and propped the book open near the antique shop's register. No wonder she insisted they go inside. Plus, Birdie knew they'd stop at the hotel. She must've set the stage with Jenny.

Birdie made her suffer through last night. Now she's waiting at the general store with an I-got-you-good-grin on her face.

But what if it wasn't a trick?

No. It had to be. She sucked in a deep breath.

That was the only thing that made sense.

Near the hotel's front entrance, she spotted a poster displayed on a wooden board.

Hesperia Hotel Ball
Saturday, June 2, 1890

Eighteen-ninety? Landing in the past? An insane, ridiculous, unbelievable concept. Her cousin got her with a phony poster.

She stepped onto the veranda and went down the stairs to the boarded walkway. A dog barked. A pair of horses galloped along the street. A blacksmith's anvil banged in the distance. How could Birdie have set this up?

No compressors running. No loud music. No screeching brakes. No noisy mufflers. Nobody wearing shorts and flip-flops. Nobody with earbuds or cell phones. Nobody taking selfies.

If this were a touristy town, it must've been built on a stretch of desert between Hesperia and Calico.

Three women strolled ahead of her in long dark skirts and white starched blouses. Why wasn't at least one person wearing a sundress? A group of cowboys wore dirt-caked jeans. They tipped their hats to her. One smiled with a blackened tooth. It didn't look phony.

She passed the Hesperia Bank. Outside the next shop, Dr. Speer's placard hung lower on the right end. The Government Road sign had bullet holes riddled in the middle of both O's. *This is crazy.*

A horse dumped stinky road-apples less than a yard from her. Gross!

She stared at the street. It matched the old Hesperia photograph her grandfather had on his office wall.

While sitting on his lap and looking at the picture, she'd seen a view of this street countless times. He'd point out the train depot, the hotel, and the church. The town's resemblance was more than a coincidence. It looked *authentic.*

It couldn't be *authentic.*

Her chest tightened. Her mind spun faster than a fidget spinner.

She found herself running past the general store and several more shops, assuming if she ran fast enough, she'd find her sanity. Instead, she arrived at a corner. On the other side of the railroad tracks, she stared at a white church next to a boxy building with a courthouse sign. The church looked identical to the one in her time, minus the peeling paint.

Main Street posted at the intersection. She recognized the enormous dome-shaped boulder. The boulder where her brother fell and later received four stitches on his forehead. With the boulder as her goal, she sprinted across the street.

"Watch out!" a buggy driver yelled.

Her pulse tripled. Bile snuck up from her stomach, and she forced it down.

Please, boulder, be fake. She touched the rock hoping it would be spongy and soft, not hard stone. As she moved to the front, she inspected the rock's sediments. Her carved initials should show in the back. Her mind said to forget about looking, but her feet took her to the spot. No initials. She let out a long, relieved sigh, while her pulse refused to settle, and her heart ticked and ticked and ticked.

If she were in the 1800's, her initials wouldn't be there for over a hundred years. Kneeling, she outlined

the bird-shaped hole near the bottom. The same
baseball-sized bird-shaped hole she'd discovered as a
kid.

Had someone relocated the boulder here? Moving
the two-ton rock would require a crane. The logistics.
Inconceivable. The last time she'd been here, the rock
was underneath the Main Street's overpass.

This was Main Street from a hundred years ago with
no overpass. Her stomach twisted tighter.

In a daze, she crossed the road and sat on a bench
under a shady tree.

Had she traveled back in time? Her whole body
became numb. There must be a rational explanation for
what she saw. Once she called Birdie, her anxiety would
disappear.

Determination marched her up the stairs to the
general store. Outside four women twirled their
parasols. She refused to make eye contact, hoping they'd
ignore her.

"Hello," a woman wearing a ridiculous green hat with
netting covering her eyes said.

"Hi." Mia's mother taught her to be courteous to her
elders, and these women had at least twenty years on
her.

"Jenny told us a single gal checked into the hotel,"
said a woman with gray-hair braided and wound on top
of her head in a bun. Might be Amish.

"I did. Love to chat, ladies, but I don't have time."
She used a domineering tone that had placated
executives.

"Gotta get gussied up for the ball tonight," a gray-
haired woman said. "Should be plenty of suitors to
choose from."

"I bet she dances with—" another lady said.

Mia hurried inside the store, relieved the door shut out the women's conversation. A pickle barrel's strong vinegary scent made her eyes water. More wooden barrels lined the wide aisle. A stick in the center of one posted: *Salt-Water Taffy-Two for a Penny*. The barrel full of pink-and-white swirled candies were individually wrapped in wax paper.

She moved to the counter and fingered a bolt of flowered fabric. Canned goods and vegetable jars stacked neatly on shelving. A brown bottle from the top of a cart caught her eye, and she examined the label. Sugar Coated Cathartic Pills. Cathartic?

This place seemed surreal.

A middle-aged owner tied back the straps of his long white apron. "Morning, miss. How may I help you?"

She dropped the pill bottle in its spot and swallowed apprehension down her throat. "I'd like to use your telephone."

"If I can get this newfangled invention to work, you're welcome to it." He went over to a wooden box on the wall, snatched a metal object that reminded Mia of a candlestick holder, cranked a knob and talked into a circular piece. "Mabel, you there? No, it's not an emergency. Mrs. Hinkle doesn't need Doc to deliver her baby yet. There's a lady who wants to make a call. Here you go, miss."

The black cylinder felt heavy in her hand and against her ear. A fluttery sensation filled her stomach. This is beyond people getting into character. Had she really landed in the past?

Everything would be fine once she talked with her cousin. It had to be.

"What's your name, miss?" The woman's voice garbled from the earpiece.

"Mia Kellogg."

"You must be the young miss Jenny talked about."

"I am." Small town gossip. Mia shook her head.

"Who do you wish to contact?" Mabel asked.

"My cousin Birdie. Her number's 760-555-4444."

Please hurry. I need to talk to Birdie immediately before I lose my mind.

"A lot of numbers. We only use one or two."

"Really?" She asked faintly as the twisting sensation in her stomach intensified.

"Where does your cousin live?"

It shouldn't matter. Okay, if this was a prank, Birdie better show herself. But Mia's gut told her this was no joke.

"My cousin lives in Hellendale."

"Helena, Montana? Out of our area. On a good day, I can connect to the courthouse in San Bernardino." Between the crackles, Mia picked out the words. "It's Helendale. The town's ten miles east of here." Cotton balls filled her mouth.

"Only places out there are the Silver Spur Ranch and the rundown Pony Express station.

Was she going freaking crazy? Maybe it's a dream. Still, her dreams were never this detailed or coherent.

"I know most folks in these parts. Who's your cousin visiting?" Mabel's personality matched the meddlesome telephone operators portrayed in movies.

"Umm, not sure. I left my cousin's address at the hotel. Sorry to waste your time." Mia spoke fast.

"Got plenty to spare," the operator said with an I-can't-wait-to tell-everyone-your-story-gossipy tone.

Mia's racing pulse told her she wouldn't talk with Birdie today.

"Mabel. This is Ronald," a voice cut in.

"Ronald owns the assayer's office, Miss Kellogg."

Where'd that other person come from? She caught herself rocking on her feet and stopped. There must be a reasonable explanation here.

"Hello," the man said.

She had to get away from this madness. "Mabel, you've been very helpful. Go ahead and assist Ronald." Her hands shook as she put down the cylinder earpiece.

The store owner twisted the waxed-ends of his mustache. "Did you speak to your cousin?"

"Unfortunately, no." A dream, a movie set, a practical joke—all legitimate explanations for her situation. But the bird-shaped hole, the town's layout, and the people, especially this telephone operator, proved her theories wrong.

Could she have time traveled back to 1890?

That's impossible.

But it had to be true. Nothing else explained what was going on. Fear filled her soul; she pinched her lips together. Tears pooled in her eyes, and she shook them off. Crying wouldn't help her.

"Anything else I can assist you with?"

"Not today. Thanks for your help." She may be losing her mind, but her mother would have a fit if she forgot her manners. She didn't have time for hysteria. Not while she had a bigger issue to deal with. Rushing outside, she waved at the old biddies, continued down the steps, and along the boardwalk.

She breathed in and out slowly several times and told herself everything would be okay. All she needed to do was think. Figure out a plan, a next step.

How would she survive? Her credit cards were useless. A dollar fifty would buy her another night at the hotel, and then what? Panic squeezed her heart.

She needed a job, a place to stay. Who would hire her?

She'd read about women in mining towns making a killing by baking pies or cooking meals. Her cooking skills consisted of using a microwave. She doubted there'd be anything to do in graphic design. Paint. Probably not much money there. Newspapers hired men, not women. Work at the hotel if they had an opening. It seemed fully staffed.

She arrived at the hotel.

Trevor relaxed on a padded bench near the entrance. "You seem as frightened as a baby bird that plum fell out of its nest."

Try stranded in another time with a bunch of strangers, scared out of her wits with no idea how to get back home.

"Care to talk about it." He patted the empty spot next to him. "Can't be worse than the oddities my sis used to spout as a teen."

As if his sister experienced life in another century. Still, an ally from this era might be advantageous, so she eased next to him.

"Promise I won't judge." Trevor took off his worn Stetson, showing gray at his temples and thinning hair on top. "Go ahead when you're ready. I'm all ears."

The cliché made her chuckle. "I planned to stay with my cousin. When I got off the train, I assumed I'd find her here. Guess I took the wrong stop." Along with arriving in the wrong century.

"Don't fret none, miss." His sympathetic smile reminded her of Uncle Al. "You know your cousin's address?"

"I had written it down, but somehow lost it." She couldn't say her cousin wouldn't be born for over a hundred years. A tear slipped down her cheek.

"Things have a way of working out if you have a little faith."

"Faith, really?"

"It helps me." Trevor's expression softened. "In the meantime, you looking for a job? If you're smart and good with kids, the Los Flores Ranch needs a teacher. That's where I work."

Teaching was her cousin's calling, not Mia's. A teacher on a secluded ranch sounded dreadful. But at the moment teaching was her best option. "I have a college degree. Think that'd be enough?"

"I reckon your schoolin' will help, but the decision will be up to the McGraw's. Me 'n Dusty will put in a good word for you if you'd like."

"Okay." A wild thought flashed in her brain. Had she been sent here to help Dusty? Maybe she could prevent him from being hanged? Trevor might have an idea who was behind his future arrest. "How long have you worked with Dusty?"

"Five years, give or take."

"Know anyone who doesn't like him?"

"Everyone respects him because he's fair." He squinted at her. "I get where you're headed. You're sweet on Dusty."

"No."

He pulled out his pocket watch and flipped up the case. "It's already three-thirty. I need to get fancied up for tonight."

"But—"

"Right now, I'm getting a haircut. See you later." He sprinted off.

This conversation ended weird.

As she headed inside, Jenny stopped her at the bottom of the stairwell, smiling. "If you need a gown for tonight, I might have the perfect one."

"How much?" Mia asked, knowing her money had to cover her room tonight.

Jenny snickered. "Not a single cent, sweetie. A patron left it behind. Still, has the price tag."

"Isn't that stealing?" It'd be her luck to go to jail for wearing the dress.

"The gown was left behind months ago. The owner left no forwarding address."

"I'd like to see it, but if the sheriff comes for me, I'll send him your way."

"You're funny." Jenny laughed. "Wait right here, and I'll get it."

The dress took her mind off her problems for maybe a second.

The proprietress rushed into a back room and carried out an emerald green gown. It had a fitted waist and a full skirt and puffed sleeves. Elaborate lace adorned the neck.

"Isn't this dress exquisite?" Jenny handed her the gown.

"It's fabulous." Mia ran her hand over the material. The luster and weight meant high-quality fabric. She looked inside for a label. "It's a Catherine Donovan."

"Is that good?"

"Amazing." In college, she had written a term paper on the woman. Donovan was a designer during this era. "The designer works in New York. This dress is expensive. I'm not sure if I should wear it."

"Nonsense. You like it, and the color accents your eyes." Jenny folded her arms. "I'll send one of our staff up to make alterations."

"Thank you." Elated over the dazzling new gown, Mia practically floated up the stairs to her room. She paced to the window and looked out, must've paced back and forth at least ten times when a knock came, and she opened the door.

The blonde staff member seemed to be about her age. "I'm Kristy, the hotel's seamstress." She helped Mia remove her dress and noticed her corset on the bureau. "You'll need to put this on for me to fit the gown properly." She cinched the corset tight.

"Please loosen it a bit," Mia swore her ribs pushed into her organs.

"How's this?"

She let out a deep breath. "Better."

Kristy slipped the silky gown over Mia's head and buttoned the back. As the seamstress took in the bodice, she understood what it felt like to be a pin cushion.

"You sure I can't tighten the corset now? Then I won't have to let out the waist."

"I prefer breathing, thank you very much."

Kristy chuckled before taking off the dress and stitching by hand.

She watched from the edge of her bed. "You're talented. Where'd you learn to sew like this?"

"Used to help my ma."

A half an hour later, Mia had the gown on. The silky material flowed to the ground, making her feel like a princess.

"You look ravishing. Now for your hair. I'm thinking a loose bun with soft strands cascading down."

"Perfect." Good thing she chickened out getting a pixie cut at her hairdresser's last month.

Kristy brushed the back and used a fancy clip. "I'm done."

She glanced in a full-length mirror, and turned, feeling like a movie star about to strut the red carpet. "Thank you."

"It's been my pleasure." Kristy glanced at a clock on the wall. "It's almost six. I'd better get ready for the ball myself." She scurried off.

The dress lifted Mia's spirits, giving her a temporary sense of happiness, until she remembered she was stuck in the past. Well, for tonight, why not enjoy the ball.

"Miss Amelia, it's me," Jenny called as she knocked.

She opened the door. The proprietress' orchid colored gown shocked Mia's eyes.

"My, aren't you fetching."

"You look stunning yourself." She lied.

"Brought your dance card. There are more men than women around here. You'll have your pick of the fellows." Jenny's brow rose. "Folk should be arriving now. Come down whenever you are ready. Can't wait to watch the heads turn."

The idea of being scrutinized made Mia uncomfortable.

Chapter Four

Mia swallowed her apprehension as she stepped into the lobby, fingering her dance card's satin ribbon. Dozens of people filled the space. The low din of conversation buzzed in her ears. Would she be able to pull off acting as if she belonged?

"Howdy." A skinny man, in an ill-fitting black suit, said.

"Hi."

A scraggly long-bearded guy moved next to her. More men pressed in closer, encircling her, boxing her in, and suffocating her.

"Gentlemen, please give Miss Kellogg room." Jenny butted in sideways and grabbed her hand. She quickly dragged her down the hall, behind the check-in counter, and out the double-doors to the patio. "Dearie, are you all right?"

"I am now. Thanks for saving me."

Jenny slowed her pace outside. Chickens scratched for feed between bales of hay. Folks kicked back at awning-covered tables. Others lounged on split-log benches semi-circled around fire pits while awaiting their slice of the barbecuing whole hog. Disgusting.

She missed her friends. Her own rules. Her life.

The orangey-pink sunset faded to dusk. Hotel workers used metal sticks with covered wicks to light the lampposts.

Jenny brought her past a long table to where Dusty and Trevor sat in chairs facing the back entrance. "The poor thing was ambushed by close to a dozen single men. Think you two gentlemen could watch out for her?"

"I'm fine." Mia said, even though she felt far from fine.

"It'd be my pleasure." Dusty gave her a lopsided grin, his shoulder-length hair had been cropped, his face clean shaven. Darned attractive.

"Seein' Miss Amelia's welfare is in check, I'd best go in." The proprietress picked up the edges of her long skirt and rushed off.

Dusty cleared his throat. "I imagine you're parched, Miss Amelia."

"A little."

"I'll get you a drink." He didn't hesitate to stand.

Her heart made an overhand loop. "You're sweet."

"Don't recall ever being called *sweet* before." Dusty walked backwards watching her and bumped into a couple near the door.

Trevor let out a loud chuckle. "Ain't never seen him do that before."

She focused on Trevor's pinstriped suit and derby hat. "Nice outfit. Trying to impress somebody?"

"Might be." The wrangler puffed up bigger than a peacock displaying all his feathers. "Lady Luck gave me a royal flush last night, so I decided to treat myself to these duds. Dusty already called me a citified dandy. Kinda liked it."

"Now I know who to ask for money."

"How much you need?" He pulled out his wallet.

"Nothing at the moment." She found this gesture endearing. Her card twirled in the soft breeze, so she untied it. "Any idea how this works?"

He held it up to the lantern on a side table. "A man will ask you to add his name. Think you could spare a dance with an old man like me?"

"Absolutely."

"If you approve, I'll take the second number." He grabbed a quill and ink bottle from a stand near the door, dipped the metal nib into the ink and scratched in his name. "May I write Dusty in for the first and last songs?"

"Yes, please."

A distinguished man in a brown suit approached the table. The town banker asked permission for a dance.

She nodded, and Trevor added his name. She liked how Trevor took over the task. In this situation, she could see her father or uncle doing the same.

Four cowboys shuffled up to her. Eight eyes stared at her like they saw a prize at the fair.

"I don't believe these fellows are here to see me," Trevor quirked one brow.

The cute one in the white Stetson took off his hat, showing off his shoulder-length blond hair. "Come on, Trevor, introduce us."

"Reynolds. Slick. Blackie. Checkerboard. This is Miss Amelia."

The slight gap between the front teeth of the *cute one* made him seem badass. He cleared his throat. "Miss Amelia, I'd be honored if you'd allow me a dance."

"You want to give Reynolds a chance?"

48

"I guess." Reynolds. The name fit the brawny cowboy.

"Name's Blackie." A dark-haired cowboy put his hat over his heart. "I'd be right pleased for a dance." In his late thirties, he seemed nice.

She nodded, and Trevor added Blackie's name.

Deep lines furrowed in the face of a short, stocky man. "Miss, if you take pity on this poor old cowboy, I promise not to stomp on your toes."

"I'll hold you to that promise," she said a little leery about his big boots.

"You'd better. Checkerboard ain't exactly light-footed," Blackie snorted.

"I'll take my chances." She nodded at Trevor to add Checkerboard.

Slick's eyes shifted back and forth. "Would you be willin' to dance with this Buckaroo?"

"Certainly," Mia said.

Trevor added his name

"A pleasure meeting you, Miss Kellogg." Reynolds tipped his hat. "See you inside."

The others nodded, touching their hat brims and left.

"You're trembling." Trevor placed his hand over hers. "Don't worry. The men will be respectful. Want me to fill in the open slots with my name and Dusty's."

"Please."

Dusty staggered toward her table, juggling three cups of punch. She shouldn't stare, but oh my, from his muscular shoulders to his chiseled jutted jaw, the cowboy oozed rugged virility.

~ * ~

Dusty offered his arm and led Mia to a spacious dance floor where dozens of couples gathered. Gazing at the spellbinding vision in green, her soft gown tapered down from her tiny waist. Her hair swept up like a golden halo. His pulse trotted, cantered, galloped. She sure was pretty.

The fiddler warmed his bow across the strings, the banjo strummed, the pianist fingered ivory keys. The musicians wore white shirts with string bowties.

"Welcome ladies and gentlemen," Bob's booming voice called from center stage, "It's my privilege to introduce Mayor Halleck and his Quicksilver Band."

Dusty positioned his left arm below her shoulder blade, grasped her small right hand, breathed in her flowery scent and longed to caress her neck. *Whoa!*

"I haven't polkaed in … um … at least a year," she said. "Hope I remember the steps."

"Good thing I'll be leading."

"I'm supposed to believe you're a good dancer?" Her voice held plenty of tease.

"Yep." He pulled her closer, surprised to find the top of her head reached his chin. "You sure are a bitty thing."

"I happen to be five-foot-two-and-a-half." Her shoulders straightened as she stood on her tiptoes.

The fiddler played a catchy intro. They glided with the lively song. She melted into his arms. Their closeness kindled a warm hankering, a hankering to hold her like this forever.

She moved in the wrong direction and trod on his left boot. "Sorry."

"Don't be." He spun her under his arm and continued with the polka. A couple stepped into their pathway, and he made a sharp right. "I'm the envy of every man in this room." He figured he sounded romantic.

"Does that line work with other women?"

"Not all of them, apparently." He kept moving. "Your wit is refreshing."

Her eyes seemed guarded. "Really? I thought—"

"What did you think?" he asked.

The song ended. "Nothing important," she said and looked around his shoulder. "Hey, Trevor."

Dusty hated releasing his hold on her.

"You had your turn," Trevor said. "Now it's mine."

"Me 'n Miss Amelia were just getting warmed up, right darlin'?"

"Not really." She peeked over at Dusty and fluttered her lashes. Pretty and sassy.

Then she waved to Reynolds off at the side in the food line.

~ * ~

Mia adored flirting with Dusty. His smoldering eyes practically devoured her. She needed a reprieve away from him to think.

Trevor was fast becoming her ally. No way would she ever tell him the real truth, but it was reassuring to have someone around who treated her like his niece.

"Ready?" Trevor asked.

"I am."

They joined a square with three other couples, and Trevor nodded to the person next to him.

Dusty wrapped his arm around the waist of his partner. The girl could be a twin for Melissa Turner from her high school—boyfriend stealing Melissa

Turner. She hoped the woman would trip and knock out her front teeth. Her jaw hurt from clenching it.

She should calm down. Dusty wasn't her ex. Her thoughts had nothing to do with him, but old wounds had opened.

"Ready for the *Texas Star*?" the caller said.

The crowd's loud, "Yes," resounded in her ears.

"Ladies meet and greet." The man's voice boomed from the stage.

She walked to the center, clapped, and sauntered back.

"Wave to your own and pass her by—catch the next girl on the fly—star promenade."

Passed to the banker, he asked, "You enjoying yourself?"

"I am." The dance consisted of quick steps.

"Scoop up your right-hand lady around the waist," the caller's sing-song voice coached. "Walk side by side in the Texas Star."

Moving up to her third partner, she heard, "This is cozy." Dusty's voice crooned like Harry Connick, Jr.

She told herself to quit swooning. "It's alright."

"And here I thought you were starting to like me."

"Pass your own and take the next," the caller chanted.

"So soon?" Dusty held her hand for an extra second, before reluctantly letting it go.

She strode forward, took Reynolds arm and promenaded around the square. "Your green gown brings out the emerald in your beautiful eyes."

"You're quite a charmer."

He pulled her closer. "I try."

No butterflies, no heart fluttering, no excitement. Nothing like a single glance from Dusty stirred. *Quit thinking about him.*

"Are you and Trevor related?"

"Not exactly," she said, keeping her answer vague. "You like working with him?"

"Trevor's right fun to be around, 'cept if he starts singing. Sorry to say, he can't carry a tune in a corked jug."

"I'll be sure to tell him."

"Please don't. I rather like the old wrangler." His words might be amiable but came out controlled.

Required to step forward, she took Trevor's arm.

Trevor wore a partial smirk. "When I looked back you seemed to be enjoying Reynolds' company. What were you two talking about?"

She promenaded with him, secure and content. "You're singing."

"Nice to know I've got admirers."

"Not according to Reynolds." The words slipped out.

"Dusty says I scare the cows, not that I ever paid him any mind." Trevor gave a hearty chuckle, and the song ended.

The banker bowed. "Miss Amelia, I believe I have the next dance. If you'd rather, we could go outside and stroll where it's cooler?"

She caught him staring down her low-cut gown. "I'd prefer to dance, thank you."

"Whatever you wish?" His sugary, deceptive smile kept her vigilant. The "Mississippi Sawyer" had her switching partners frequently, so she didn't hold the banker's arm for long.

Song after song played. Blackie bumped her into a couple during the two-step. Checkerboard's enormous boots stomped on her toes three times. So much for his promise.

Trevor approached her. "Is something wrong, Miss Amelia?"

"My feet hurt. Mind if we sit this one out?"

"Not at all." He brought her outside to a cushioned bench.

The slight breeze cooled her warm cheeks. Trevor fanned himself with his hat.

"Tell me about Los Flores Ranch." Several years back, she had dated an architect who was remodeling a home for the owners, but in her time. She'd admired how the river snaked through the tranquil and secluded property. Acres of emptiness was not her idea of paradise. And once given a tour the stables, she asked to be taken home. Horses terrified her.

"Reckon the best words to describe the place, pretty and peaceful."

Might as well say boring unless you're into hiking with bovine. She tried not to think about the isolation because she planned to speak with the McGraw's about a job. Maybe it wouldn't be as horrific as she imagined. Maybe the school would be located far from horses and creatures. Maybe she'd lost her mind.

The music stopped, and people gravitated outside. Dusty appeared, and Trevor waved him over. "You mind keeping company with Miss Amelia? I'm dying for a drink and hate to see her out here all alone, fending off suitors."

She would've jabbed Trevor in the side if he were her uncle.

"I'd be honored." Dusty bowed.

Trevor hurried off, caught up with an attractive brunette and escorted her inside.

Dusty eased into the wooden seat and placed his arm on the edge of the bench around her shoulders.

"Think you're sly?"

"Guess you caught me, darlin'." His former redheaded partner pranced past, and he eyed her. "I see Rebecca finally has Mitch's attention." The kerosene lamplight enhanced Dusty's chiseled features. "You have a bone to pick with her?"

In her head, she was back in high school, battling for her boyfriend. Could she explain her exasperation without appearing juvenile? She'd be truthful—kind of.

"Rebecca reminds me of a girl from my home town. Um ... we weren't exactly friends."

"Not friends with you? Hard to believe."

She laughed. "I know."

"Appreciate your honesty."

Honesty. If she told the real truth about herself, she'd be locked up. Asylums weren't pretty in this century.

Dusty snatched two glasses from a waiter's tray.

A whiskey nip laced her drink. She downed her glass, relishing in a pleasant euphoria.

"Who's your next partner?"

She opened her card and scrolled to the middle. "Reynolds Butler."

"I'd rather you'd dance with me." He gulped down his drink and coughed. "It's spiked."

"Thought it tasted odd." She hiccupped. "Warmed my insides a bit."

He put his hand over hers. An electric shock arced back and forth.

Reynolds strolled up to her. "May I have the honor of this dance?"

She fanned her face with her dance card. "Of course, Mr. Butler?" She thought of Rhett Butler in *Gone with the Wind*. When she peeked over at Dusty, he didn't smile.

"Mr. Butler makes me think of my father. Call me Reynolds, please." His deep husky voice matched his masculine features.

"Only if you call me, Mia."

"Sure thing." He led her to the ballroom floor, and the waltz began. Reynolds held his right arm between her shoulder and waist and took her hand. His breath smelled like tobacco and whiskey. Not an unpleasant scent, but not, well, not Dusty.

"Do you plan to stay around town much longer?" Reynolds turned to the left.

"I'm not sure. It depends if I get a job teaching at the Los Flores Ranch." She prayed for a miracle. A personal locomotive to bring her back where she belonged.

"I'll put in a favorable word for you. My uncle owns the ranch." His voice came out strong and confident.

From her perspective, men who liked to flaunt connections were usually insecure. His cuteness factor dropped by a million.

~ * ~

Dusty stepped up to the counter separating the ballroom from the dining room. An older woman ladled punch into a crystal glass. "Nice to see you, Mabel."

"My, oh my, if it isn't Dusty Mann." She batted her eyes and handed him a glass. "You find yourself a good woman yet?"

"I've tried, ma'am. The problem is you're already taken."

The woman blushed. "Charming as ever, just like your pa and granddad."

His pa died when he was four, so he barely remembered him. His grandfather died six years ago leaving Dusty with bitterness and regret. Dwelling never did much good.

He gravitated toward the bar. Suds splashed as the bartender slid a glass of beer down the polished mahogany counter to a big man in a plaid shirt and pants with black suspenders. The man caught the thick handle and held up the mug.

"What'll it be?" The bartender puffed his cigar.

"Coffin varnish." Dusty downed the whiskey and spotted Mia on the dance floor. Reynolds spun her, and she gave him a flirty smile.

Dusty motioned the bartender for another and allowed the liquid amber to send a slow burn to his gut.

Checkerboard came up. "Buy you a beer?"

"Be obliged." Dusty's eyes drifted to Mia laughing as she danced the round.

"You interested in her?" Checkerboard asked.

"I reckon."

His friend finished his beer and left. Dusty thought about heading outside. He polished off his brew and spotted her polkaing with Trevor.

The woman churned his emotions.

"Folks, it's time for our last number," the caller announced.

His turn again, finally. "Shall we dance?"

She took a step back, and her lips pressed into thin lines. "You like to drink?" Her voice held a mad-dog yip.

"On occasion. Needed a smidgen of courage to dance with you again."

"You're impossible." Her eyes didn't judge, they twinkled amusement.

"Been called worse." He bowed a *how do you do*. She curtsied. He caught a glimpse of her calves, and his pulse quickened. He *dos-si-doed* around her. Promenading, he pulled her closer, gazing into her bewitching green eyes.

"First couple balance swing," the caller shouted. "Down the center and divide the ring."

Dusty stepped over to the men's row. She stood in the women's line on the opposite side. She clapped as couples joined hands and glided down the middle and took their place at the end. The line moved up until he and Mia reached the front for their turn. They met in the center. She froze. Dusty pulled her forward.

"Sorry." She sashayed across the floor with him. "Must've been zoning."

"Zoning?" Whiskey addled his thinking.

"Um, not paying attention."

"Your citified talk can be mighty confusing." She might not mean to make him feel ignorant, but her manner of talking proved they were leagues apart in their upbringings.

"I don't mean to be."

They finished their jaunt and took their separate lines.

"Promenade," the caller said.

Mia was his partner again. With his arm around her, he appreciated her slim waist no bigger than a loaf of bread or two. "I could get used to this."

"Not a very original line."

"No line, the truth."

His boss waved from across the circle. "There's Westin and his wife, Sandy. They own Los Flores."

Her steps faltered.

"They're right genial folks." He hoped to put her at ease.

"That's what I've heard." Instead of her shoulders relaxing, her whole body stiffened.

Dang. He'd never been much good at comforting.

The song ended. One whiff of her perfume and impure ideas captured his mind. To get his thinking under control, he silently thought about the color of horses. Chestnut, bay, palomino, pinto.

"You planning to spend the night in the middle of the floor?" Her comment shocked him into action.

"Nope." He entwined his fingers with hers—dainty and smooth.

The band packed up to leave. People stopped and gathered their sleepy children. Others converged in the center of the room.

As he and Mia entered the lobby, he planned to whisk her outside on the veranda, but Jenny waved them over.

Dusty whispered, "Hoped for some time alone with you."

She gripped his hand as firmly as he gripped his lasso as they continued.

"Westin, Sandy, this is Miss Amelia Kellogg," Dusty introduced her.

Her top lip trembled a might, showing worry. Her confidence switched in the time it takes a flea to bite a dog.

Westin tipped his hat. "My nephew says you're a teacher. Would you consider teaching at our place?"

"I may be interested in the position." She shifted back on her heels.

"What's your background?" Westin folded his arms.

"I ... I attended college in ... Los Angeles. Graduated with honors."

"Where have you taught?" Westin asked.

"In the city." She kept her answers vague, a trick Dusty often used.

"May I ask why you left?"

"I needed to take care of my grandmother." She blinked, her words tumbled out slow and steady.

Sandy whispered in Westin's ear.

"Our last teacher eloped in January, so we'd like to hire someone right away." Westin kept his gaze steady on Mia. "Since it's summer, the classes end before lunch. Salary's two dollars a week. Includes room and board. If you work out, it'll go up to five dollars, come fall, when the children attend full days. You interested?"

She flinched for a mere second, then pasted on a smile. "Yes."

Dusty wanted to shout, "Yippee," but with her being a refined lady, he figured it best to keep quiet.

"Our buggy's full of supplies or we'd take you to the ranch ourselves." Westin said, and turned to Dusty, "Think you can escort Mia after church tomorrow? Maybe take Trevor with you."

"You've got it."

"Pleasure meeting you, Miss Kellogg," Westin said.

"I'm looking forward to working with your children," Mia's voice cracked.

Why was she nervous? It might be she'd never been employed away from the city.

Westin and Sandy left, but not Jenny. She planted her hands on her hips. "Don't worry none with Trevor or Dusty. They'll get you there safely."

"Of course, we will," he snapped, riled at the notion the proprietress planted.

"Better supervise the cleanup of this ball." Jenny scooted off, her orchid gown swishing.

"Care for a moonlight stroll?" Dusty asked.

"Not tonight. I'm pretty exhausted."

Not the least bit tuckered, Dusty hid his dismay. "Then may I see you to your door?"

"That would be nice." She yawned.

He escorted her up the stairs. Shadows cast from the lamps lighting her perfect profile. "Church is tomorrow at nine. I'd be more 'n happy to take you." Unbelievable. Of all places, he'd asked to escort her to church. They reached her door. "See you at breakfast."

"Make sure there's plenty of coffee."

"Coffee?" He'd expected her to change her mind or rush inside.

"Without my caffeine fix, I can't think."

Figuring caffeine was a fancy word for brown gargle, he chuckled. "Seems we have something in common."

She smiled, her full lips practically begging him for a goodnight kiss, but it'd be improper kissing her so soon.

"See ya in the mornin'." He reckoned it'd be a long night.

~ * ~

Mia floated inside her room daydreaming about Dusty. *What a hunk.*

She flopped on her bed, swooning over a cowboy, a doomed cowboy. A man who belonged in another century—she belonged in the future. A man who thrived on wide-open spaces and a simple life—she thrived on fast food and shopping malls. A man who raced his horse—she raced her BMW.

Nothing wrong with breakfast. But church? A sacred place. She valued honesty. Her survival here depended on being deceitful. From her experience, liars usually got caught.

She shivered. Okay, focus on something else.

Today is June second. According to the article, Dusty hanged on July fourth.

One week, the ninth. Two weeks, the sixteenth. Three weeks, the twenty-third. Four weeks, the thirtieth. Twenty-eight plus four equals thirty-two. Thirty-two days to try to stop Dusty's demise.

A loud whistle sounded.

She ran to the window. A locomotive slowed at the station. *Is it here to take me home?*

She doubted she'd get on, but curiosity made her want to see for herself if this was the same train. She grabbed her purse off the bed, scrambled down the hall, and snatched a lit lantern hung on a hook near the outside stairwell. Slipping on the first step, she held tight to the railing, rushed to the ground and across the street. Yellowish shadow-creatures formed from the lantern. An owl's hoot made her uneasy.

Her ring got warmer by the second, and she twisted it.

She reached the bottom of the depot's stairs, sucking in a ragged breath. The engine's firebox glowed red-orange. A billowing black smoke cloud enveloped around her. The whistle blasted.

"All aboard," the conductor yelled.

Another whistle announced its departure. The engine rumbled and chugged forward and kept moving. Yards from the caboose, her eyes stung from the thick smoke, and she couldn't tell if this was her train. The urge to remove her hot ring tugged at her, but she kept it on. As much as she wanted to go home, Dusty would be a a goner if she left. Still might be if she couldn't figure out a way to keep him from the hangman. The smoke disappeared as did the train. Somehow, this must be her portal back to her time.

She tripped on a loose board and fell to her knees. The lantern slipped from her fingers. It shattered making the stars above seemed brighter. She picked out the Big Dipper. The constellation seemed like a sign that eventually, she'd make it home.

But what if she missed her only chance to get back? Could she be stuck here forever? Not her idea of fun.

With no idea how much time had passed, she stood and brushed off her clothes. Under the soft moonlight, she trudged toward the hotel's flickering lights—alone, uncertain, optimistic.

Chapter Five

Beep. Beep. Beep.

Sunday morning Dusty stood in line at the side counter, piling his dish with sourdough bread, scrambled eggs, bacon, fried potato wedges, and flapjacks. He waited along the wall on the end. Mia walked by him.

"Hello, darlin'." He tipped his Stetson.

"Hey." Pink crept up her cheeks. With her hair in a loose bun, her white collared-blouse accentuated her slender neck. She seemed distracted; her eyes had lost their sparkle; her step lacked energy.

He led her to the dining room. "You okay?"

"Sure." Her refusal to look at him contradicted her reply. Where was that wit, quicker than the first rattler out of a box?

A funny line might change her temperament. His mind drew a blank. He put his plate on the closest table to the entrance and pulled out her chair on the opposite side. The server poured each of them steaming coffee.

Adding a generous portion of cream, she used her spoon to stir and stir and stir.

"Think the cream is plenty mixed."

She released the spoon like it was blazing hot. "Suppose you're right." Her melancholy tone and restrained demeanor chaffed his pride a bit. It was as if she didn't want to be sitting with him. As he passed the crystal butter dish closer, his fingers brushed hers. "Pardon me." The brief contact ignited sinful sensations.

"You say something?" She sampled a slice of melon and ran her tongue along her upper lip. A blush colored her cheeks.

"Just said you look beautiful."

She giggled.

"Are you questioning my integrity?" He believed in acting honorable.

Westin and Sandy McGraw approached their table.

Mia froze, reminding him of a mouse caught under a cat's paw.

"Since you'll be at our ranch this afternoon, I'll make sure your room's aired, and there's fresh linen." Sandy gave a friendly smile.

"Th-anks." Her answer hitched. She acted nothing like the lively, confident gal he danced with last night.

The couple left, and she let out a deep breath.

"You're different today, disconcerted."

She sipped her coffee. "Well, starting a new job makes me nervous."

Now he understood. "Don't let the jitters get to you. Those kids are lucky having such a pretty and smart teacher."

"What a nice thing to say."

He caught a hint of vulnerability. Had she mourned the decision to accept the job?

"You know, my last teacher named the dunce corner Dusty," he said, keeping the conversation light.

"Bet you were the teacher's pet."

He couldn't help chuckling. "Maybe when I was six."

~ * ~

Mia held Dusty's arm and leisurely strolled along Government Road's boarded walkway. On a creosote bush, birds chirped and leaped from branch to branch. She longed to feel as carefree.

A horse and buggy kicked up dust. She removed her arm from his and rubbed her right eye.

"That'll only push the dirt in deeper." He offered a clean white handkerchief from his shirt pocket. "Try this."

Men in her day never carried hankies or acted this considerate. Dabbing the cloth to her eye, she got out most of the gunk. If only her ability to return home could be solved as easily.

They turned left and paused at the railroad tracks. The same railroad tracks where hours earlier she watched the train disappear. Her ring sparkled, and she twisted it. Exhaust fumes caused her eyes to water. Tires squealed. Cars sped past on the paved street.

Blinking, the scene disappeared. No cars, no tires, no paved street. Only dirt and dust, Joshua trees and creosote bushes.

They continued toward a white brick building. The Old Hesperia Church. Not old—modern for this era. They followed a couple up the stairs to the entrance. Inside, she stepped on a creaky floorboard. People turned and stared.

Not one to crave attention, she'd love to be invisible.

"Smile, darlin'," Dusty whispered, "Folks are as fascinated by you as I am."

She pasted on a parade-like smile and pretended she belonged in this church.

The back pews were full, forcing her and Dusty to head to the front.

"Over here." Jenny motioned to the empty seats by her.

She scooted next to the woman, making room for Dusty near the aisle.

"Heard Trevor eloped last night after the dance," the proprietress looked to Dusty.

"So he finally got up the nerve." Dusty shook his head.

"He's been sweet on Dottie Dolton for some time."

"Is that the tall brunette I saw him with?" Mia asked.

"Sure is. Means I'll be losing a good hand. He's mighty handy with a rope."

"Won't he come back?" Mia liked having Trevor around.

"Not likely. Seems Dottie recently inherited some property near Los Angeles." Jenny scooted closer to Mia. "This weekend was eventful. The dance. The elopement. And you, Miss Kellogg, were quite a sensation last night."

"She sure was." Dusty's hand brushed the side of hers. Her whole arm tingled at his touch.

The pianist played "Amazing Grace." Six women in robes sang along.

A short, stocky man with mousy brown hair and round glasses stood behind the pulpit. The preacher belabored the importance of virtue. "Devious and deceptive conduct will bring you to eternal damnation."

It seemed as if the man of the cloth communicated to her personally, and she squirmed. She didn't like pretending to be a teacher, pretending to belong. Packed in close on the hard bench, Dusty's thigh pressed against her leg creating urges that shouldn't be burning while inside a house of worship.

Light shimmered through the stained-glass Jesus. His crown of thorns made her think of death. Dusty's death. A supposed God-fearing patron might implicate him. Glancing over her shoulder two rows behind her, Reynolds noticed her and winked. The wink made her stomach clench. Next to him, Slick's Stetson covered his face.

The congregation sang a few more hymns, and the service ended. People filed toward the foyer exit. The banker smiled at her. Others waved as she stood in the reception line.

Jenny pushed ahead of her. "Pastor Thomas. This is Amelia Kellogg, the new Los Flores teacher."

The pastor grasped her hand. "I'm honored to make your acquaintance and hope you'll visit here again soon."

"I will if I'm in town." If she had her way, she'd figure out how to keep Dusty from hanging and be back to her own time soon.

The preacher focused on Dusty. "Been a long time, Harold."

"Yep." He placed his hands on her shoulders and ushered her down the stairs.

"What's your hurry?" she asked.

His strides got wider. "Need to get moving."

"The truth?"

"I like that you don't mince words." He paused, looking at the ground. "Church makes me as jumpy as a bit up old bull at fly time."

"You're funny." His diction tickled her. He should be cast in a western movie.

"What'd you think of the service?"

"It was tolerable."

"You didn't pay attention, did you?" His boyish grin made her heart pound. "Pastor's voice usually puts me to sleep right away, but not today."

"Why?"

"You were mighty distracting."

Thoughts tumbled wildly as she glanced at his rugged face. Her heart pitter-pattered instead of being sensible. Unable to ignore his charm, she said, "You're hopeless."

"You don't seem to mind." He pressed his lips to her forehead.

The simple move made her wonder what it'd be like to kiss him.

They paused at the railroad tracks. She twisted her ring, hoping for another image of her time.

"Is there a problem?"

An enormous, inconceivable, forsaken problem. She didn't want Dusty to hang. "Um, no." She fiddled with the handle of her purse. "Just adjusting my pocket book."

"I'm right pleased you'll be working at the ranch." Dusty drawled low and sexy.

The ranch. The remote ranch. The non-modern ranch. How would she ever persevere?

She clutched his arm as they stepped onto the walkway. Women in their Sunday best spun parasols in front of the general store. Cowboys, with checkered shirts and vests, Stetsons and holstered pistols, headed toward the saloon. Children chased and tagged each other. "You're it."

"Since Trevor's gone off, suppose I'll be bringing you to the ranch by myself." He removed his hat, combing his fingers through his cropped hair. "If it's okay?"

Nothing about traveling to the ranch without a car and air conditioning was okay, but being without other options, she nodded.

He tipped his hat. "Be back within the hour."

Gorgeous, charming cowboy. In her experience, not a good combination. She strolled inside and up the stairs to her hotel room.

Packing took all of two seconds. A book, *Compliments of the Hesperia Hotel,* lay on the dresser. Thumbing through it, she found every page blank.

Might as well draw. She brought the journal to a table by the window, dipped a nib into an inkwell and sketched an oval. Added penetrating eyes, dimples, a square chin shaded with day-old beard, a black Stetson.

Dusty.

The guy invaded her mind and now her art.

A soft knock rapped on her door.

She hid her sketchbook under an embroidered towel on the dresser and opened the door. "You're fast." Her eyes met the round face of Jenny. "Oh."

"Figured you might like lemonade after your jaunt to church."

"Thanks." She took a sip. "This is delicious."

"I've enjoyed having you as a guest. You'll come back soon, won't you?" Jenny's eyes crinkled.

If only she could stay at this hotel with room service, running water, a general store within walking distance. She ingested her plea and tasted trepidation.

"You must come to our Independence Day celebration next month. It's great fun."

The day of Dusty's hanging. She somehow managed to choke out, "I'll think about it."

"Please do."

Was there a way to change the newspaper's story? Movies about time travel portrayed how changing one event creates disruption in the future. This new life isn't fiction or some type of game, it's reality.

"I'll save you a room, just in case." Jenny eyed her with optimism.

"Thanks. How long will it take to get to the ranch?" If only she could drive her BMW M6.

"Couple of hours. It's fairly flat most of the way."

The buggy seats better be well-padded.

"Have a pleasant journey." Jenny hugged her and left.

Mia slipped her sketchbook inside her purse, took out her Gucci sunglasses and modeled them in the mirror. Damn. Plastic had yet to be invented, so she slipped them inside her bag.

The heavy knock must be Dusty. She opened the door.

Lean hips, broad shoulders, and a black Stetson— a man belonging on the cover of *American Cowboy*.

"Ready?" He picked up her bag.

She nodded.

Outside they stopped at a post where two horses were hitched. "You'll be riding Half-Pint."

Dusty's gigantic stallion snorted and flared his nostrils.

Her legs trembled. She backed up several steps. "You're joking, right?"

"Nope." He tied her bag to a ring on the saddle.

She held her stance. "Borrow a buggy. I'm not riding on that—that monster."

"No time for dawdling." His strong hands encircled her waist, lifting her, forcing her legs to straddle the saddle. He secured her feet in the stirrups and handed her the reins, swung onto his own mount and both animals lurched forward.

I should've caught that train. "Damn cowboy!" she shouted.

He had the audacity to laugh.

Chapter Six

As the horse trotted on uneven ground, Mia fought to stay on. If she lost her balance, she'd plummet into cacti, tarantulas, scorpions, rattlesnakes, and other creepy desert dwellers. Tugging and jostling the reins, she shouted, "Turn around you blasted horse."

The smelly beast snorted and whinnied. It better not stretch its head and use its gigantic teeth to take a chunk out of her leg.

Dusty's stallion picked up his pace. Her idiotic horse galloped faster, slamming her pelvis into the unforgiving saddle. Up and down, up and down, up and down. Sweat sheened on her forehead and dripped into her eyes. "Stupid horse—asinine cowboy."

He slowed his steed and fell in next to her. "If I could give you one piece of advice, follow Half-Pint's gait. You'll have a smoother ride."

She'd give him the finger if she weren't afraid of letting go of the reins and falling. "If you were a gentleman, we'd be in a buggy."

"Never said I was a gentleman."

If he were closer, she'd throttle him, make him beg for mercy.

"We'll take a break up the hill at the summit."

"Yes, master," she said in her most sarcastic tone.

"I like your spirit." He kicked his horse to a canter.

"Don't you have a brain of your own?" She yelled at her mount. The insipid horse increased his speed.

Dusty slowed his mount at the top of a hill and stopped. Her horse did the same.

"Isn't this sight spectacular?"

"It's passable." So what if she saw a panoramic view of the entire valley? Her mind struggled between agitation versus giving into curiosity. Curiosity won, and she looked around. No housing tracks where homes were built so closely together, you could reach out your window and shake hands with your neighbor. No hazy brown pollution from cars and factories. No tall telephone poles connected by thick wires.

Hesperia's main drag passed for the miniature buildings from her brother's train set. Unpaved roads trailed in both directions. Bushes and grass outlined the wide, twisting Mojave River. Cabins, buildings and livestock scattered along the hillsides.

In another century, most of the pristine loveliness would be mowed down in the name of progress. She'd taken this area for granted, speeding by without much thought. As impressive as this sight had been, she refused to give an inch to Dusty. Not after her atrocious ride. "It'd be prettier from a buggy." Her voice sliced through the silence.

"Not according to your eyes." Crap. He'd read her thoughts.

"You're mistaken." She sat tall in the saddle. Her back ached, but she refused to admit weakness.

"Am I?" His mocking tone annoyed her.

The ride continued. Each jarring trot rattled her spine. The rigid pommel between her legs rubbed her sensitive areas. "Jerk, asshole, idiot, brute, cowboy." She shouted every derogatory word she could think of.

Either their horses' clomping hoofs drowned out her language or he ignored her. She figured the latter. As they gradually descended, she relaxed her grip on the reins and flexed her throbbing fingers.

Hours underneath the sun scorched her neck. How stupid? She'd left a partial tube of sunscreen in her purse. Reaching for the saddlebag, she kicked the horse's side.

The animal made a horrendous squeal and bolted.

"Stooooop!" If she fell at this speed, she'd break her neck. She gripped the horn with both hands, squeezed her leg muscles and struggled to stay on. "I don't wanna die." The horse galloped toward a tree. Low branches scratched her arms as she held on with all her might.

"Whoa!" Dusty rode up alongside her horse. Like a circus stunt, he reached over to grab the reins and slowed the horse to a stop.

Her body rippled with fear.

He dismounted and helped her to the ground. "Are you alright?"

"Not after that monster tried to kill me." Her legs buckled.

"I'm sorry." He swept her into his arms, forcing her to cling onto his neck to steady herself. Gently, he placed her on a grassy knoll and lowered into a spot close to her. "Half-Pint's gentler than a pet rabbit. Only bolted 'cause your kick told him to run."

"Really? You're siding with a horse? Horses terrify me." And she'd spent two hours in the saddle. "Told you when we first met."

"Reckon your pretty face distracted me."

75

She groaned. How did she ever find him charming? Right now, she rated him as equal to a horse, no, make it a swine.

He gave her a don't-be-mad-at-me smile. "During our first encounter, you were scared of one particularly large horse, didn't reckon you meant all horses."

"You assumed I'd be cool riding. When I asked for a buggy, you threw me on that horse like a barbaric caveman. My bottom aches as if it's been whipped with a wooden paddle." She sighed. "You're nuts. Absolutely certifiable."

He closed his eyes. "Everybody around here rides, and so should you."

Her blood pressure must've shot to over a zillion. "I'm not like everyone else." Hot and perturbed, she undid the top button of her blouse. "I've had it. I can't take any more of you."

She stood and kicked the ground scattering stones, stomped on the rough terrain ignoring her aching legs and chapped thighs. Her pointy shoes pinched. The heel stepped on a squishy spot. A brown lizard scurried away. Under her foot, its wiggling tail remained. "Serves you right you loser lizard."

"You're pretty when fired up." Dusty stood in front of her, stepped closer and brushed his fingers along her cheek.

She slapped his hand away. "Leave me alone."

"That's a nasty scratch."

"Blame it on your gentle as a rabbit horse who charged me into a tree."

"I'm right sorry 'bout his manners." He spoke low and soothing. "Now come along. Don't want your cut festering."

She let out an I-give-up groan. Without penicillin, an infection could be deadly.

He guided her to the grassy area. "I'll be right back."

"Like I care." She shouldn't watch his long strides or his form-fitted jeans accentuating his muscular thighs. She closed her eyes and twisted her ring. *Please Mr. Wizard, take me home.*

Of course, nothing happened.

And he had the nerve to whistle. His spurs jingled as he strutted back. "Did you miss me?"

"Nope." She let him spread out the plaid blanket by himself.

"Have a seat."

She plunked down.

He must've seen her wince because he dropped to his knees. "I'll take care of your scratch."

"Fine. If you hadn't thrown me on that horse—," she said with clenched teeth.

"Quite a firebrand, aren't you?" He used his canteen, poured water on a soft cloth, and carefully cleaned her left cheek. His caring manner made it hard for her to stay livid, but she wouldn't let him know that.

"This may sting." He dabbed foul-smelling salve on her cheek and arm. Tracing the side of her face with his index finger, he said, "You're tough for such a pretty little gal."

Okay, she liked tough, but not the little part.

He inched closer. "Got lemonade to sweeten the deal?"

She shrugged. "Better be sweeter than sarsaparilla."

He took out a canteen from the basket and poured the drink into a metal cup. The cup might be made of lead. Thirsty, she guzzled the lemonade anyway. "The drink's sweet. Could be cooler."

Dusty unwrapped an oilcloth and offered her a piece of fried chicken. "I made a mistake. Most likely make plenty more."

She crossed her arms not quite ready to succumb to his effort to apologize.

"Darlin', have you ever made an error?"

"Nothing I care to admit."

"Someday, I hope to know all your secrets."

Yeah. If she said she's from the future, he'd have her committed.

"I'll share something nobody else knows." He took a bite of chicken. "Not much scares me 'cept scorpions. Stung as a kid, got sick, nearly died."

"Scorpions aren't as bad as my twin brothers' pet tarantula."

"Don't mind spiders."

"You would if you woke with one crawling on your pillow." She shivered. The hairy arachnid had been next to her cheek. Her brothers were relentless with their stunts.

"Might." He opened a wrapper and offered her strawberries. His eyes stayed focused on her mouth. "Sweet, red, tempting." Leaning in, he traced her lips with his thumb.

She hadn't fully forgiven him. "Red, huh. Like the red spot on the underside of a black widow."

"What an absurd notion." He chuckled as he poured her more lemonade, polished off two more chicken legs, and she ate a chicken breast.

"If you're up to standing, I'd like to show you the ranch from here." He guided her to the edge of a ravine.

"You thinking of throwing me over?"

"Never, darlin'." With his arm around her, she breathed in his musky scent. "See the house to the right."

She nodded, way too aware of him.

"That's the Campbell spread."

"Is your ranch far from here?"

"An hour's ride." He pointed south. "The buildings forming a horseshoe shape are part of Los Flores."

"Cool."

"Cool?" He leaned down pressed his lips against her cheek.

"I'm still mad at you." Kind of.

"Don't be."

"Easy for you to say. You're not the one with the sore bottom." She tried to move away.

He held her firm, but not demanding. "I'll do my best to make it up to you." His steadfast gaze caused her mind to turn to mush.

"See the black horse kicking up her heels?"

She squinted. "I think so. It looks like a black spot from here."

"That's Bella. She's a thoroughbred. The boss owns about ten now."

"You own many horses yourself?"

"Just Thunder."

Did she hear sadness in his voice? "Something wrong?" she asked.

"Not with you in my arms." A big eared jack rustled in the bushes and hopped past. She found it cute. "Over yonder, you can faintly make out Cedar Springs. The tall point is the top of their church."

"The town is underneath Silverwood," she stopped. Now was not the time to tell him about the twenty-first century. "I mean ... um ... is that a silver-crested ... hawk flying over us."

He glanced up. "All I see are a couple of buzzards." Tracing her cheek with his forefinger, he said, "You're a heck of a lot more enchanting."

"Than buzzards?" She couldn't help laughing. "I should hope so."

"If you're up to it, we'll head for the ranch."

She would prefer going back to town. As they went toward their picnic area, they passed Half-Pint chomping grass on a hill. "Don't make me get back on that monster!" Her heart thudded loudly in her ears.

"I won't. You're riding with me." After he'd tied Half-Pint's reins to the pommel of his stallion, he carefully placed her in the saddle.

She remained motionless. "Get me off. I hate heights. I'll walk."

He mounted behind her. "I won't let you fall. You're safe with me."

"Hardly."

He stiffened. "Don't you trust me?"

"Not much."

"I may be ornery at times, but you can count on my honesty." His prickled pride came out in his tone.

He might be honest, while she'd been forced to be less than truthful. "Why are you telling me this?"

"Figured you oughta know." He pulled her against his rock-hard abs and tightened his hold. "Close your eyes. We'll be at the ranch within the hour. I'll take it slow while you nap."

The rocking motion made her sleepy. She saw Dusty on a horse under a large oak tree. The hangman put the noose around his neck, and she yelled, "Don't hang him. He's innocent."

"Shh, darlin'." Hands softly shook her awake. "You're having a nightmare."

"Dusty?" She opened her eyes. "It seemed so real."

"You're trembling. Who hanged?" His warm breath blew along her neck.

"You." She couldn't stop shaking.

"For making you ride Half-Pint?" He gave a dismissive snort.

She hit his arm. "You're not funny."

"Suppose not," he drawled. "Obviously you're upset. Reckon I'd be a bit rattled at such a dream, but there's no need to fret. I have no intention of getting lynched."

"It could happen. Please be careful." She had to warn him.

"Yes, ma'am." He acted like she was joking. Typical cowboy—exasperating, hard headed, never listened.

"We're on Los Flores property. Ten minutes and we'll be at the house."

"Oh." She wouldn't survive. Breathe. In and out. *I have to do this.*

Along the trail, she spotted a cluster of quail. "It's adorable how the mother quail and her chicks bob in synch with each other."

"Adorable." His tone said otherwise.

Cattle bellowed. The horse plodded on a bridge over the Mojave River. Water lapped along the shore.

"I envy the duck. His only concern seems to be those coots invading his space." Nothing like her current dilemma.

"Prefer them plucked and barbecued."

"Thanks for ruining my fantasy."

"You can always fantasize about me."

"No way." She leaned back into his broad chest. They moved toward a pentagonal-shaped red barn.

A young boy rode up alongside them on a black spotted pony. "Howdy, partner," the child called.

Dusty wore a wide grin. "Hey J.J. You shoot any rustlers lately?"

The boy made a fake gun with his fingers. "Only a couple—bang—bang." He kicked his horse, galloped toward the ranch house, jumped off, and shouted, "Ma—Dusty's got a lady with him."

Chapter Seven

Cami snagged her puffy pink jacket from a hook on Mia's legs operated like Jell-O as she met the McGraw's outside their ranch home. She missed having Dusty's arms wrapped around her, giving her a false sense of well-being.

Westin pushed his boy forward. "Son, this lady is Miss Amelia Kellogg."

"Howdy." The boy spoke with his two top teeth missing.

"She's your new teacher," Sandy said matter of factly.

J.J.'s smile vanished. Proof he didn't want to attend school. The other kids would probably act the same.

"I'll help you tend the horses," Westin told Dusty. "Come along, J.J."

"See you at dinner." Dusty grabbed his horse's reins and followed the boss.

Her impulse was to run, but she had nowhere to go.

"It's been a long journey. Let's go inside where it's cooler."

As she stepped into the spacious parlor, the open wood-beamed ceilings gave the room a modern style. Scattered area rugs covered polished oak flooring. Sandy sat on an overstuffed couch.

She took a floral-covered chair and focused on the massive fireplace. Knickknacks and framed photos lined the wooden mantle. "Your house is beautiful, Mrs. McGraw."

"It's Sandy. We're not formal around here."

"Then call me, Mia." She loosened her grip on the chair's arm.

A large woman in a starched white apron held a silver tray with glasses and a plate of muffins.

"Thank you, Cookie," Sandy said. "This is Mia, our new teacher."

"Hi." Out of habit, she held out her hand and remembered to drop it to her side a nanosecond later. Women didn't shake hands in this era.

"Heard Trevor got hitched. Gonna miss that man," Cookie said. "Always had a ready smile and a kind word to say."

"Westin's lost a good hand." Sandy's eyes softened. "But I'm happy for him."

Mia tried not to be selfish, but she really needed him to advise her. He made her feel safe in this crazy old-fashioned world.

J.J. came running in. "Mom, Mary Bell's kittens are here."

"James John McGraw. Apologize to Miss Kellogg for interrupting our conversation." Sandy used a harsh tone, opposite to her expression.

"My apologies, ma. Ma'am."

Sandy tilted her head. "Shouldn't you be helping your pa?"

"Pa said I got underfoot." J.J. gave an impish grin. "And then I found the kitties. You've gotta see them."

"Finding newborn kittens is exciting," Sandy said. "But Miss Amelia is weary from her long ride, and I need to show her to her quarters. After I get her settled, you can show me."

"Ma, please—"

"It won't take long."

Sandy ruffled J.J.'s hair.

"I'd like to see the kittens if it's all right." Kittens she could handle. Maybe one of them would look like her tabby, Tiger.

"Sure, if Ma says so."

Every step along the pathway caused her muscles to ache, but she refused to let the ride get to her. They passed outdoor corrals. A horse whinnied. Trepidation shimmied up her spine.

"Bella Sheba's like a princess. She's a thur-bread," J.J. lisped.

"Thoroughbred." Sandy corrected.

"That's what I said." J.J. pointed to the filly. "Pa says she'll win the Can't Derby."

"Kentucky Derby." Sandy gave her son a warm smile. "Can't wait to see how fast Bella runs in a few years. She's spirited and fast like her sire, Midnight Thief."

The filly frolicked around her pasture. Mia didn't mind the animal as long as it didn't come any closer. Then she remembered the stories about a thoroughbred, Allysheba, who won the Kentucky Derby in the 1980's. The horse had once been stabled at this ranch. Bella might be an ancestor.

"My husband's mighty proud of our new stable. Insisted on forty stalls, each rigged up to the watering pump."

Mia followed her inside and heard snorts and nickers. *Horses, please keep your distance, and I promise not to scream.*

"The kittens are in the last stall." The boy skittered toward the end.

She stayed in the middle of the aisle, praying she'd be free from danger.

The boy stopped at a stall near the door. "They're on the blanket," he shouted, covered his mouth, and whispered, "shh, we don't want to scare them."

The child was freaking adorable. She peeked inside. Fresh hay without any horses. Squinting, she noticed a striped cat camouflage with the cover, she picked out six fur balls nursing.

"Better let them sleep." Sandy patted her son on the head.

"Aw, can't we stay a little longer?" he said with a high-pitched-please-give-in tone.

"Not today."

He nodded but didn't throw a fit.

They exited from the opposite door and headed along a dirt road.

"We keep the mares and older colts in the outside stalls." Sandy stopped by a rusty-brown horse. "Hey, Elsa." She pulled out a carrot from her pocket and passed one to J.J. He fed a black horse in the next pen. "This is my mare. You want to feed her."

She backed up and shook her head. *Hell no.*

"Forgot you're worn ragged." Sandy's horse chomped the carrot.

Its enormous teeth could take off a finger. She would've run to her room if she had any idea where it might be.

They continued by the center of the horseshoe-shaped thoroughfare with shady trees, assorted flowers, and handcrafted benches. "That's my favorite spot to read," Sandy pointed toward a wagon wheel bench.

Tethered to hitching posts, horses whinnied and neighed. She moved on the other side of J.J., as far from the dreadful creatures as possible.

"There's the bunkhouse." J.J. pointed to a two-story building next to the stables. "Pa says I'm not supposed to bother the cowboys." His smirk suggested he'd snuck in a time or two.

A white-picket fence surrounded a tree-swing, teeter-totter, and rectangular building.

"The schoolhouse is in front. Your quarters are in the adjoining room at the back." Sandy led her up three steps, pulled a key from under the mat and went inside. "You'll find towels and sheets in this cupboard. Fresh water is right outside at the pump. The outhouse is straight ahead."

Porta potties were bad enough—but an outhouse? A stinky, dirty, unsanitary outhouse with bugs and rats and other creepy creatures lurking inside.

Sandy opened a battered wardrobe. "Feel free to wear anything you find in here. Previous tenants tend to leave things behind."

Mia hadn't brought much clothing with her, so she'd better be gracious. "Thanks. Everything's great."

"Supper's served at five in the dining hall behind our home. Gives you 'bout an hour to get settled." Sandy left.

No five-star hotel. Sparse, the room passed for fairly clean, except for the dust blowing in from the screenless opened window. She stood by the dresser, dipped a white cloth in the water basin, and washed her face with the bar of smelly soap. The fabric became brown with dirt. Picking up the heavy pitcher, she poured more water into a basin, wrung the soiled cloth, and wiped her face again. She sloshed water on the floor as she went to the porch, throwing the dirty liquid over the railing onto the ground. Never again would she take running water for granted. She missed the modern luxuries from her time. What if she never made it back? She sucked in a deep breath.

Her blotched red face reflected from the beveled mirror. She plunked on the edge of her bed. *Ouch,* her butt hurt.

She broke her pointer fingernail unhooking her shoes, ruining last week's French manicure.

Peeling off her stockings, blood caked onto her blistered heels. She crossed the planked floor to grab a clean towel out of the cupboard. At least a splinter didn't wedge into her foot.

She poured water into the basin, lugged it on the floor, and stuck her feet in it. Water made her open blisters throb. The soap stung. She fell back on her mattress in agony.

Her thighs were on fire. Unlacing the top of her petticoat and tossing it on the bed, the insides of her legs were red. Chafed raw.

Again, she got up and threw the filthy liquid off the porch. Pouring the last of the water in the basin, she dipped a fresh cloth with the stinky soap and wiped between her thighs. She screamed as her muscles spasmed.

~ * ~

Dusty stood outside Mia's door feeling jittery. Odd, he could tame the meanest stallion, but one little gal had him practically shaking in his boots. The first half of the ride to the ranch had been fast paced. He wouldn't be surprised if she took one look at him and slammed the door in his face. Still, after holding her in his arms, he yearned to be near her. He knocked three times.

"Coming." Strands of hair strayed from her bun as she opened the door. The covers lay rumpled on the bed. "Give me a minute."

He pictured her sleeping, her long locks fanned against the pillow. His body stirred. "I'll wait outside 'till you're ready."

A mocking bird swooped and chased a sparrow, as he leaned against a tree. A chipmunk chittered and scattered a couple acorns onto Dusty's boot.

Mia tapped him on the shoulder. "Let's go." She wore a simple cotton gown that accentuated her tiny waist and flared around her hips.

"Do I have dirt on my nose?"

"Not a speck. You're gorgeous." It'd be easy to lean down and kiss her. Instead, he offered his arm, and they strolled along the path, she limped.

He stopped by a bench. "You'd best sit, and I'll get you some salve."

She batted her eyes. "If my pain becomes unbearable, you can carry me." Not berating him for being a brute, her teasing eyes tempted his control.

"Anywhere, in particular, you'd like to be carried?" He imagined bringing her to the meadow overlooking the river and—"

"I'd prefer a buggy and return to town."

"Just when I thought you might be sweet on me, you talk about leaving." He tried to keep his tone unaffected, while inside her words stung.

She pointed to a rundown cabin, its front yard full of tumbleweeds. "I take it nobody lives there."

"Not since Tex passed. The six-foot cowboy had an ornery personality, one that surpassed his size. Heard his ghost still haunts this place."

"Do you believe in ghosts?"

"Not sure. Figure I'll have to wait 'till I take my final ride out to the big ranch in the sky."

"Big ranch in the sky. You're nuts." They continued along the wide path. "What are the larger cabins for?"

"Cowboys with families."

"Is the rent more on those houses?"

"Nope, it's one of the ... " his throat closed, "well, privileges of being—"

"Married?" Her eyebrows raised.

"Yep." Not something he planned to do until he secured a ranch of his own.

They wound along the path toward the rear of the ranch house. The low mutter of voices grew louder as they neared the backyard. The savory scent of hickory and smoke drifted. "You're in for a treat. The boss' barbequing flank."

A couple dozen men, women, and children mulled around a table under the eaves of the building. Dusty gave her a plate. He piled on steak, potato salad, watermelon, and green beans. She took meager portions. No wonder the gal's so bitty; she ate like a robin.

Curious cowboys crowded 'round her.

"I'd better introduce you, or they won't leave us alone." She might feign confidence to the others, but Dusty recognized her nervous smile. The same nervous plastered-on smile she gave when she first met the McGraw's. "Men. This is Amelia Kellogg, the ranch's new teacher."

"Wish my teacher'd been purdy like her," he heard one of the men say.

Cowboys tipped their hats.

Dusty scanned the faces. "You've already met Blackie and Checkerboard."

"Nice to see you again." She nodded in their direction.

"The young pup's Scotty."

"Not that young, turned twenty last spring." The cowboy gave her a crooked-toothed grin. "It's a pleasure making your acquaintance, Miss Amelia."

Dusty escorted her to the only empty spots at the end of a picnic table across from Slick and Reynolds.

"You're mighty fetching today." Reynolds touched the rim of his Stetson.

"You're too kind." Did she just simper?

A surge of protectiveness hit Dusty, but he held back acting on it.

Children giggled from behind him. He turned his head. J.J. stood with two friends.

She pivoted sideways in her chair. "How are the kittens?"

"Eyes are open now. Once they get bigger, I'll talk ma into letting me keep one in my room."

"Good luck with that." Had she tried a similar tactic as a child?

"Won't need luck," J.J. said, giving an innocent grin of certainty.

"Who are your friends?" she asked.

"Norma and Ben."

She looked each one in the eye. "I'm honored to meet you."

"Do we really got to go to school in the summer?" the young, curly-haired Ben whined.

"I'm afraid so. I'll try to make it fun."

The boy backed up two steps. "Ain't sure I'll be there. Ma's counting on me catching fish for supper."

Norma twirled a ringlet around her finger and wrinkled up her nose. "I hate fish. They smell."

Dusty figured Mi held back a snicker.

Norma's mother came behind her little girl. "Hope she hasn't been bothering you."

"Not at all. I'm Mia Kellogg, her new teacher."

"Sandy told us 'bout you. Said you went to school in a big city."

"I did." She sat a little straighter.

"I'm mighty glad you'll be teaching my little girl."

"Me, too," Norma cut in. "I'm gonna be her helper." Her mother took her girl's hand and left.

Dusty concentrated on cutting his steak, chewing without paying attention to the taste. He'd prefer to taste Mia's lips.

"Poker game's starting." Slick said to Reynolds.

Reynolds stood, his eyes riveted to Mia. "Have a pleasant evening."

"Good luck, gentlemen." Did she have to smile at Reynolds?

"Gonna need it." Slick followed his friend.

She pushed her green beans to the side of her plate.

"What's the matter?"

"I don't belong here." She forked patterns in her watermelon. "They'll probably tar and feather me when they find out I'm an imposter who never taught a day in her life."

"That's cow dung."

"Did you call me cow dung?"

"No, darlin'. Called your misgivings manure."

Her glare made his tongue stumble. He had to get back on her good side. "I-I mean, well ... watching you with those youngins makes me wish I could be in your class."

"Even if I put you in the dunce's corner?"

"Wouldn't mind a bit." Shadows grew longer on the horizon. It'd be dark within the hour. "Care to take a stroll?"

"Promise you won't throw me on the back of a horse."

"You have my word."

"I wouldn't mind a short walk."

He led her outside, past the barn, and over a short narrow bridge to a dry gully. She walked stiffly. She could've whimpered, could've grumbled, could've censured.

He might apologize for being tough on her earlier today. Never been much good at the likes. He motioned to a worn wooden bench. "Let's sit underneath the tree."

She picked up the sides of her dress and eased into the seat. He settled next to her, brushed his fingers along the scratch on her cheek. "You're mighty special." His mouth lingered close, and her warm inviting lips parted.

A rock thudded against the bench. Another skidded off a tree. He yelled toward a spot where creosote bushes rustled. "Whoever's back there better show his face?"

A dark-haired boy ran between two creosote bushes. Dusty sprinted and caught him by the scruff of his collar. "Billy, I'm certain your pa taught you better manners." He pushed him toward the bench. "Apologize to Miss Kellogg."

"I'm sorry." Billy's high-pitched voice croaked, and he hid his slingshot behind his back.

"Try anything like this again, and I'll tan your hide. Be sure to tell your friends not to mess with Miss Kellogg, or they will be seeing me." Dusty let the boy go.

"Yes, sir. Sorry again, ma'am."

If she hadn't been watching, Dusty would've kicked the kid in the butt. She brought out his chivalrous side.

"Boys never change," she said with a sigh.

"Reckon it's true. I'd best take you to your quarters." Dusty tried to sound convincing.

"Can we stay here a little longer and watch the sunset?"

"If that's your fancy." He'd stay all night if she asked.

"The orange shades blend with pink like we're in a romantic mov ... um ... story."

"You're way prettier than any sunset." A spark ignited in a part of his brain, the part with clogged cobwebs. He stretched his arm behind her neck and leaned down, pressing his lips against hers and reveling in the softness. Her breath hitched as he claimed her mouth with a slow, deliberate kiss.

Her arms ringed around his neck. Her lips parted with a quiet mew, and he explored until sanity brought him to his senses. Pulling away, he gazed at her deprived expression, an expression matching his own thoughts. "As much as I like it out here with you, it's getting late. We don't want to give folks any fodder for gossip."

"I don't care if people talk." Attitude made up for her small stature.

Her lips tempted him, but he rose and helped her up. Using the last rays of dusk, they took the trail behind the barn, stables, and past an outdoor stall. A horse snorted, and she shivered. "Don't worry. The horse is secured and well behind the fence."

"Fences can be broken. Then what?"

"Suppose someone like me'd have to fix it. No need to fret none." He grasped her hand and escorted her up the steps to her cabin. "Can I give you a tour of the ranch tomorrow afternoon?"

"Only if we walk."

"Why don't you care for horses?" He needed some insight into her troubles.

Her mouth quivered. "Two years ago, my grandfather was killed by one of those vicious brutes."

Dusty pulled her into his arms. "What happened?"

"He went trail riding on an unhinged stallion. It threw him into a fence and stomped on his body." She shivered.

"A mustang killed my friend. Still bedogs me, but darlin', you can't work a ranch without horses."

"I'm not working a ranch. I'm teaching children."

"Then I suppose I'll have to prove to you not every horse is meanspirited."

"You're impossible." She pushed him away, fled inside, shut the door.

Wooing her wouldn't be easy.

Chapter Eight

"Did you think your deception would remain unnoticed?" Sandy stood so close to Mia's face she could smell her maple syrup breath.

"But—" What did Sandy know?

Her boss held up her mascara. "Virtuous women never brush kohl on their eyelashes." Bam. She slammed her hand on the dining room table.

Bam, bam, bam. "Miss Amelia, it's time for breakfast."

Was the nightmare a premonition?

"Missy, you need to wake up," a woman's voice called.

"Cookie?" Mia opened her eyes and glanced around her narrow room. A porcelain pitcher and basin on a table. A battered wardrobe. Darn, she was still at the ranch. "I'm awake."

"Good. Hurry over and get some grub." Cookie's fading footsteps meant she was gone.

Not much of a morning person, she figured it was the crack of the dawn early. Did she teach today? She inhaled and exhaled, inhaled and exhaled. No. Not for two more days.

She opened the curtain partway and let in some light. The dresser needed paint as did the dingy walls. Not her biggest concern at the moment.

Might as well get dressed. Since her only clean item left was her fancy ball gown, why not help herself to the clothing in the closet? She flipped through the wooden hangers to a faded cotton dress with daisy material. Loose in the waist, the frayed hemline dragged on the ground.

Maybe this outfit would get Dusty to quit distracting her with those sweltering hot kisses.

She focused on her red and blistered feet. Unable to wear yesterday's tight-fitting shoes, a pair of battered pink cowboy boots peeked out from the bottom of the wardrobe. She slipped on clean stockings and carefully slid her feet inside. Loose, not huge, they'd suffice.

Her purse lay on top of her dresser. The nightmare reminded her to hide her items from the future. Where? A drawer? The closet? Under the bed? Dropping to her knees, the dust made her sneeze. Nobody'd think to check there, so she pushed her purse against the wall. The items inside her bag could wait until later.

A long yawn told her she needed caffeine and fast. No Keurig available in this room. Not even a cheap coffee maker. She hurried to the back door of the kitchen and knocked.

"Sweetie, you don't need to knock. You're part of the help now. Miss Sandy's out riding. Said she'll stop by the schoolhouse later." Cookie pointed to a square table in the corner. "Have a seat. Want coffee?"

"Oh, yes, please."

The woman brought her a cup.

Mia poured in cream and took a sip. "This is heavenly."

"Glad you like it." Cookie set a plate in front of her heaped with buttered pancakes drenched in syrup. A trillion carbs.

"I'll never finish all this food."

"Try." The cook used a cloth to wipe down the stove. "If you ask me, you could use some meat on your bones."

She called her skinny. Not meant as a compliment, Mia took it as one anyway. "Have you worked here long?"

"Since Westin and his brother were youngins."

Westin had a brother? Interesting. Did he live here too? And what about the parents? Now, didn't seem like a good time to ask.

"Sandy says you lived in the big city. Seems odd a pretty girl like you would take on a job like this one. But if you're looking to get hitched, I suppose a ranch is as good a place as any to find a husband." Cookie kneaded bread as she talked.

"I'm not looking for a husband." In this era, men pretty much owned their wives.

"Hope you're not into that suffrage movement. From what Sandy's been telling me, the whole idea of women being equal to men don't seem natural."

She held back her opinion, took another bite of her pancakes, finished off her coffee, asked for a refill, and headed for the schoolhouse with her cup in hand.

The schoolhouse could pass for the one from the TV show, *When Calls the Heart*. Not much larger than her living room at home, she didn't expect to see a potbellied stove. At least it wasn't winter, or she'd have to chop wood. Probably not. If all cowboys had immense muscular biceps like Dusty's, she'd find plenty of willing wranglers.

Hopping up on a sturdy wooden chair, she pulled down four books from a shelf above the desk. Teaching had always been her cousin's calling, never hers. Since it was summer, thankfully the kids left at one. She should be able to fake her way through a few hours.

Behind the books, coal pieces filled a copper container in the shape of a gravy boat. Perfect for drawing.

In the bottom drawer of the desk, she found colored powder in jars. "Paint pigment." She'd loved using this stuff in college. As she reached in for a red container, a mouse poked his head up.

"Stupid mouse." She backed away. The brown critter jumped and skittered up her arm.

"Geeeeeet off!" she screamed.

The terrible creature hopped onto her shoulder and chittered.

Sandy ran inside. "Never seen a mouse do that." She flicked the rodent off with her finger. It squeaked as it hit the floor and ran into a mouse hole.

Panic seized Mia's brain. She had to get away from the flea bitten rodent. She got on top of the closest desk and pulled her knees to her chest.

Sandy seemed unfazed. "Sure was a pesky one."

"It tried to bite my face and could be rabid." A cure had yet to be invented. Her mouth got dry, her stomach knotted.

"You're afraid of a little mouse? I've heard they have rats the size of rabbits in the big cities."

"That's an exaggeration." A good line came to her. "Besides, my cat, Tiger, kept my place vermin free."

"Want me to grab a cat from the barn?" J.J. asked.

Sandy smiled. "The orange one's a pretty good mouser."

J.J. sped out of there quicker than a blink.

Mia hated being helpless, not in control. "Sorry to be such a bother."

"You're far better than the last teacher we hired. Five miles into the buggy ride, she changed her mind about the position. Said the hills were too brown. Said she had standards. Demanded we turn back to town immediately."

At least the woman got to ride in a buggy. Mia doubted her poor thighs would ever heal.

Sandy pulled a jar filled with blue powder from a drawer. "What's this?"

"Pigment." Elation bubbled inside at the thought of using paints. "You mix the color with egg yolk and water. Where'd this paint come from?"

"Near five years ago, we hired a teacher from San Francisco. He insisted we buy the paint and have it here when he arrived. Also asked for half a dozen brushes. The man stayed maybe a year. He painted a picture or two, but never with the children." She passed a brush to Mia.

Handmade, the coarse whiskered bristles might have come from a pig. She preferred camel's hair, but these brushes would be perfect for teaching kids.

J.J. waddled in struggling to hold a scruffy orange cat almost as big as him. He kicked shut the door behind him and dropped Whiskers. The feline perused the exterior, pounced close to the desk, held a mouse under his foot, let it go, pawed it, played with it, and ate it whole.

Disgusting!

Sandy opened the door to Mia's bedroom. "Give the cat an hour. He'll rid this place of every varmint."

Varmint. She envisioned a possum with razor-sharp teeth.

The cat headed into her bedroom. To think she could have come face to face with a rodent under her bed.

"Thanks for sharing your cat, J.J.," she said, appreciative he'd been quick to grab the animal and fix her dilemma.

"Tweren't nothing." He flashed an adorable smile.

~ * ~

Dusty tapped on the classroom door and nudged it open. "Need any help?"

"No." She wiped her hands on an apron. Dirt streaked across her nose.

"Finished my chores early." He stepped closer. "I'd like to take you on a buggy ride around the ranch if you're willing?"

"Are you asking me on a date?"

"I reckon. Be much obliged if you said, *yes?*" With her eyes downcast, he couldn't read her mood. "Even had Cookie pack us a picnic."

"You've thought of everything." Her voice rose a notch, hopefully, impressed.

"It pays to be prepared. Now about the buggy ride, will you go?"

"Give me a sec to clean up." She sauntered to her room, swaying her hips. His throat went dry.

Needing to divert his wayward notions, he leaned against the stove and read the teacher's duties poster.

Fill the lamps, clean the chalkboards, and sweep the floors daily.

Mop the floor at least once a week with hot soapy water.

Never dress in bright colored clothing, wear at least two petticoats.

Petticoats. He'd caught a glimpse of her petticoat at the dance. The idea heated up his desire for her. He kept reading.

A teacher who is dishonest or marries will be dismissed.

Dusty wasn't the marrying kind. Another suitor like Reynolds would make her his wife. Dusty slammed his fist into the wall.

"What'd that wall do to you?" She wore a big straw hat and a pink dress a might too short.

He sucked in a growl. "Nothing." He helped her down the stairs. She took cautious steps at the side of the buggy. The horse whinnied, and she backed into him.

"Don't fret, I'll protect you." He walked between her and the horse, assisting her onto the leather seat, and jumped in on the left.

The horse snorted.

"Pay no mind to Old Bessie." He placed his hand over hers. The touch made his pulse beat like a fast drummer. "Ready?"

"No."

He clicked his tongue and shouted, "Giddy-up."

The horse lurched forward. She gripped the bench.

"You're doing fine."

"I'm trying." She eased her hold. "How'd you get the name Dusty?"

Good. Talking should help her relax. "Learning to ride I fell off plenty, usually landed on my face in the dirt."

"You weren't born in a saddle?"

"Hardly." He kept the horse's pace slow. They took a bridge and crossed over the river.

"Isn't the fawn precious?"

He didn't mention he preferred cooked venison. On a distant hill, wild horses galloped. "See the appaloosa stallion leading the pack. I've been trying to catch him for the last year."

"Either he's stubborn, or you need to work on your roping skills?"

"You vex me." He unintentionally brushed his fingers along the outside of her skirt. A sizzle charged and nearly knocked him for a loop. It took watching a hawk swoop and catch a mouse to reason rationally. "You enjoying the ride?"

"Much more than being on Half-Wit."

He couldn't help chuckling. "His name's Half-Pint. Now, back to how much you love being in my company."

"You wish."

He found her comment odd. Probably something big city folks said.

"Those cattle gathering under the tree remind me of cliques at my high school."

"Clicks? Chickens cluck. Cows moo." Did she not know this?

"I was comparing those cows to some of the groups or cliques at my high school. They didn't think, just followed the crowd." She might as well call him unworldly, inept, a bit uncultured.

"And you prefer to take a different path?"

"As an artist, I tend to see things differently from most people." She pulled her hat down, blocking her eyes.

"Nothing wrong with being different. Cowboy's happen to have their own unique views on life."

"Such as?"

Typically, he'd button up when it came to feelings, but he wanted to let her in. "Don't believe in fretting. Take things as they come. And if you can catch the eye of a beautiful woman, you count your blessings and enjoy the moment."

She exhaled a little croon. "You're a romantic at heart?"

"Only when I look at you."

"You're crazy." Her blush said she'd been flattered.

Around the bend, four cows blocked the road and forced him to stop the buggy. He jumped down and yelled, "Shoo. Get." The bovines mooed their complaints and headed to a field of grass to the west.

He caught her staring at him as he hopped in.

"I can't believe you got those two-ton cows to move."

"Doesn't always work. Cattle can be obstinate." He took her hand and brought it to his mouth. "The opposite of you."

"You're trying to charm me. What do you want?"

"Hmm—" He kissed her cheek. "That'll do for now."

They curved northward on the road. "You wanna drive?" he asked.

"No way."

"Bessie's easy, honest. She can't hurt you from where you sit."

Tilting her chin, her eyes widened.

"I'll teach you the commands. *Giddy-up*—Bessie walks. *Whoa*—she stops. *Step up*—she trots. *Gee*—turn left. *Haw*—turn right. Now make her stop?"

"Whoa," she said, and the horse stopped.

"See, Bessie's already listening to you." He positioned his arm around her shoulder.

"Change your mind about me driving?"

"Nope, just admiring the natural view." He glanced at her.

"Oh, brother."

"Trust me. I'm not your brother." He welcomed holding her close. "Secure the reins between the index and third finger. Loop the extra strap."

"Like this."

"You're an expert. Bet you're buggy racing before this week ends." He released her hands and kept one arm around her shoulder. It felt right. "Keep your wrists and fingers loose. Now tell her to giddy up."

"Giddy up," she said in a soft voice.

"Louder."

"Giddy up," her voice clamored. The horse lurched forward.

Neither spoke as the horse continued along the straight, flat trail. Her sumptuous lips pressed together as she concentrated. "Ready to go faster?" he asked, anxious to be alone with her at a picnic spot.

"Not on your life."

He spotted a shady area on a hill, one he'd visited a time or two. "I need you to turn left at the fork."

"Gee," she shouted. The horse turned down a less worn path.

"You're an ace."

"Not even close." Her light tone said otherwise.

The skinny road led to a flat acre at the top of the hill.

"Whoa," they called out at the same time, and the horse stopped.

She glanced around, taking in her surroundings. "It's pretty here."

"You sure are." He helped her down and took the basket from the backseat. "I'm right glad you came today." He spread out the checkered tablecloth with her assistance.

"Surprisingly, I am too." Still a little stiff, she lowered herself and fanned her full skirt around her.

He took out a canteen and poured two glasses of lemonade. "Told Cookie to make our drink plenty sweet."

She sipped slowly and gave an oh-so-delighted simper. "Not bad."

He placed crusty bread and hard cheese on a wooden board. Taking out his holstered Bowie Knife, he cut several slices of cheese and added them to a plate. "Help yourself."

She smiled. My, she was pretty when she smiled. She tore off a chunk of bread and added the cheese. "Delicious."

He wanted to kiss her something fierce but knew he shouldn't. "You go on many picnics?"

"Maybe once or twice a year."

Could be men in the city didn't use picnics to court? The idea of another man with her badgered his jealous streak. Best switch topics. "You mentioned twin brothers. Have any other siblings?"

"An older sister, Nancy. And you?"

"I've got a younger sister, Josie. Rarely see her since she lives with her pa." Talking about her brought up old memories.

"You said her pa. What about your dad?"

He tried to hold the anguish rising up his throat. "I was six when he died."

"Must've been hard. My father's awesome."

"You city folks shore have some peculiar sayings."

"So do you cowboys. Anyway, where does your sister live?"

"Riverside."

"It's not far." She made it sound like a jaunt to the barn. "She's family. You should make an effort to see her. She should visit you, too."

"Been telling myself to go, but work keeps me busy." Gloominess hit him like a snowstorm in the middle of the day. "Her father won't let her come here. Thinks my side of the family is no better than pigs in a sty."

"You have any other family?"

"No. Everyone's gone." Pain wretched his heart.

"You poor thing." She scooted closer. "Care to talk about it?"

"I'd rather do this." Hunger drove him to brush his lips against hers. As she wrapped her arms around his neck, he couldn't resist deepening the kiss.

Her soft little whimper brought him back to the present. He broke away, gasping for air and gazing at her well-kissed lips,

She had a reason to not smile, a reason to be upset. A man married a gal like her. Spoiled her with gems and do-dads. What could he offer? His only possession—his horse and saddle.

"You mad at me?"

"I shouldn't have kissed you." He'd treated her like a saloon girl.

"Probably." She walked to the edge of the hill, picked up a stone, tossed it, and watched it roll down.

His gut twisted, aching worse than if it'd been punched. He needed to make amends.

She let out a slow-sad breath. "Why must things be so complicated?"

"Somebody else courting you?" His mind cooked up Reynolds kissing her, and Dusty's jaw clamped tight. He wanted to be the one courting this woman. She may have a stubbornness that matched his own, but the feisty gal fired his desire to be near her.

She moved closer. "I like you, but it's wrong."

Jealousy roused more suspicions. "You married?" Of course, a pretty gal like her would be married. "Running from your husband?"

"I've never been married. Not sure if I ever will be."

His head twirled like a ready-to-throw lasso. "Why?"

"Let's talk about you." Her eyes were wide and uncertain. "Be careful. I don't want you to die."

The dumb dream about him hanging surfaced again. "Don't need to be concerning yourself with me." He crushed his mouth on hers, showing her he was very much alive. Her lips were glistening and red, her hair unkempt. He'd gone too far. "Next time we go anywhere, I reckon we should bring a chaperone.

"A chaperone? That's insane."

He came within a second of pulling her into his arms and kissing her senseless.

~ * ~

An hour later, Dusty raced Thunder along the wash and across a meadow. Too long without a woman, he'd take a trip to the Golden Horseshoe Saloon as soon as possible and find a pretty blonde with green eyes.

Mia belongs in the city—he belongs in the country. He doubted she'd be happy living as a foreman's wife, but after the closeness they'd shared, he desired a relationship.

If he could get her to trust horses, maybe she'd stay. His grandfather used to say, *Never will you find a friend truer than a horse.* She liked kittens. Foals were similar, but a bit larger. Why not show her the foals?

He strode to the dining hall and saw the back of Mia's blond hair. Across from her, Reynolds flirted, raising a brow, his smile wide.

Jealousy hit him like an unwanted guest. Good thing the scent of Cookie's fried chicken made his stomach grumble. He filled his plate at the side bar and took the empty seat on the right of Mia. "Evening, darlin'."

She said nothing, fidgeted with her napkin.

"My uncle Westin gave me a prime piece of land. I'm building my place on the south end of the ranch. Got a view of the entire valley," Reynolds said.

"Sounds nice." Her voice was polite, agitated, and had a sarcastic bite.

Reynolds gazed at her like a lovesick cow. "I'm more 'n happy to show you tomorrow afternoon."

"No thanks, Reynolds." Her eyes were downcast.

"The offer's open whenever you're ready. I'd be honored to accompany you on a stroll this evening."

"Listen, Reynolds, you should know I'm keeping company with Dusty," her words were controlled.

Dusty almost shouted, *Yippee!*

"I aim to change your mind." Reynolds' eyes glinted fury, and he masked his rage with a quick smile. "But for now, I'll get to playing poker. You in Slick?"

"Yep."

Reynolds touched the brim of his hat. "Evening, Miss Kellogg."

Both cowboys left.

"You handled that well."

"No, I didn't. Reynolds may have disliked you before," she groaned. "He hates you now."

"It's not true. The man's never liked me from the get-go."

"Any idea why?"

"Doesn't matter." He'd prefer to get her alone and steal another kiss. Two families remained in the hall. It'd be best if he thought about branding.

"I'm going for a walk before the sun goes down," she whispered. "Mind escorting me?"

Reynolds already offered her a stroll, and she chose him. "Why, Miss Amelia, I'd be honored."

She laughed. "You sound like a woman."

"Do I look like a lassie?" he said in a high voice.

"Not one bit."

He led her outside to the trail.

"Besides Reynolds, who else doesn't like you?"

"You're not still fretting about your dream." He wished she'd forget this nonsense.

"An awful feeling inside me says someone is out to get you and you'll get arrested. Framed for something you didn't do." She stepped closer to him. "You'll be careful, won't you?"

"Yes, miss."

Her ring sparkled in the light.

"I think your ring's stones match the one on my belt buckle."

"Let me see." She held her ring alongside his buckle. The proximity of her fingers seemed a bit naughty on his end. "I think I like garnet better set in silver than gold."

He gave a half-hearted laugh. "How'd you know it's not ruby?"

"The color's deeper red."

"Once thought my buckle was ruby. As a boy, I found a treasure box in the attic—filled with necklaces, buckles, rings, even a timepiece. Grandpa had everything appraised. Garnets aren't worth much more than a few pieces of penny candy." Regret filled his lungs. "I'd be running our family's ranch right now if the gems were rubies."

"You lost your ranch?"

"Not important. Happened a long time ago." They went up a hill toward the same bench as last night.

She adjusted her skirt. Sunlight flickered on her ring.

"My ma wore a ring similar to yours, but hers had only three stones."

"Do you ever see your mom?"

He fought the bleakness climbing from the pit of his stomach. "She died." Just like his dad. He remembered being five when she married, left her father's ranch, and moved with her new husband to his Riverside Ranch. She'd told him to stay and help Gramps.

"I'm sorry." She gently squeezed his hand.

He fought off the melancholy bubbling inside, traced her bottom lip with his thumb. "I'll be done with my chores by mid-afternoon tomorrow and would like to show you the foals."

"Okay."

"Might even coax Cookie to fix us another picnic."

"Think she'll add strawberries."

"If I ask, I reckon she will." He cupped her face and kissed her. "Then I'll teach you to ride?"

"Not in a million years." She reminded him of a stiff wooden sawhorse. "I'm staying where it's safe."

"Darlin', be reasonable'. It's vital to know how to ride out here."

"Not gonna happen." She ran down the trail.

He followed her at a slow pace. When he saw a light in her room, he wished he'd been attracted to a less determined woman.

Chapter Nine

If that cocky cowboy thought he'd be teaching her to ride tomorrow, he was mistaken. Mia fluffed her pillow. Apparently, he'd forgotten the horse she rode to the ranch could've killed her.

"Oooo-m." She used a yoga chant to try and clear her mind. It didn't work.

"Oooo-m." It hurt to sit crossed legged on her bed. Getting under the covers, she attempted to sleep, but her mind kept recalling Dusty's hot kisses.

She shifted to her stomach. Damn handsome cowboy. Might as well go through the alphabet and make up adjectives for Dusty.

A—aggravating. B—bossy. C—cute. D—dogged determination. E—elegant. Not quite right. She settled for exasperating.

Yawning, she struggled to keep her eyes open.

Suddenly, she found herself standing in a crowd in front of a wooden structure. An old man next to her shouted, "String him up."

And then she saw Dusty, solemn as he progressed up the gallows steps. Thick metal handcuffs secured his wrists.

"Don't dawdle," the executioner's voice echoed from the side of the platform.

"He's innocent. Let him go." She attempted to shout. No voice came out. She remained frozen, unable to go to him.

The sheriff nudged him from behind. "Move along. It's time."

Dusty's muscular build had thinned. His checkered shirt no longer molded to his brawny arms. His jeans fit loose. He took the makeshift stairs, slowly, one at a time, and stepped up to the scaffold. A rope slipped around his neck.

"Don't do it!" She screamed, and her own voice woke her. Sweat beaded on her forehead as she glanced at her wind up clock. Seven a.m.

"Miss Kellogg," a high-pitched voice squeaked from outside her room.

"Who is it?" Her fuzzy mind tried to think. *Where am I?*

"J.J. Ma said since ya weren't at breakfast, I was to bring over a plate."

Still in the past. *Shit.* Throwing on a robe, she accepted the food with a thank you. Sitting at the desk, she took several bites of egg, skipped the bacon, and polished off a freshly baked raisin muffin. Like Dorothy from the *Wizard of Oz*, she clicked her heels together, twisted her ring and said, *"There's no place like home. There's no place like home. There's no place like home."*

She twisted her ring again and waited. Nothing happened.

Disappointed her silly action didn't work, the alarm clock ticked.

Twenty minutes later, she unlocked the connecting door to the classroom. Thankfully, she had one more day to plan. At least she'd volunteered in her cousin's fourth-grade class and had a clue how to muddle through. Maybe.

She picked up a McGuffey Reader, impressed by the cover's intricate ink print of children. The table of contents listed fifty lessons, varying from basic spelling to literature. The story, *Two Dogs,* had detailed vocabulary work for the first hour. With only one math book, she was forced to write the problems on the board.

When she was little, she struggled to learn her numbers until her mom turned the shapes into animals. She picked up a stick of chalk from a wooden holder, drew a straight line, and incorporate a giraffe's head on the slanted top of number one. Two turned into a duck with the beak on top and a tail feather on the bottom. Before long, she'd created cute animals for all the numbers. Taking a step back, she admired her creations. "Perfect."

On the top of the board, she copied addition, subtraction, multiplication, and division problems. That'll take care of the first hour or two. Then what?

~ * ~

"Hello," Dusty called from the door. "May I come in?"

"Sure." At least she didn't glare or kick him out. But she did cock her head and stare at him.

"Hisssss." A mangy orange tom scampered toward the bedroom.

"Where'd this cat come from?"

"He's my bodyguard." Her mouth quirked up.

"Bodyguard? You mean he's your protector?"

"You better believe it."

"Thought that was my job. Last night I never meant to get you riled." He braved looking at her.

"You're not talking me into riding." Hands on her hips, her curt speech proved she wouldn't budge.

"You still want to see the foals?"

"Sure." Cautious, her eyes flickered a hint of forgiveness. At the door, she took his arm.

They passed an outside corral with an adjoining fenced-in pasture. A bay colt's head went over the railing, and the horse neighed. She backed against Dusty. His arms wrapped around her trembling body. "He won't hurt you. Sarsaparilla was born curious."

"Sarsaparilla?"

"Brown like the fizzy soda." He tried to put her at ease.

The horse snorted and cantered off.

"See, nothing to fear."

"Right? Bet he's as gentle as Half-Wit."

"You mean Half-Pint." He loved how she joked. Not loved, appreciated. "Bella's next to the big tree on the left. She's the yearling feeling her oats and frolicking."

"How big will she get?"

"A smidgen taller. Fifteen to seventeen hands."

Her body stiffened. "Sandy said Bella's a thoroughbred. Isn't the breed expensive?

"Can be. A few years ago, Westin won four thoroughbred mares and paid stud services for a purebred stallion with papers." Not just any stallion. Until his grandpa lost the horse in a card game, Midnight Sheik had belonged to Dusty.

"Why isn't Bella housed in the stables at night?"

"It's better to keep her outside. Gives her plenty of room to run. If she gets into any mischief, I can see her from my bedroom window."

"Westin should be the one watching her."

The comment irked his cowboy pride. "I'm the foreman. Westin trusts me to handle the ranch's livestock."

"Of course, he does," she mumbled. They reached the stables. "Can we see J.J.'s kittens first?"

"Sure thing." He brought her into the stall with mewing sounds. Wobbly-legged balls of fur took uneven steps.

"Aren't they precious?"

"They're mighty small." He picked up a striped kitten and gave it to her. She stroked its chin, rubbed noses and reluctantly put him down.

How he envied the little guy. "So, you like cats?"

"I do."

He grabbed a black one. It wriggled out of his hold.

"I could stay here all day." She knelt to pet the three remaining kittens. "Still I think I'd like to see the foals."

He offered his arm and guided her toward the newest foal five stalls down. A horse whinnied.

Her fingernails dug into his arm.

"You're safe with me."

She stayed in the middle of the aisle. "How many horses are in here?"

"No more than a dozen mares, plus the foals."

"That many." She took a deep, unsteady breath.

A few stalls further, he opened the top gate. "Rock Sand isn't more than a few hours old?"

The spindly-legged foal took three steps toward their voices and rushed to its mother.

"Oh my gosh. He's adorable! If only horses stayed this small."

"If they didn't grow, we'd be stuck walking. I happen to prefer riding." He accompanied her to the next stall. "Renegade's another one of Midnight's colts."

"How many thoroughbreds are on this ranch?"

"As of this morning, we've got over a hundred saddle horses. They're a mix of mustangs, quarter and cow ponies." He showed her more mares and their offspring.

"They're not so bad from a distance," her voice came out clipped.

"Horses tend to be gentle. Like people, there can be an occasional bad seed."

They stopped at the entrance of an open stall. Inside, a red-and-white-checkered tablecloth had beenspread on top of stacks of hay.

"You did this for me?" She pushed to her tiptoes and kissed his cheek.

"Why wouldn't I? You're worth a heck of a lot more" He tried to hold her gaze, but she'd already seated herself and opened the basket.

"Help yourself." He sat close to her.

She took out a steel canteen. "What's in here?"

"Lemonade." He reached into the basket and pulled out two metal cups. "Allow me." He unscrewed the cap and poured her a glass and one for himself.

Taking a sip, she smiled. "This is refreshing." The enticing woman may prove to be his undoing.

He opened a wrapper filled with strawberries. "Want one?"

"Yes, please." One bite and strawberry juice colored her lips.

"I can't resist you." His arm looped around her neck, breathing in her tangy essence of strawberry and sin. He teased her lips with his tongue, moved his mouth over hers slowly, exploring. Her hand pushed against his chest. He stopped, releasing his hold on her and backed a few steps. Dammit, he'd been too forward.

Her eyes flashed alarm. She blurted, "I don't want you to hang."

Here he thought she'd been terrified of him. "Not the nightmare again?"

"It's way more than a nightmare. This will sound weird, um, I know it'll happen."

"Why are you so obsessed with my death?" He was annoyed.

"Because I want you to live." She scooted closer. "If I allow you to give me a half-hour riding lesson, will you do something for me?"

"I suppose. What do you want?" Now she peaked his curiosity.

"I'll tell you after the lesson."

~ * ~

Fear quavered through Mia's body as huge horrid horses whinnied and snorted, galloped and neighed. If there really were time-travel gods, the deities definitely have a warped sense of humor.

Dusty had the dreadful Half-Wit tied to a post. Agreeing to learn to ride. Dumb, dumb, dumb.

A shadow appeared near the bunkhouse. A blond cowboy lurked between the building and Dusty's cabin. Was it Reynolds?

Time to Save a Cowboy

Her mount snorted and bared his teeth. "Changed my mind. I'll stay here."

"Think of Half-Pint as an overgrown cat."

"By a thousand percent."

He rubbed the horse behind the ears. "Wanna pet him."

"No."

"Your loss." Lacing his fingers together, he boosted her up.

"This is lunacy." She swung her right leg over the saddle.

He secured her boots in the stirrup. "It's natural to be scared." Unlooping the reins, he brought her inside a circular arena and walked her and Half-Wit around.

She clutched the saddle horn so tightly her knuckles ached.

"Concentrate on the location of your hips. If you look to the left, your hips move slightly and so will your horse. Sit up tall, put your legs forward, and allow the horse to stretch its head."

She did as told.

"That's it." He rewarded her with a charismatic smile.

"Easy for you to say when you're on the ground."

"Follow the gait." He ran alongside holding the reins. "Perfect. Squeeze your thighs, and you'll bring him to a canter."

She stared at Dusty's muscle-toned backside. Her insides quivered, as she relived how his thighs pressed against her as his warm lips set her body on fire. Knowing that she didn't belong in this era, this attraction needed to be squelched.

He gave her the reins. "Your turn."

"The half-hour's up."

"You've got another fifteen minutes," he said with a soothing, deep voice. "You'll be fine. Use your thighs to encourage Half-Pint to go faster."

She walked her horse, pressing with her thighs to get him to trot.

"You're doing great." His smooth and sexy voice encouraged her.

She cantered, lost her balance and landed face-first in the dirt. Worried the horse was about to take revenge and stomp on her, she got up and sprinted for the railing.

He caught her. "Where're you going?"

"I'm done."

"No, you're not." He picked her up by the waist and dropped her into the saddle.

"I hate you." She seethed, livid because he put her back on the horse.

"Once around the ring, and you're done."

"No, we're done now." She dismounted, running down the path full bore until she reached her cabin, and he heard her door slam.

~ * ~

Dusty should've been gentler when he threw Mia on the mare. Still, if a person falls off a horse, he gets back in the saddle. Apparently not with her, because she turned as sour as a lemon. Well, seeing as he hadn't done anything wrong, he refused to apologize. Then he imagined her flirting with another cowboy, and his gut ached something fierce.

Women confused him. Horses he understood. At an outdoor stall, he gave a loud whistle. A black thoroughbred galloped over and stopped at the open gate. "Come here, Bella," he cooed, holding an apple.

The filly trotted inside the stall and accepted the fruit, munching it down. Dusty fastened the latch on the interior gate, securing the animal for the night.

Outside the stables, he heard shouting.

"I won't do it." Reynolds' voice reverberated, loud and menacing.

Dusty rushed inside. "Keep your voices down, or you'll scare the foals," he whispered. Reynolds and Slick knew better.

Both cowboys stopped. Reynolds bore the kind of glare that'd make a coyote hault in his tracks.

Slick shrugged. "Sorry."

"He won't swap chores and let me bring in the hay." Reynolds whined worse than a younin'. "The numskull says he's too old to muck out the stables. Guess he's forgotten Westin's my uncle."

"If you're so damn important, how come you're living in the bunkhouse," Slick snarled.

"Enough." Dusty had no patience for nonsense. "Quit griping."

"Well, it ain't right. How's a man 'spose to go courting wearing horse shit cologne?"

Would Mia go out with Reynolds after their spat? Exasperated, Dusty grunted, "Take a bar of soap out to the river."

"Don't think I won't tell my uncle about this." Reynolds scowled and stomped off.

Slick lifted one of his bushy brows. "You courting Miss Amelia?"

"I reckon." After their recent fiasco, she might not even acknowledge him.

Westin rushed into the stables. "Blackie says the fence is down at the northwest border. See that it's fixed."

"Sure thing." Dusty turned to Slick, "Get Reynolds, saddle up, and meet me at the hitching post."

Slick hurried away.

Scotty walked along the dirt trail behind the barn.

"Need you to mend fences, "Dusty said. "See if you can round up Checkerboard."

In a short time, the men rode along the wash and over the bridge leading north. "Keep your eyes peeled for the downed fence," Dusty shouted.

"Over here, boss." Checkerboard stopped at the northwest corner. "Four sections have been cut."

Dusty dismounted and picked up the end of the barbed wire on the ground. "Wire's been snipped. Deliberately."

Checkerboard shook his head. "Hundreds of cattle tracks."

"Rustlers." A deep anger etched through Dusty's mind. He and his grandfather once lost close to fifty head due to theft. Their ranch never recovered. Lately, he'd noticed little things that pointed to cattle thieves here.

"You sure these prints ain't from the last roundup?" Scotty asked.

"Nope, we used the central gate." Dusty went to the back of his saddle and untied a small spool of wire.

"You really think there's rustling?" Scotty asked.

"Appears that way. One thing I can't stand is a thief. If someone's been helping themselves to our cattle, believe me, I'll hunt them down."

The cowboys grabbed pliers and wire cutters and mended the broken sections. Dusty worked alongside the men, and they quickly finished.

He inspected their labor. "Good job. In case somebody comes back, I'll camp out here tonight." Even though he didn't like missing supper with Mia, being the foreman meant sacrifices.

"I'll stay too," Slick offered.

"Much obliged."

Scotty, Reynolds, and Checkerboard mounted and rode off.

Slick collected stones for a containment ring. He added kindling, wood, and sticks to the fire pit, and flicked a match. "Too bad you're stuck with me, 'stead of the purdy gal."

"Sure is." Dusty liked sleeping outdoors, but tonight an odd longing hit him, one where he cozied up to a gorgeous blonde. He set a pot on top of the fire, filled it with canteen water and coffee grounds. In no time, he spread out his bedroll and gazed up at the dusky sky. The golden rays spread like Mia 's flaxen tresses, the pink strip the color of her blushing cheeks.

In less than an hour, Reynolds would woo her with promises of a big house and security. What could he offer? A worn saddle and a cowboy to match.

The sky turned dark. A shooting star left a glistening trail. He took the streak as a sign his ma, pa, and grandfather watched over him from above. Why'd they all have to die?

Slick added more dried brush into the fire. "A summer night like this gets a man thinking about the choices he's made." He sounded wistful as he picked up the dented pot and filled a tin cup. "I almost married once."

"You?" Surprised, Dusty couldn't picture Slick young and in love.

"Seems she didn't want to be a cowboy's wife, wanted me to work in her pa's store." Slick shrugged. "Decided I ain't got the disposition."

"Reckon I'd do the same." Dusty would never make much of a greenhorn.

"Can't go back anyhow, so there's no sense fretting." Slick stood. "You go ahead and catch some shut eye. I don't mind taking the first watch."

"Sounds good." He gazed at the sky, picked out the Big Dipper and Orion's Belt. The wind whooshed, as he closed his eyes. Restless, it took quite a while to settle. He dreamed of waltzing with Mia, holding her close, whispering, "I could get used to this." Happier than he'd ever been, he never wanted to let her go.

"You're sweet." He loved her melodic tone.

"My turn." Reynolds cut in, grinning from ear-to-ear as he snatched Mia out of Dusty's hold.

KA-KRRRACKKK!

What was that? He opened his eyes and sprung for his rifle. Now wide awake, he heard a click.

KA-KRRRACKKK. A bullet zzzzzzzzz by his ear.

Based on the deafening noise, the gunman must be close. Where was Slick? Dusty fell low to the ground, scooted behind a spindly creosote bush, and waited.

No more shots.

Another few yards up a hill, he spotted Slick leaning against a Joshua tree, not moving.

He crawled toward him. Had someone shot him?

Slick grabbed his gun and held the butt end against his shoulder with his finger on the trigger. Had he lured Dusty into a trap?

"It's me, Dusty." Fear caused his legs to shake as he stared into Slick's eyes. Cold, dark, emotionless. He held the barrel pointed at Dusty's chest.

"Put the gun down," Dusty said slow and steady.

Slick blinked and lowered his gun.

Dusty wanted to shout, "You could've killed me," but didn't wish to rile Slick. "You hear gunfire?" he asked.

"Sounded more like blasting. Could've come from one of the mines in the mountains."

Not when a bullet whizzed by Dusty. Had Slick shot at him? "It's near midnight. I'll take my turn at watch."

"Appreciate it." The older cowboy walked to his bedroll while still holding his rifle.

Mia said to be cautious. His hand shook as he poured himself coffee, thick cowboy brew.

A distant coyote howled; his mate returned the call. Pairing up with Mia came to mind. He wanted to makeup with her. Hell, he wanted to kiss her senseless.

He pondered about a future with her. He longed to breed horses. Have his own place. He'd heard property in Montana or Wyoming wasn't much. Might have enough saved for a ranch, not enough for stock.

The day broke, and he woke Slick.

They headed back. Dusty appreciated the desert's wide-openness filled with sagebrush and Joshua trees. Cattle bellowed. The Mojave River rushed over rocks. Cicadas sang their irritating buzz.

He rode past the red barn and left his horse in an outdoor stall. Washing up outside, he dragged into the dining hall on time for breakfast.

"You ever visit New York City?" Scotty asked Mia,

"After I graduated, I visited there to see the museums. There are so many people it's hard to walk down the street." She reminded him of a queen surrounded by every single cowboy—her subjects.

Dusty took the empty seat to the left of her. "Darlin', sorry I missed dinner last night."

She wouldn't look at him.

Ding. The clock signaled the half hour, and she stood. "Excuse me, gentlemen. I'd better hurry. Don't want to be late on my first day." Her skirt swayed as she scurried out the door.

Reynolds dropped into the chair where she had been. "Miss Amelia and me are courting." He gave an I'm-superior-to-you sneer. "Taking her to see our future house this afternoon."

"She'd rather hightail it with a greenhorn—" Dusty stopped. No need for name calling.

"Like your ma did?"

Dusty's hands fisted, ready to reach across the table and punch the loud-mouthed road apple. Nobody says derogatory things about his mother, even if she did marry a wealthy rancher after his pa died. Reynolds strutted out like the main cock in a henhouse.

"Don't let him get to you, boss," Checkerboard said, "being related to Westin's wife don't give him no right to act uppity."

"He doesn't see it that way." Dusty would always be the undeserving hired help in Reynold's eyes.

Chapter Ten

Mia glanced out the long narrow window to the schoolyard. Two girls sailed up and down on a teetertotter. Boys kicked a can or played ball like a Norman Rockwell picture in 3D. An object flew towards her. She extended her arm up and caught a hand-stitched leather ball. Baseball she could manage.

"Great catch, Miss Kellogg," a gangly teenage boy shouted.

"Thank you." She threw the ball underhanded and rang the cast iron bell mounted on a bracket above the schoolhouse door.

Two girls bounded up the wooden stairs.

"Morning, girls." She did her best imitation of a teacherly voice. "J.J., how're your kittens doing?"

"Look like rolling fur balls when they play. The gray, Ash, purrs all the time. Licorice, the runt, is kinda shy."

"Glad they're doing well." Mia cut in. "Better find your seat."

"Yes, ma'am." He headed inside with the other younger children who filed into the front two rows.

"Billy, you're looking well." She recognized him as the boy who shot rocks at her with a slingshot. His ears turned red. He and two friends, each a foot taller than her, found seats in the back.

She pulled her shoulders back and stood straight. "Welcome class. I'm Miss Kellogg. Since I'm not from ... around here, how do you usually begin your day?"

Ben raised his hand. "We start with the pledge of all-a-giants?"

"Close, actually it's allegiance."

"That's what I said."

Sighing, she asked, "Billy, would you like to lead?"

"Darn right." He jutted out his chin as the children stood. "Ready, begin."

She joined in. "I pledge allegiance ... for which it stands, one nation under God."

The class stopped and stared.

Norma shrilled, "Miss Kellogg, don't you know the real pledge?"

These kids were ruthless. "Of course, I do," she said, a bit miffed she had to defend herself to a group of children.

"God ain't never mentioned." Billy scoffed.

Since when? "It's the newly revised version," she covered, hoping her ruse worked. When they said the Pledge again, she mouthed the words.

She did a quick peruse of her lesson plans. "Get out your reading books and practice with the person next to you."

Norma curled a ringlet around her finger, acting either obstinate or clueless.

"Is there a problem?" Mia asked.

"I don't got a book."

"I'll share with her," Bonnie, her neighbor, offered.

Mia grabbed a reader from the shelf and gave it to Norma. Two older boys whispered. She stood behind them, and they pretended to read silently. She stayed there for maybe a minute and decided to head to the front.

Over an hour had gone by. "Put away your readers," she called. "It's time for math."

"Weaving mats is for girls." The nasally tone sounded like Billy.

"It's M.A.T.H." She placed her palm on her forehead willing away the onset of a headache. "My college professor called arithmetic, mathematics or math."

"Can't have three r's without no rith-maw-tic." Billy made sure his voice carried clearly.

"Your point is taken." She pasted on a smile. "I wrote problems on the board for the older students to complete."

"Who's passing out the slates?" Norma asked.

"You." Mia said, and motioned to the younger children, "Please come to the floor."

Four students sat with their legs out straight, holding boards on their laps and slate pencils in one hand.

"To help you remember numerals, I have decided to turn the lines into animals."

"I like the giraf-ee," Norma squeaked.

"It's also the number one. Draw a straight line." She pointed from the top of its head down its long neck to the feet. The slate pencils created a horrendous noise akin to fingernails on the chalkboard. "Let's move on to two." One by one, she associated the rest of the numbers with animals and had them practice writing.

"You're a good draw-er." J.J. gave an impish smile.

One of the older kids snickered. People assumed teaching would be a piece of cake. They were wrong. Keeping classroom order was difficult.

She sent the children to their seats.

"Ben, collect the books and put them on the shelf."

"Yes, ma'am."

Being called ma'am made her feel like she was ninety, not twenty-five.

Around noon, she said, "I saw coal in here," and trembled at the memory of the ornery mouse from the other day. "Does anyone know where it is?"

"You don't need to light no fire." Billy laughed, and so did his friend.

"We're using it to draw." It took effort to keep her voice from sounding snarky.

"We've got some inside the stove." J.J. jumped up, slid open a drawer near the bottom, and produced a piece of coal. The piece would do for now. She grabbed an apple from her desk and set it on the windowsill. "See how this apple looks round or circular."

"Does circular mean a circle?" Little Norma asked.

"It does." Holding a piece of blotter paper with her left hand, she drew a charcoal circle with her right. "And boring, wouldn't you say?"

Several students nodded.

"What color is the apple?"

She heard calls of red, pink, orange, as she shaded in black. "Even with the lack of color, you can create its beauty." In minutes, she'd completed her drawing. Everyone clapped. An ebb of happiness fluttered inside. This must be why Birdie taught.

"It's like magic." Ben's words made her gasp.

Magic? Fear trotted through her mind. She was pretty sure burning witches happened a hundred years earlier. "This isn't magic—it's art. Now, it's your turn to create masterpieces."

The students smiled. Even the older boys seemed happy.

"J.J., pass out the old pulp scraps." She spotted the container of coal on a shelf above her desk and handed it to Norma. "Give each person one piece." She walked around and monitored the students, smiling at the simple lop-sided circles from the younger children. An older girl grasped shading and light, reminding her of herself at a young age.

J.J. shaded his apple soot black. He ended up with a line of charcoal down his cheek. "This is real fun."

She bit back from correcting his grammar.

"Ma says Miss Kellogg won't last two weeks 'fore she gets hitched," Billy said to his friend.

Marry? Not her. In this century, a wife became a man's possession. Then her thoughts shifted to Dusty and his red-hot kisses.

"Too bad. I think Miss Kellogg's nice," a boy said, reminding her to quit daydreaming.

Clang.

Saved by Cookie's lunch bell.

"It's one. Put away the supplies and straighten the desks. Then you're dismissed." The kids were like efficient machines collecting items. Ben swept the floor.

"Good job today. Take your drawings with you. You're excused." She let out a long breath.

As the room emptied, Sandy came in. "J.J., did you paint your face?"

"I drew a apple." He gave his mother the picture. "See!"

Sandy held it up to the window light. "Sure is round and dark. Now run along and clean up at the pump outside." She picked up a slate pencil from the floor and put it on a desk. "How'd your day go?"

"Not bad."

"Reckon I'll hear plenty from J.J." Sandy walked to the door. "By the way, the men are branding this afternoon, so it'll be quiet around here."

No riding lessons. Relief filled her for a blink. Worry quickly followed. If she didn't see Dusty, she'd never get to convince him that his life was in jeopardy.

"Come for lunch when you're ready."

"Thanks, but I'm full from breakfast."

"If you change your mind, the offer stands," Sandy said. "Otherwise, I'll see you at dinner."

She went into her bedroom and flopped on the bed. Her mind conjured up Dusty riding his tall steed and lassoing a bronco or a bull. Serious, rough, confident.

Lasso, rope, hanging.

He's going to die.

She must persuade him to leave and do it today.

Meowing came from outside her door. She let Whiskers in, and the cat leaped onto the bed. "You miss me?" She petted him, and his soft rumbling purr lulled her to sleep.

The noise of children playing outside woke her. She glanced at the wind-up clock.

Four. An hour until dinner.

In a normal day, she'd check for messages or work on a project. With neither available, might as well draw. She pulled out her journal and sat at the table. Whisker's curled up in the center of the bed. Dipping her pen in ink, she drew him.

The cat jumped off and rubbed against her legs. She picked him up and pointed to the animal's portrait. "Aren't you handsome?"

Not impressed, he squirmed out of her arms, bounded onto the floor, and meowed to be let out.

Ink was a pain, so she went into the schoolhouse and grabbed a piece of charcoal. Seated in a hard-wooden chair, she turned to the next blank page. Drew an oval head, large eyes, filled in the iris and bushy eyebrows. She added a nose and mouth with a quirky smile. She managed to capture Dusty's mischievous gleam, his dimples. Dimples made him disarmingly attractive, so did the jagged line on his square chin. The final touch—his Stetson.

Again, she found herself mesmerized by the man. Next time, she'd pick a different subject. Sketch the river or the schoolhouse. If only her runaway fingers would comply.

Dusty told his nerves to stop twitching as he waited in the dining hall for Mia. His eyes darted to the door for what seemed like the hundredth time. At least Reynolds hadn't arrived yet. He was in no mood for that cowboy's nonsense, especially since the lazy good-for-slacking-deadbeat snuck off during branding.

Mia took a seat next to Dusty. "Hi." Based on her prim mouth, she remained miffed.

He refused to say, *I'm sorry I forced you back on the horse.* "How was your day?"

"Dandy." Her eyes were guarded, lacking the usual ritzy flicker.

"You still mad at me?"

No answer.

Getting her to smile would take a whole heap of his charm. "Had you on my mind all day. Because of you, almost ran a cow into a ditch."

Her lips turned up at the corners, amused.

"May I take you on a stroll after dinner?"

She shrugged, avoiding his eyes.

Scotty plopped into a seat across from them. "Did ya find out who cut the fence?"

"Nope."

She tilted her head. "Cut a fence?"

"Might be rustlers." Blackie took the seat next to Scotty.

"Rustlers? Sounds dangerous," she gasped. "Any idea who?"

"Hard to say." Blackie looked at her bemused. "No clues, other than the cattle's hoof prints."

Dusty shrugged and his hand brushed her knee. His pulse sped.

"You don't get it," her breath huffed as she spoke in his ear. "You're in danger."

"Not me."

Reynolds took the empty spot to her left. "Miss Amelia, you're quite fetching this evening."

"Thanks." She inched closer to Dusty, uneasy and ramrod stiff.

Reynolds glared at Dusty, then her, and stormed to a seat on the other side of the room.

"Heard a bullet whizzed by your ear, Dusty," Scotty said.

Damned cowhand needed to keep his trap shut.

"Someone shot at you, and you're not worried?"

"No need to be." He took in a long breath. "Why don't you tell us 'bout your first day? I'm sure everyone's curious."

"It was all right. I can't believe you're not scared," she said into his ear, hushed but chastising.

He didn't reply, concentrating on finishing his meal. She picked at her food.

An older cowboy moved toward the side of the room. "Checkerboard's playing piano tonight," Dusty said and put his arm around the top of her chair. She didn't push him away, but her glare proved she remained peeved.

Checkerboard played *Old Susana*. Everyone sang; she joined in. Her shoulders relaxed, her posture eased.

For the next song, Checkerboard sang, "If Whiskey Were a Woman, I'd Be Married for Sure."

Dusty leaned closer and whiffed her sweet floral scent. "You could be my whiskey."

He expected her to sigh, not give a throaty laugh, and say, "I don't think so."

"Okay, I'll settle for you being my gal."

She bit her bottom lip and glanced around the room. "You have to take any threat you get seriously."

"If I do, will you admit you still like me?"

She pressed her lips together and looked toward Checkerboard.

"Camp Town Races" played.

"Going to rut all night. Going to rut all day. I spent my money on a bonny whore. To pass the night away." Blackie sang loudly, changing the chorus.

Scotty jabbed Blackie. "Ladies and children within earshot."

"Sorry, miss. It's the only version I know."

"Guess that's it for tonight," Checkerboard announced. "Got a card game calling."

The room cleared with only a scattering of folks remaining. Dusty needed to be alone with Mia. He needed to hold her hand. Who was he joshing? He needed to kiss her. "Ready for our walk?"

"It's not safe."

"Sure, it is. I'll protect you."

She folded her arms. "I'll go, but only because we need to talk."

As he led her up the hill to their special place, she didn't hold his hand, and he figured kissing was out. She cupped her hand above her eye and squinted at the pasture to the south. "Is there a cowboy in Bella's stall?"

He stood behind her. "Looks like Blackie or Reynolds. Wonder if there's a problem. Nope. He's leaving."

"Dusty, be vigilant. If you get arrested, they'll hang you."

"You seem to think someone's after me. Forget about the dream." He turned her to face him, caught her hand, and placed it over his heart.

"You've seen the way Reynolds glares at us. He's out for revenge."

"The guy's harmless. Quit thinking about him and enjoy our pleasant evening." He motioned to the bench, slid in next to her, and snuck his arm around her shoulders. "Westin's Great Grandfather built this bench for his new bride." His fingers swept a strand of hair from her eyes, he pressed his forehead to hers.

She pushed away. "I need to say something. Promise me you'll listen before you respond."

Listen? How could he listen when he longed to sample her lips? "If you promise me more kisses." He leaned in and pressed his mouth to the curve of her neck.

"Stop that." She stood, folding her arms.

"Darlin', please sit down. I'm all ears."

She sat and jiggled her foot. "This is hard enough to say without—"

"Did something happen today?" He tried to gaze into her eyes, but she glanced at the ground.

"I'm, not ... not from here." Why did her bottom lip quiver?

"I know. You're from Los Angeles."

She folded and unfolded her hands. "How do I tell you this and not sound crazy?"

"Just say it. I won't judge."

Her foot swung back and forth. "Like I said, this will sound insane, but it's true. Well, um, before last week I lived over a hundred years in the future."

She must be jesting, but her lips pinched together, and her eyes lacked amusement.

"You're from the ... future?" Future stuck to the roof of his mouth. "Quit joking."

"Think about it. When we first met, didn't I seem a little odd?"

She had plowed right into him. Odd, but not when she said the Belgian Draft scared her. "Being terrified of a horse doesn't make you odd."

"I only had one bag with me. Didn't you wonder why?"

"You said your trunk had been lost. Did you lie?"

She nodded. "Only out of necessity."

Dishonesty rubbed him wrong, even coming from her. "If you're from the future how'd you get here?"

"I boarded a train in Rialto."

"Heading for?"

"Victorville, I mean Victor." She scowled. "Is this an inquisition?"

"Don't rightly know what an inquisition is. I'm just setting my mind straight."

She remained as still as a windless night.

"Go on," he said.

She didn't look at him. "The train crested past the Cajon Summit. I placed this band on my finger. The metal became hot, and I turned and twisted and tried to take the ring off. Then my vision blurred, and I wound up here in eighteen-ninety Hesperia. I must've gone through some portal or window of time."

"That's impossible!"

"It happened." Her eyes were wide, frightened, fragile. "Now for the worst part. I saw your sketch in an old newspaper article. The headline said, *Hesperia Horse Thief Hanged.*"

He got up and paced. She sounded crazy. "This can't be true."

"I wish it wasn't." She stood in front of him and took his hand. "You're a good man. You don't deserve to die young for something I know you'd never do."

"I need to think. We'd best head on back." He had to get away, take Thunder on a long ride.

"You don't believe me?" Tears filled her eyes.

"I don't know what to believe." He offered his arm.

"I know it's a lot to comprehend."

She couldn't be from the future. Had to be pulling his leg.

"Time's running out. You must leave this ranch before it's too late. Like tonight." Her voice became high and frantic. He kept their walk slow and steady. They passed his place, and he opened the gate into the schoolhouse yard and escorted her to her door.

Using his bandana, he wiped away her tears. "We'll talk tomorrow, darlin'. I promise." He kissed her forehead and left, unable to kick off this ominous feeling turning in his gut.

Chapter Eleven

Unable to sleep, Dusty punched his pillow. Mia's comment rattled through his head. *I'm from the future.* Had her beauty blinded him, making him weak north of his ears? But a little voice in his head said she was telling the truth. When she spoke about the newspaper article written in the future, she never flinched.

Plus, there'd been questionable things happening lately. The barbed wire fencing had been snipped, a bullet nearly killed him. Somebody wanted him dead. Reynolds despised him as did Slick. He wouldn't put it past either one to go after Mia, just to get to him. She must be protected.

He settled in his bed, closed his eyes, and drifted off. Like a voyeur, he watch himself mount a horse under a tree. White's Hanging Tree. What the hell?

"Dusty, let's get this over with." The sheriff, Flynn Law, prodded him from behind.

Assisted onto a horse, the hangman held a coiled rope. It seemed real.

"String him up," somebody yelled from the packed crowd. Off to the side, families spread out blankets and picnicked. The morbid scene reminded him of Old Man Griffith's necktie party. He recalled watching the man's neck snap, his legs wiggle and stop. The awful death still sickened Dusty.

"Any last requests?" The preacher's horrid breath washed over him.

"Stop the hanging. I'm innocent."

"That's what they all say." The hangman hit the horse's rear, and shouted, "Yaaaahhh."

Dusty lurched forward and fell to the floor. He woke holding his neck, gasping, powerless.

The dang nightmare had him far too perturbed. He picked up a pitcher from the table next to the stove. Filling a glass with water, his hand shook. Mia's foreboding put this deranged notion about hanging into his mind.

Dawn's glow filtered through his windowpane. A rooster crowed his morning call. No sense trying to sleep. He dressed and stepped onto the porch.

Roar.

What was that?

Snorting. Chuffing. Bellowing. Another bull must've gotten out.

The noise came from the road behind his cabin. Dusty bolted to the edge of the trail.

"Dammit, Rampage is out," he grumbled. "Not again." The hulking two-ton bull snorted. Its ears pinned back. Lowering its head, it stomped its hoof on the ground. Blackie walked past the barn. The beast raised its tail and charged.

"Watch out, Blackie!" Dusty shouted.

The stocky cowboy sprinted, grabbed hold of the top of a fence post, catapulted over the barbed wire into the pasture, and safely circumvented the bull's wrath. The animal huffed as it stood on the trail between the cabins and the fields.

Ace rushed out of the bunkhouse.

The enraged bull turned and frenzied forward, hooking its horn into the front of the cowboy's waist. The bovine picked up Ace like a stuffed bear and threw him several feet in the air. The cowboy landed inches from the fencing. The bull chortle-wheezed and galumphed along the dirt path toward the main entrance.

"Ace's injured," Dusty screamed and dropped next to the crumpled form on the ground. "You alright?"

"Been better." A deep red stain of blood grew above the cowboy's belt line.

Blackie hopped the fence and stood by Dusty. "That should've been me."

"Count yourself lucky." Dusty tried to slow his thumping pulse. "Fetch doc."

Ace sprinted off.

"Scotty get Westin. I'm going after Rampage."

Checkerboard stood next to Dusty. "So am I."

More wranglers rushed from the bunkhouse.

Dusty grabbed his saddle from the stables, called for Thunder in his pen, and mounted. He glanced at the schoolhouse. Mia would be sleeping in her room. He imagined her long hair fanning her pillow. Forget her for now. Concentrate on catching the dang bull.

Dusty and Checkerboard rode half a mile to the front entrance. "Some idiotic chucklehead left the gate open," Dusty grumbled.

Checkerboard nodded. "Somebody's got the brains of a grasshopper."

"There's Rampage—heading towards Cedar Springs," Slick said, as he caught up to them where the road forked.

They came within ten yards from the bull, and it bounded.

"Rampage, will you quit playing chase," Slick yelled.

The bull roared and sped further.

"You dumb bull." Checkerboard kicked his horse to a gallop.

They chased the bull down the dirt road. It stopped. The men inched closer; the animal sped off.

"Dammit." Dusty's agitation rose.

The bull ran across the bridge over a wash, slowed, turned his head, chuffed and kept going.

About noon, it turned up the road leading to Cedar Springs, trotted through a section of downed fence at the O'Malley's farm, and charged toward a renegade heifer and mounted her. Mating took ten seconds at most.

Dusty laughed. "Guess Rampage's got a girlfriend."

Finished with the act, the bovine turned around and trotted in the direction of the Los Flores Ranch.

"Hope she was worth it." Checkerboard chuckled as he rode next to Rampage, roping the now tame as a puppy, bull, and trotted it to the ranch's main entrance and onward.

"Close the gate," Dusty said to Slick.

They went past the bullpens. Sure enough, Rampage had knocked out a section.

"Tornado's old pen oughta hold him." Dusty figured the pen in the middle of two fields would confine the bull. No way would he chance anyone else getting hurt.

Slick opened the front gate and then the middle.

"This time stay put, Rampage," Checkerboard said and released the bull from the rope inside the second enclosure. It bellowed and ran off.

By late afternoon, Dusty made it to the stables.

Blackie greeted them on the path. "Ace's darn lucky. Only ended up with a gouge in his side. Nothing serious. How'd the bull get out anyway?"

"Knocked down a fence." Dusty led his horse to the stall, his thoughts on Mia.

Scotty rushed up to him. "The mare, Stormy, is in labor."

"What's she doing?" Dusty followed him inside the stables.

"Keeps huffing, making odd noises, won't settle down."

Dusty rushed to the stall and examined the restless mare. She kept lifting her tail and walking in circles. Damn wretched timing. He'd have to wait to see Mia. His patience cinched tight.

"Think it'll be quick?" Scotty asked.

"I doubt it, but you'd best get Westin from the dining hall. And if you see Miss Amelia, tell her I'll see her as soon as I can."

Nothing in Dusty's life ever was easy.

~ * ~

Mia paced inside her room. An hour until dinner, and Dusty wasn't back yet. If only she'd seen him at breakfast. The bull caused her hours of grief.

Why'd she tell Dusty the truth last night? As if she had much choice. In less than three weeks, it would be the Fourth of July. Her nerves frazzled worse than the time she'd lost her passport in Tijuana. She walked to her porch, checking Dusty's cabin and the trail leading from the stables to his place.

146

No Dusty.

Frustrated, she went inside and parked on her bed. The right side of her dress hiked up, displaying a pocket at the bottom of her petticoat. Pushing two fingers inside the four-inch-long rectangle, she found no holes at the bottom. Perfect spot to hide her license and debit card. Tonight, she'd show Dusty these items. Maybe then he'd believe her and leave the ranch.

The dinner bell clanged, and she rushed down the trail and into the dining hall.

No Dusty in sight.

Reynolds waved. He'd seen her holding hands with Dusty, kissing him. The man couldn't get it through his caveman-like brain she wasn't interested. He must be one of those guys who took a woman's rejection as a challenge. Probably figured she'd change her mind about him once he straightened out her thinking.

A chill coursed through her veins. Would Reynolds setup Dusty? She walked to the side counter, ladled beef stew into a bowl, and took a seat kitty-corner from Sandy and Westin.

"Rampage's secure." Westin had a sullen expression. "Hate it that Ace got hurt."

"Doc says he'll be fine." Sandy placed her hand on her husband's shoulder.

Where was Dusty?

"My boy ain't complained about goin' to school in the summer." Ben's dad, a big burly man, said from beside her.

"You said if I went peaceable-like, I could fish all day Friday."

Mia snickered; the father laughed full and hardy.

147

Scotty hurried into the room straight to Westin. "Stormy's ready to foal." He turned to her. "Dusty said to tell you he'll see you as soon as he can."

"Tell him I'll be waiting." Could it be too late to save him? She had no idea what date he was arrested or how long the trial lasted.

"Let's go," Westin said, and the two left.

"How long does it take for a foal to be born?" she asked Sandy.

"Hard to say. It's the mare's second birth, should be fairly quick. Three hours at most."

Three hours sounded like an eternity. A low burn filled her stomach. "I'll go to my room and read the next chapter in *Little Women*. Thanks again for loaning me the book."

"You're more than welcome. See you in the morning."

She stopped at the door. Reynolds watched her and tipped his hat.

Wary, she rushed down the path. Footsteps crunched behind her, kicking up gravel, and skittering pebbles. She picked up her pace, unlatched the schoolyard gate and glanced over her shoulder.

"Miss Amelia, please wait," Reynolds called.

She sprinted up the stairs to her room. Her fingers grasped the doorknob.

Reynolds stepped in front of her. His back blocked the door, forcing her to face him. "Heard you and Dusty arguing last night."

He'd been spying on her. Aggravation surged from within. Why wouldn't this guy leave her alone?

"Got a hunch you two are through, and I aim to court you." The cowboy ensnared her hand and lifted it to his mouth. His hot, breath disgusted her.

She pulled out of his grasp. "Reynolds, please move so I can go inside."

He traced her cheek with his thumb. "Only if you promise to have breakfast with me tomorrow."

"Honestly, Reynolds. Dusty's courting me." It might not be true.

"I know how fickle you women can be. I'll save you a seat in case you change your mind." He walked away whistling.

What a prize. She wasn't fickle—she chose Dusty.

She slammed her door and leaned her body against the inside frame, breathing fast. She locked it, primed to find a weapon in case the creep decided to return. Hangers, boots, and dresses in her wardrobe, the brush, and her drawing book wouldn't protect her. The lamp on her desk might do. She picked it up. Too awkward to hold.

There should be something in the classroom, and she went through the connecting door, she picked up a glass jar. Not quite. Two hornbooks. Not heavy enough. On the wall, a flat wooden paddle. Excellent!

She had to see Dusty. Talk to him. Convince him of the danger. Get him to leave. Once the mare gave birth, Dusty would be home. If not, she'd wait outside all night if need be. She pulled back the schoolhouse curtain, checking to see if Reynolds lurked around. No sign of him or anyone else. Paddle in hand, cautiously, she opened the door and stepped out.

Neighing, crickets chirping, laughter from the bunkhouse.

Not yet dark, she glanced to the right, to the left, back to the right. With nobody in sight, she dashed to Dusty's cabin.

She knocked once. No answer.

A mouse scurried along the windowsill. No creepy mouse would ever intimidate her again. "Go away." She stomped her foot. The mouse dropped down and scrambled under a bush.

She banged on the door. Nothing.

Peering inside his window, she spotted an old battered table, a pot-bellied stove. No sight of Dusty.

Why not wait inside? She gripped the doorknob, started to turn it, and chickened out.

Dusty said they'd talk.

She pulled a weathered chair away from the building, propped her feet on a bench, and whispered, "Dusty, please come home soon."

Chapter Twelve

Rhett and Michael attended a rancher's meeting in
Dusty was standing inside the mare's stall when her
water broke. The head and front feet presented. Minutes
ticked into hours. Finally, the foal made its grand
entrance. Its coat was covered with slime. The mare
proudly smelled her foal resting on the ground and
licked away the sticky substance.

"Got a name picked out?" Dusty asked.

"Ben Sheik." Westin smiled. "Figured it's a fitting
name for a thoroughbred."

The foal gave a quiet whinny.

"Sounds like he agrees." Dusty stared at the spindly
legged animal who tried to stand. He'd never tire of
seeing new life.

"You've been up since dawn. Can't thank you enough
for going after Rampage and helping Stormy. Go on
home. Scotty and I will take it from here," Westin said,
still seated on a bale of hay inside the stall.

"Thanks, boss. Appreciate it." Dusty grabbed a lit
lantern from the wall and headed for his cabin.

Someone slept in his porch chair. Small boots
propped on the bench. Shapely calves. Blonde hair.
Mia?

Crouching next to her, he said, "Darlin', wake up."

"Dusty. You're back." Her eyes flitted open. "What time is it?"

"After midnight." He kissed her forehead. "Did something happen?"

"I've been on edge all day." She grasped his upper arm. "Can we go inside, talk in private?"

"But your reputation?"

"The hell with my reputation," she snapped, purpose glowed in her eyes. "I can't chance anyone hearing us."

"What if they fire you? They might even force us to marry."

"I'm okay with either one." She stood.

"So am I." A warmth settled deep inside him at the thought of coming home to her every night.

She sat in a chair at the kitchen table. He placed the lantern in the center.

Usually poised, her lower lip quivered. "I-I don't want you to die."

He dropped into the other chair. "Neither do I."

"What if we could change fate?" The dark shadows under her eyes proved she'd done plenty of pondering.

"Can't wish the grim reaper away. He comes when he's called." He leaned over and kissed her. "Your lips taste sweet."

"And you're avoiding the obvious. A million kisses won't change anything," she said through clenched teeth. "I *am* from the future, over a hundred years from now. I'm not insane."

"Never said you were." But he considered it plenty.

"Maybe this'll convince you." She raised the edges of her skirt to show white stockings, pushed the material up, and gave him a clear view of the bottom of her bloomers below her knee.

He whistled. "Figured you had gorgeous legs, and you've confirmed my suspicions."

"Quit gawking." She pulled out a card from a hidden pocket and pressed it into his palm. "This is my driver's license."

"Nobody needs a license to drive."

"They do in the future. Hold it up to the light. My photo's in color. Color photography won't be invented for another thirty or forty years."

He stared at the wording. "What's DOB mean?

"Date of birth."

He shook his head. "That's over a hundred years away.

"I know it seems impossible. When I first came to the hotel, I resisted the idea I'd gone back in time."

He rubbed his finger along the card, flipped it over, tried to bend it. "Can't place the material. Kinda feels like rubber."

"It's plastic." She gave him a blue card with an orange and blue circle at the bottom. "Here's my debit card. It works like a line of credit."

Dumbfounded, he struggled to fathom the things she showed him.

"The article said you'd hang on July Fourth—in eighteen days. If you leave the ranch today, you might be saved." Her eyes seemed clear and lucid.

"You say you're from the future. You know the day I'll die. Could you be wrong?"

"I wish I were." She stood, tilting her head. "Since you don't seem to believe me, I've got more items in my room to show you. You coming?"

"Not sure if it'd be proper."

"Really, Dusty. It's no worse than me being alone with you in here." She held the door open.

He followed her down the path and up the back step of the schoolhouse that led inside her room. She sat at the end of her bed and sifted through her luggage on the floor. He leaned against the dresser, awkward and out of sorts.

"Please sit down." She patted the bed. "Looking up at you kinks my neck."

He took a spot on her right. She continued searching inside her bag and pulled out a pair of odd footwear in the brightest of pink shades. "Ever see shoes like these?"

"Nope."

"They're neon pink."

He examined one shoe, lighter than any footwear he'd ever held, and dropped it into her bag. "Color hurts my eyes."

"I guess it would. How about keys like this?" She handed him a small coated object with a hard tar-like substance.

"Nope, but—"

She dug into her purse, gave him a small rectangular box and squeezed in next to him. "This is a telephone. It won't turn on, or I'd show you how it works."

"A telephone this small?" Her closeness made it hard to concentrate.

"Yes. You won't believe some of the inventions in the future." She pulled out a book and flipped through pages with sketches of cats and kittens and turned to the next page.

He stared at his own likeness. "You've been drawing me?"

"Can't seem to stop myself."

He leaned in and feathered tender caresses along her neck. "I can't stop thinking about you either."

A tiny smirk lifted the corner of her mouth. "You're incorrigible." She took her book and sat at her desk near the window. "I'll sketch what's in the future."

Stationed over the back of her chair, he massaged her shoulders.

"Cars, carriages that run with motors similar to a train, will replace horses and buggies," she said as she continued drawing with charcoal.

"Please say horses still exist."

She blinked. "There's plenty of horses around. Most people ride for pleasure or watch them race."

He focused on her art. "How'd you learn to draw like this?"

"Practice, lots of practice." She kept sketching. "Electricity will light lamps in maybe ten years. This reduces the number of fires from kerosene."

"Electricity's like lightning. Lightning spooks me something fierce." A friend of his grandfather was struck down dead, and the idea still haunted him.

"In time, scientists get the bugs out."

"Bugs?"

"Problems." She had a glint in her eye. "Life's easier. You'll buy all your food from a grocery store."

"I don't get it. You need cattle for steak, chickens for eggs, cows for milk."

"There's plenty of ranches and farms left in rural areas." She sketched an object with wings. "This is an airplane. It's sort of like a big carriage. I've flown from here to New York in less than a day."

"Does the thing flap its wings?"

"It has an engine similar to a train. I can't explain how it gets in the air. It somehow does."

"Sounds plain loco." He'd never set foot in one of those contraptions.

"It's true."

"Shh. I hear voices outside." He blew out the lamp, pulled her to the floor on the side of the bed, and covered her mouth with his hand.

"Keep your trap closed and wait here." A man shouted from below her window. "I could've sworn Miss Amelia's lantern was lit. Must've just turned in." Boots stomped up the stairs.

Dusty was ready to get up and cold-cock whoever was out there, but she whispered, "Stay down."

Rap, rap, rap.

"It's Reynolds." Another knock. "Sweetie, I hope you're awake, and we can talk." His voice slurred.

"Bet she's playing possum."

"Shut up, Slick," Reynolds' voice came out gruff. "Miss Amelia ain't like that."

"Well, I'm leaving," Slick shouted.

"Wait for me." Boots clunked down the steps and crunched on the gravel and faded off.

"Has Reynolds been bothering you?" Dusty's teeth jarred together as he pushed himself up and stood.

"The guy won't get it through his dense brain I'm not interested." The bed squeaked as she sat on it. "He heard us arguing last night."

Irritation coursed through his blood. "He's been eavesdropping on us."

"Sit and chill." She patted the bed.

He fumbled his way next to her. "It's awfully dark in here. Think I'll light the lantern."

"This is better." Click.

A light beam hit his eyes. "What in tarnation?"

"It's my flashlight." She shut it off. Darkness. Click. The light returned. "Try it. Push the button on the side."

She placed a small cold cylinder in his palm. He clicked. On, off, on, off, on, off, on. "Amazing. Why isn't it hot?"

"It uses batteries for energy in here." She pointed to the knob on the end of a two-inch cylinder. "I'd take it apart, but then we'd have to light the lantern."

"Such a puny thing making a bushel full of light." Pressing a tiny button on the end, a blue light shone. He held the light on her face. "This is an awful lot to reckon."

"You believe me, right?" She wrapped her arms around herself, her eyes narrowed.

"Either that or I've gone loco." This little lady needed him, needed his comfort, needed his reassurance, so he draped his arm around her. "Did the article say who wanted me out of the picture?"

"I don't think so."

"Do you know the date of my arrest?" The sound of his thundering heartbeat thrashed through his ears.

"No, but you're supposed to hang on the Fourth of July." She shuddered. "It's night. We can leave now, and nobody will see us."

"If we sneak off and one of the thoroughbreds ends up missing, we'll both look guilty. Folks will suspect you're my accomplice. Could never live with myself if you were arrested."

"Is saving me worth risking your life?" Her voice shrieked despair.

"Absolutely. You're worth a whole heck of a lot more."

"Come on, Dusty." Her right eyebrow lifted. "Don't let pride get you killed."

"From where I stand, pride is a good thing."

"My God, you're stubborn," she huffed.

"Already told Westin I'm taking you to town on Saturday. I'll see him at first light and say we're heading for town tomorrow afternoon."

"Dusty, this is serious. My intuition says it'll be too late."

"I'll be okay." He pulled her closer. "Today's June thirteenth. We still have three weeks."

"What can I do to change your mind?" She stroked his arm.

"Fate didn't send you here to watch me die." His thumb grazed her chin, lifting her face to gaze at him. "Before we met, I saw visions of a woman. Think it might have been you."

"You did?" Her voice sang with wonder.

"Yes. Over the years, I've seen a blonde in the distance picking wildflowers at the fork of the Mojave River. She always faded and disappeared. I wished she was real. Figured it must be a figment of my imagination."

"I've picnicked at the fork plenty of times and picked flowers. Sometimes my cousin and I looked for frogs."

"Frogs? Horses terrify you, but not slimy frogs."

"Frogs are little."

"And you're full of surprises. Must be why I find you alluring." He kissed her cheek. "Anyway, it's no coincidence we're together. Reckon we should enjoy every minute we have."

"Quit acting so darn charming." Not an ounce of flirt came with her line. Instead, she put her hand on his knee.

He jolted upright as her touch kicked in desire.

"I'm begging you to leave tonight. Please."

"Tomorrow, we'll go anywhere you want. Even have a little money saved."

"I don't care about your money, I care about you. I care about you staying alive." Using her arms to encircle his neck, her lips touched his. "Let's go."

She was mighty enticing. "Tomorrow." He pulled her on his lap. "Destiny's already changed. We're together. That must mean something."

"Please listen. This is serious."

"It's difficult when you're so distracting." He teased her mouth, and his tongue lingered along her lips.

She pulled away. "It's hard to believe we've known each other for only a couple of weeks."

"Best weeks of my life." He'd fallen fast.

"You have to believe I'm from the future." She clicked the flashlight off and on two times and dropped it on the floor. It lit the bed, but not as brightly as a lantern would. "And what I'm feeling is wrong, I've tried hard not to—"

"Was I too forward?"

"No." She gasped in a quick breath.

"Don't you know you can tell me anything?"

"This problem is big, gigantic. I knew better than to—" She paused for one, two, three seconds.

"Say it. Whatever it is can't be so bad."

"I-I can't help it—I shouldn't—"

"Shouldn't what?" His heart slowed. What could be so dreadful?

"Love you."

"You love me?" He cupped her face. "Darlin', do you mean it?"

"Yes. I couldn't stop myself. You're kind and handsome, principled and stubborn."

"You love me because I'm stubborn?"

"You're willing to put other people and even animals before thinking about what you want. You've been patient with me, taught me to ride, even when I fought you." She sighed. "You're a good guy—too good to die."

"You love me? You really love me?"

"It's wrong." The gal who lassoed his heart gazed at him with wide-eyed trepidation.

"Not wrong. The best thing I've ever heard."

"Loving you is a disaster." She pushed to get off his lap, but he encased his arms around her.

"Not hardly." He removed her hairpins. Her locks flowed past her shoulders, and he brushed the hair from the nape of her neck. His mouth had access to her sensitive skin, and he skimmed kisses along her shoulders and collarbone, lingering to give her a quick nip on the side of her neck.

"Ummm," her moan drove him on.

He nibbled her exposed throat, her jaw, and upward toward her mouth. His bulge straining against his pants.

"You're beautiful," he moaned into her mouth. His meandering tongue met the softness of her lips. Her mouth opened, allowing him to glory in her taste.

Her tongue sent hot little sparks throughout his body. Her fingers played with his hair, as he slowly deepened the kiss. Drowning in illicit sensations, a groan shuttered through him, and his breathing became labored. "I'll never tire of kissing you." His mouth brushed caresses along her neck.

"Your whiskers tickle."

Her hands slipped underneath his shirt, her fingers riffed along his back.

"I like it when you touch me," he managed to whisper.

"I need you to touch me."

With her still on his lap, his large fingers struggled with her delicate buttons on the front of her blouse. He removed it and untied her lacy camisole. His hands brushed along her skin, the smoothness reminding him of velvet. He outlined a breast with his thumb. His body was on fire. His craving couldn't be satisfied until he perused every inch of her. She undid all the buttons on his shirt until her fingers traced his bare chest. They fell back onto the mattress lying on their sides kissing.

A voice inside told him to stop. "I really should go."

"Stay." She called to him like a deck of cards calls a gambler.

"You sure?"

She pulled his mouth to hers, igniting searing kisses.

He kissed her slow and leisurely, treasuring every moan and croon she emitted as he continued devouring her mouth.

His body hummed with tension. He toyed with her nipple between his thumb and forefinger until it became a hardened pebble. Burying his face in her neck, he took a love bite. Her hands massaged his back.

He removed her skirt, exploring every luscious curve along her waist, her smooth stomach, the slight indentation of her belly button. His tender kisses became hot and demanding. An inferno raged between them as they kissed, ravenous for each other. Her fingers roamed along his waistband. She unbuckled his belt, unfastened the top snap of his pants, and his erection hardened

It took every ounce of discipline to pull away. "You sure 'bout this?" He'd leave if she asked.

She answered by placing his hand on the drawstring of her pantaloons

"You want these off," his voice croaked.

"Uh-huh," she gave a barely audible lilt and continued unbuttoning his pants.

Somehow, his shaky fingers undid her tie. She lifted her bottom and pulled off her pantaloons.

"We need to even the playing field." Her voice came out breathy and sensuous and desperate as she pushed his jeans down to his thighs.

A thunderbolt of awareness made him pick up his speed to undress. He sat up, yanked his right boot off, his left, unintentionally kicking the light under the bed as his pants fell to the floor. His length grew, throbbing for release. Dark, he relied on touch. Sweeping his hand along her belly, to her breast, he cupped the right globe and gave a gentle squeeze. His mouth covered the left nipple, teased and taunted, teased and taunted, teased and taunted.

"Oh, Dusty." She gave a low, feminine murmur.

"You like that?" He gently touched the corner of her mouth and caressed her slow and tender. Once he deepened the kiss. Her little mewing sounds stoked his cravings. Her kisses matched his own yearning for more. His heart drummed wildly as he slid his palms up her inner thigh and parted her legs. His finger dipped inside her core, finding her wet. Her nails raked across his back as he moved one finger in and out. Longing to taste her sweet dew, he hesitated.

"Dusty, make love to me." She sounded as desperate as he felt. Her hand slid along his manhood, triggering his loins as she squeezed his length.

"Are you sure?" he had to ask.

She gave a breathy, "Yes!"

His body said, *take her now*, but his mind said, *take your time*.

He rose above her, his pulse ricocheting, wishing he could see her eyes. His fingers linked with hers as he entered her slowly, filling her, as her slick core molded around his shaft. "Am I hurting you?"

She wriggled a little bit, her body rocking against his hips.

He pulled out. Heat spiraled as he flexed his hips, rocking her, keeping their rhythm slow. The pleasurable aching built a timeless bond between body and soul. Each giving and taking, pushing and pulling, touching and arching, and loving.

"Faster," she moaned and wrapped her legs around his waist, moving with him and demanding more.

Raw need consumed him as he thrust into her over and over. Excitement heightened. It was like a fire forging out of control, generating heat. He pumped harder increasing his pace, feeling her orgasm close, and holding back his own need for completion. Her body wound tight, spiraling until she shattered.

Her climax triggered his own release, erupting in rippling waves of intensity.

With his breathing ragged, he rolled to the side and pulled her into his arms. "Darlin', I love you."

"You don't have to say that,"

"I mean it." He lay there boneless, enjoying the cool air. "Besides being gorgeous, you didn't run when things got tough. Got a stubborn streak that matches my own, and the gumption to take a chance on me. But it's your tender heart that gets to me every time. How can I help but love you?"

"That's the most romantic thing I've ever heard." She placed her head on his chest. "So we can leave now?"

"Hmm." They'd made love, and he'd make an honest woman out of her. "Seein' as you're the most passionate, desirable woman I've ever known, marry me. Be my wife."

"I don't belong here."

"Yes, you do. You belong with me." She made his life complete. "I'll be a good husband, well, can't promise I won't get flustered at times, but I'll do my best to make you happy."

"What if one day I disappear?"

"We'll take things as they come," he said, hoping she didn't feel him wince. He gently caressed her cheek.

"I'll marry you, but only if we elope tonight."

"I reckon that can be arranged." He kissed her with a fierce determination.

"Just so you know, I can be difficult."

"You?" he laughed.

She slapped his arm.

"I'd say you're challenging and well worth the chase." He feathered kisses up her neck and nipped her ear.

"Good to know you get me." She moved off the bed. Must've crawled under it to get the flashlight because when she got up, he could see her nude body. Sexy, she stirred his passion, and he wanted to pull her back into his arms.

She threw him his clothes. "Now, get dressed."

"Yes, ma'am." He tugged on his pants, buttoned them, put on his shirt, and lit the lamp. "Can't wait to see Blackie's expression when we wake him to get hitched."

"Blackie does weddings?" Her jaw dropped.

"Also, gives Sunday services here in the winter."

"Wouldn't it be better to go to town while we still can?" She slipped on her pantaloons and camisole. "We'll slip away quietly and not tell anyone."

"Works for me. Let them think we eloped." He admired her rosy cheeks and well-kissed mouth. "You need any help?"

"Nope. And I know what you're thinking. We're not making love again until we're far away from here. Turn around."

"You're mighty fetching."

"You have to wait," her voice came out sassy.

"Don't mind. The next time we share a bed, I want it to be as man and wife." He watched her fasten her blouse. Her breasts were covered, but he vividly recalled how her nipple responded to his mouth. His manhood stiffened. He stepped into his boots and stared at her as she put on the same clothing he'd helped remove not long ago, causing a groan to escape from him.

"Is there a problem?" she asked in a husky voice.

"Nope. Just wanted to say you look gorgeous." It took every ounce of resolve to not throw her back on the bed and have his way with her, so he pulled back the curtains and glanced out the window. It couldn't be dawn already.

"I'm almost done." She sounded happy.

Hell, he was ecstatic. In another hour or two, they would be legally wed.

Her boots clicked on the floor, and he swiveled to her. Her long hair tousled, her cheeks tinged pink with afterglow from their lovemaking. She brushed her hair and braided it into a ponytail. "Come along, cowboy. I'm ready to be Mrs. Dusty Mann."

"Impatient little thing." He walked to the door.

Clang, clang, clang.

"Fire in the stables!" a man shouted. "Wake up everyone!"

Clang, clang, clang.

"Darlin', I've gotta go. We'll get married after the fire's out."

"Please don't leave me." She rushed to him and anchored her arms around his neck.

"I'm sorry. I couldn't live with myself if someone dies because I didn't help."

"Don't be so damn heroic. There's plenty of others who can help with the fire."

"I love you." He kissed her one more time and peeled her arms off from around his neck.

"If you insist on acting heroic, go on." She held the door.

From his view on the porch, red-orange flames flickered. Dusty dashed toward the stables, barely visible through the thick smoke. If the wooden structure went like a tinderbox, the barn would be next. Boards crackled and sizzled.

A cowboy threw a bucket of water at the bottom of the door.

"Think the fire's out," Scotty said. "Do I need to pump any more water?"

"Fill ten more buckets," Checkerboard grabbed a full one and handed it to the closest person in line.

Westin rushed up. "What the hell happened?"

Scotty raised a brow and glanced at Dusty. "Saw the glow from my bunkhouse window and got the others to come running."

"Anybody inside?" Dusty open the double doors.

"No people. Horses." With a lantern next to him, Scotty kept pumping water and filling buckets.

"Stormy and her foal need to get out of the smoke." Dusty had to get to her.

"Take my bandana," Checkerboard dipped it in water.

Dusty tied the cloth over his nose and mouth. "I'm going in."

"Right behind you." Westin threw open stalls, slapped horses' flanks, and shouted, "Yaaaaaah!"

Inside Stormy's stall, Dusty talked slow and smooth. He slipped a rope around her neck and led her outside. "It's all right, girl. Come on." The spindly-leg Ben Sheik followed. "Stormy and Ben seem to be unscathed," he told his boss.

"That's a relief." He called to the people gathered outside. "Men, thanks to your quick action, the fire's out. Now round up any mares with foals and bring them to the old stables.

Stormy snorted as Dusty kept walking. The light of dawn was barely visible through the layer of smoke.

Mia ran up to him and wrapped her arms around his waist. "Let's leave now?"

"Darlin', I can't." He kissed her cheek. "Let me take care of the horses. Shouldn't take much time to get them settled. I'll see you at breakfast."

Niki Mitchell

Chapter Thirteen

Mia scanned the dining hall and didn't see Dusty. Her crazy, responsible cowboy had to stick around and put his life in danger.

Maybe he was right. Destiny wouldn't allow him to die. They both deserved a life together. If only worry would quit gnawing at her brain, telling her history can't be changed.

Reynolds stood inches from her. "You're mighty fetching this morning." He smiled a tad too wide. "I'll save you a spot at the table next to me."

"Not necessary," she said.

Reynolds strutted off with a cocky swagger. God this guy had nerve. She'd like to knock the arrogant no-good cowboy down a notch. Not watching, she turned and umphed into a hard, warm chest.

"Hello, darlin'," Dusty drawled. "Looking for me."

"You promised we'd leave."

"Don't worry, you'll soon be my bride." His voice reverberated.

Talking ceased. Silverware stopped clinking. Everyone stared. Mia wanted to leap into the Mojave River and float away.

"Relax, darlin'," Dusty whispered. He addressed the crowd. "Me 'n' Miss Amelia are getting hitched."

Hollers filled the air. Two cowboys put their heads down. Reynolds glowered.

"When's the wedding?" Blackie asked.

Without thought, she said, "This afternoon?"

Everyone laughed, except for her and Dusty.

Sandy cut in. "Make it next Saturday, and we'll have the shindig here."

Today's June thirteenth. Seven days—the twenty-first. Fourteen would be the twenty-seventh. Twenty-one days until July Fourth. Dusty's hanging. "It's nice of you to offer, but we're getting married today."

"Folks, my intended's mighty anxious to get hitched," Dusty chuckled and winked at her.

"What's the rush?" Sandy pressed her lips together.

She probably thinks I'm pregnant. It was possible since neither one even thought about birth control. The idea thrilled Mia. "I'm not getting any younger." She bit her tongue to stop from saying, *"Dusty needs to leave before—"*

Laughter surrounded her, irritating, obnoxious laughter.

"The whole town will want to see our handsome ranch foreman marry our school teacher," Norma's mother said.

Dusty turned to Westin. "I'd like to take Mia to town this morning."

"The fire's got everybody spooked. Since I don't know who started it, you need to ride fence and make sure the ranch is secure." His boss wore a serious, I won't-give-an-inch, expression. "Can't chance anybody else sneaking around and causing more trouble."

"Can't you please get somebody else to do it this once?" Mia said, determined to keep Dusty safe.

"There's nobody I trust more than him." Westin nodded to Dusty. "Figure you'll be done by eleven at the latest."

"Leave now, before it's too late." she whispered into Dusty's ear.

"I'll be fine."

Westin turned to his nephew. "You're lead this weekend."

Reynolds glared hatred in her direction; her skin prickled.

"Will school be cancelled?" Billy's eyes gave a mischievous glint.

"We'll end at ten-thirty," Westin said and smiled at Mia as if that would appease her.

"Yippee!" Children whooped and hollered.

"Surely, someone else could cover for you." She followed Dusty to the breakfast counter.

The silhouette portrait on the wall reminded her of a shadowy grim reaper. The angel of death pointed his bony finger at Dusty. She shivered.

"Quit fretting, please." Dusty filled his plate from the side counter. She took a slice of buttered toast. She and Dusty sat on a bench on the opposite end of the room from Westin and Reynolds.

"Smile, darlin'," Dusty whispered in her ear, "we're leaving today."

"It should be now." The toast tasted like cardboard. She washed it down with coffee. At the thought of Dusty behind bars. her hunger vanished.

Dusty shoveled in his food and quickly emptied his plate. "Walk with me outside." Past the dining hall entrance, he pulled her into his arms and kissed her, long and loving. "I'll be back soon, I promise, and we'll be on our way."

"Don't go."

"I gave my word." He kissed her again.

"I love you." She said, tired of arguing.

He leaned in for another kiss. "Can't wait to make you my wife."

She held onto him tight. "Be careful."

"I will, darlin'." He headed down the trail and behind the stables.

~ * ~

For the tenth time, Mia checked the wind-up clock on the dresser. Ten-forty-five. Waiting on her porch, she paced back and forth, back and forth, back and forth. *Hurry up, Dusty.* If only he could text her to say everything's okay.

Cookie waved as she walked up, carrying a basket lined with yellow checkerboard material. "I packed you a lunch for the road."

"You're sweet."

"Ya hear 'bout Bella?"

"What happened?" Her heart sank to the floor.

"Near an hour after breakfast, Westin couldn't find her in her stall."

"Oh."

"A couple years back, one of the saddle tramps Westin hired was a horse thief."

A horse thief like Dusty in the newspaper article. Mia swallowed hard. "Do you think someone stole Bella?" Her voice came out unsteady.

"Don't know." Cookie put the basket down on a chair. "Your hands are trembling."

"I'm good." She lied. "Just anxious to see Dusty."

"Was in love once myself. Lost my man to the California Gold fever. You're fortunate Dusty ain't that sort."

Hard working, loyal, responsible. His principled traits might become his downfall.

"Dusty's a good man." The cook hugged her. "Glad to hear you two's getting hitched."

Blackie ran up the steps, breathing hard. "Dusty tried to steal Bella and got caught."

"This can't be." Her greatest fears came true, and her heart sped a hundred times normal. Lightheaded, she sucked in several deep breaths. To plan her next steps, her mind needed to be sharp.

"Not Dusty. He'd never do that," Cookie said, her eyes wide.

"Honest to God, it's true." Blackie held up his right hand.

A chill rippled through Mia.

"Westin went to work with Bella this morning, but she wasn't in her corral. Anyway, the boss and Reynolds found Dusty's spur in Bella's stall. That's when I walked up. Reynolds swore the spur hadn't been there yesterday."

"Could've been planted." She wanted to wring Blackie's neck for the false assumption.

"Could have. Still folks've been saying Dusty acted like he owned the filly." Blackie sighed a bit too long. "When she turned six months, he insisted on putting her in the stall behind his cabin. Said he wanted to keep an eye on her."

"That doesn't make him guilty, just conscientious."

"I reckon. He's always been a good foreman, but how do you explain the bill of sale found in his saddlebag pocket? Westin said it wasn't his signature."

"Are you suggesting Dusty forged the document?"

Blackie shrugged. "Don't know. Anyway, Reynolds called for a California collar on the old hanging tree."

"They didn't—" she couldn't say the word.

Blackie shook his head. "Nope. Westin wants a proper trial."

Panic surged through her brain. "Where is Dusty? I need to go to him."

"Westin and Reynolds are bringing him to town."

Her pulse raced fast, too fast. "Please Blackie, take me to Dusty."

"I know you're upset, but what you're asking to do ain't right." Cookie put her hands on her hips and gave her a no-you-won't look.

"She's right. It's best for you to stay put."

"I can't. If you won't help me, I'll saddle a horse myself and find my own way to town."

Blackie squinted at her. "Since you're so determined, reckon I'll escort you."

"I don't like it," Cookie growled.

"Well, I'm going."

"Since you're so insistent, grab your things. I'll get the horses ready." Blackie left.

Hollow inside, Mia picked up her valise and secured her purse strap on her shoulder.

Cookie stepped in front of her. "This hasty decision might come back to haunt you. Me 'n' Sandy's heading to town tomorrow. Ride with us." Cookie put her arm around her. "It's for the best."

No way would she let Cookie convince her into
staying. "I have to be with Dusty." She rushed by her,
passing Dusty's cabin to the stables.

Blackie saddled Half-Pint. "You sure you wanna do
this?"

"I am." She tried not to tear up. Dusty forced her to
learn to ride and helped her to deal with her fear.

Blackie boosted her up and mounted his own steed.
She grasped the saddle horn. The horse galloped at a
jarring pace. Ideas about who might frame Dusty
bounced in her head. Whoever had been behind the
setup must be an insider—most likely someone
employed at the ranch.

Reynolds hated Dusty, maybe hated her.

Slick had been on watch the night someone shot at
Dusty.

Scotty, the young cowboy appeared sweet and
sincere. In mysteries, the nice guy often committed the
crime.

Riding for at least two hours, a pair of jackrabbits
hopped across the road. Her horse neighed. She
startled, and her body got off-kilter, but she managed to
stay on.

Blackie rode his horse closer to hers. Let's take a
break under the trees over there." He motioned to a
secluded copse a distance from the road.

"No thanks. The sooner we get to town, the better."
The inside of her legs rubbed raw, her back spasmed,
and her fingers throbbed. Still, she refused to stop.

At the top of a ridge, the distant town came into
focus. She kicked Half-Pint into a gallop and passed the
mortuary sign. Mathew O 'Brady: Tailor and
Undertaker. O'Brady would measure Dusty for a casket.

His lifeless body placed inside and dropped into a deep hole and covered with soil. Repulsion crept up her throat.

A bit further, a boulder marked the edge of the town. She slowed Half-Pint to a trot along the main drag.

A two-seater buggy pulled in front of the dentist's office. Three boys threw a stick to a barking dog. A young man drove a wagon from the opposite direction and waved.

She waved back and stopped in front of the Hesperia Hotel.

"Good luck, Miss Kellogg." Blackie waved.

"Thanks for escorting me here in one piece." Watching him leave, she sucked in air, dismounted, and prayed her unsteady legs held her. They did, barely.

Robert came over and took the reins. "I'll take your horse to the livery."

"Thanks." She entered the lobby. The same lobby where she'd met Dusty. Her eyes misted. It seemed like years ago, not weeks.

Jenny strolled up. "I've known Dusty for years. Never thought he'd resort to stealing."

"He didn't do it." She balled her fists at her sides. The proprietress sure loved to gossip.

"It's been a long ride. I'd like a room to freshen up."

"Of course, dearie," Jenny called over a porter. "Take Miss Amelia's luggage to the Rose Room."

~ * ~

Inside the jail cell, Dusty fretted. The small, dingy jailhouse smelled like old leather, rotten food, and urine. He hated the stench, hated being locked up, felt suffocated.

Flynn Law, the sheriff, snored with his feet propped on top of his desk. The door creaked open, and a woman's heels clicked on the planked floor.

Mia.

Guilt had him staring out the cell's barred window at the back, embarrassed, shamed, useless.

She cleared her throat. "Good afternoon, sheriff."

The front legs of Ed's chair clunked to the floor. He pushed his hat in place and sat up. "Miss—Miss Kellogg. How may I assist you?"

"I'm here to see my fiancé."

"Dusty?"

"Dusty, you have company," he called.

"Tell her to go away." Dusty turned to the wall.

"Sorry, miss, Dusty don't want to see you," Flynn said.

"Tell that stubborn mule I'm not going anywhere." She once said she liked his stubbornness.

Dusty thought about their future marriage. The battles. The glorious ways they'd make up all night long. "Come on over, darlin'."

Her fingers pushed between the iron bars and reached for him. "I love you." She beckoned him like a lariat, looping around his drowning heart.

"It'd be best if you didn't." He stood and took her dainty hand in his.

She turned to Flynn. "May I go inside?"

"I can't rightly leave a single woman alone in a cell with a prisoner, even knowing you're his intended." The lawman brought a rickety wooden chair and placed it close to the bars.

Dusty moved his seat closer. "How'd you get to town so fast?"

Smug determination lit her eyes. "I rode Half-Wit."

"Unbelievable. Weren't you terrified?" His sweet gal conquered her own fears to be with him.

"Only about you getting arrested."

She must've had a rough ride, and yet he'd been her only concern.

"Sheriff, may I borrow a pen and ink?" she asked, batting her eyelashes.

"Sure. Call me Flynn." He pushed a poker table over to her, giving her a quill and a full bottle of ink. She took out her journal.

"Just like you said would happen, I was framed." He'd been a fool not to leave this morning.

"I'd like to hear your side. Mind if I listen in?" Flynn asked.

"I reckon, "Dusty thought back to the time three older boys jumped him in an alley behind the general store, and the sheriff ran the bullies off.

"As long as you promise to keep what's said here confidential." She eyed him warily.

"You've got my word."

"What happened after I saw you at breakfast?" Her eyes met his.

"Started riding inside the property line. My mind drifted back to this morning." He stretched past the bar to touch her shoulder.

She blushed. "Stick to the story."

"Near an hour later got to the northeast end. Found barbed wire severed. On the other side, Bella Sheba gnawed on grass. Couldn't believe my eyes."

"You mean the ranch's prize filly?" Flynn rubbed his chin. "Don't sound natural."

"It wasn't. Instinct told me to fetch her. Came near to roping her and the filly sprinted. Took four tries to get her lassoed."

Flynn chuckled. "Reminds me of courting my wife. Not that I'm complaining'. Found myself a good un'."

"Me and Miss Amelia planned to elope last night." Dusty glanced at Mia, and she smiled. "Then the stables caught fire. I think it may have been arson."

"The fire and Bella. Something fishy's going on." Flynn filled his pipe, tapped it on his desk.

"I agree. Anyway, I heard riders, found rifles pointed at me, namely from Reynolds and Slick's guns."

"Oh, Dusty." Her eyes filled with tears.

"Darlin', it's been a long day." He hated seeing her upset. "Why don't you head over to the hotel and get some rest?"

"Absolutely not."

"Darn strong-willed woman," Dusty told Flynn. "Makes me love her even more."

She traced her fingers along his wrists. "The cuffs cut you. Flynn, do you have any salve?"

A little scratch wouldn't hurt Dusty. "Don't bother."

"Humor me this once."

"Okay."

"Here you go, miss." Flynn handed her a ceramic pot. She dipped her fingertips into the ointment and applied it. "Finish the rest of your story."

"You won't like it."

"Honestly, Dusty. There's a lot I don't like about this situation. You need to tell me anyway. I'm stronger than you think."

"I know you are, but the next part's gonna make you madder than a wet hen." Dang. He despised repeating the story. "Reynolds implied we faked our engagement to skip town early. I set him straight, called him a jealous liar." He stood and faced the barred window. "This whole thing's hopeless."

"No, it's not," Flynn said. "I've known you since you were knee high to a grasshopper. Can't reckon you'd ever steal a penny candy, much less a horse. Folks 'round here know you've got integrity. Just like your pa and granddad."

He thought about standing at his grandfather's gravestone and choked on remorse.

"We must find Dusty a lawyer," she chimed in. "Any good ones in town?"

"No. Only one in the area's Sandy's cousin." Bitterness filled Dusty. "The guy swindled plenty of folks, myself included."

Flynn nodded. "In my opinion, the guy's lower than a slithery snake."

"There has to be someone else." Her eyes showed a stubborn gleam.

"Wish Old Man Jacobson still practiced." The sheriff grimaced. "The poor guy went blind nearly five years ago."

She stared at Dusty, her wheels inside her brilliant mind turning. "His brain's still working, right?"

"Yep, but he can't read anymore." Dusty might as well give up.

"Well, I can read, and Dusty, so can you," she gazed into his eyes, "I think?"

They knew so little about each other. "Yes, I can read."

"Good." She pressed on. "Now back to my question. Where does Mr. Jacobson live?"

"I don't reckon seeing the lawyer is a wise idea." He took a deep breath and tried to remain calm. "Whoever framed me will stop at nothing to keep you from snooping. Could you hand me your book with the quill and ink?"

"Why?"

"Please give it to me."

"Here." She shoved it through the bars.

He wrote:

June 14, 1890

I, Dusty Mann, being of sound mind, bequeath all my assets and money in my bank account to my intended, Amelia Kellogg.

Dusty Mann

He handed it to her.

"Dusty, I don't want your money." She threw the journal on the table. "I won't take it."

"Darlin', please. There's enough for you to get by for months, maybe years."

"The only place I'm going to visit is that lawyer." She gave him a don't-bother-quibbling stare. "What is Jacobson's first name? I know it's not Old Man."

"Randy."

"Tell me where I might find him, or should I ask somebody on the street?"

"Love your gumption, darlin'." With Mia on his side, he couldn't lose.

Chapter Fourteen

On the window glass, *Mark C. Jacobson, Dentist*, had been painted in gold leaf lettering and outlined in black. The slogan below read: 'Specializing in Extractions without Pain.'

Mia stepped into the narrow alcove and eyed two Queen Ann style chairs and a leather couch. An old-fashioned dentist chair and a metal table with dental instruments filled a side room. She recognized the round mirror on a long rod, the double-ended picks, and toothbrushes. The metal thing might be a tooth-extractor. Poor people. How'd they ever survive without Novocain?

"Hello." A short man wearing wire-rimmed glasses greeted her. "Are you Miss Kellogg?"

"I am."

The man's cheeks tinged a pink shade. "Pardon me for my lack of manners. I'm Mark Jacobson. Saw you at the dance, but we were never properly introduced. If the rumors are correct, you're engaged to Dusty Mann."

"He's my fiancé."

"Heard Dusty stole McGraw's thoroughbred horse."

It irked her that people believed such slander. "It was a setup."

"Really?" He pushed his glasses up the bridge of his nose. "You know this for sure?"

"Yes, I do. I'm here to speak with your dad. Is he in?" She crossed her fingers.

"I'm expecting him any minute. Maybe I can help you?"

"Dusty needs a lawyer."

"My dad no longer practices, but knowing his determination to see justice, he'll be willing to assist you. Have a seat." He motioned to a russet colored sofa.

A few minutes later, the front door opened, and a white-haired man walked into the room tapping his cane back and forth on the floor. The older man prodded to a chair and sat in it with dignity. "I smell the delightful fragrance of rose petals, and I know it's not you, Mark. We must have a visitor."

"I'd like to introduce you to Miss Kellogg. She's here to speak with you."

"Me?" he said flashing a warm, amiable smile. "Now, miss, what's on your mind."

"If you've heard about Dusty's arrest, you're aware he needs a lawyer. Would you represent him?" He had to say, yes.

Randy's eyes failed to focus in one direction. "I don't practice law anymore."

"I'll help you. I'm a fast reader, a quick learner. I'm willing to do anything to save him." She talked fast, maybe a bit too fast.

"He deserves a better lawyer than me." Randy slumped in his seat.

"Don't use Marvin Kincaid." Mark frowned.

"Since I lost my sight, the townsfolk are stuck with Kincaid." Randy twirled his cane and hung it on the arm of his chair.

"Must've been tough to quit." She felt for the lawyer.

"Any challenge the good Lord gives us makes us stronger. If only my sight had lasted long enough to settle Dusty's estate. It's such a shame he lost the family ranch."

"What happened?" Mia scooted to the edge of the couch, curious about Dusty's past.

Mark closed his eyes. "His grandfather fell behind in taxes."

"I would've loaned him the money, but my friend's honor was at stake." Randy's face reddened. "Instead he gambled Dusty's horse and lost Midnight to Kincaid."

"Poor Dusty." Her heart ached for him; he'd been through so much. Midnight? He'd mentioned the stallion's name before.

"His grandfather never seemed the same." Mark shook his head. "I'm quite certain shame and humiliation drove him to his maker."

"Folks suspect Kincaid cheated in that card game. He's been known to have a card up his sleeve." Randy pounded his cane on the floor. "Can't stomach that beady-eyed conniver."

She opted for sarcasm. "Sounds like a real gem."

Randy laughed. "Probably the nicest thing anyone ever said about Kincaid."

"Kincaid loaned the stallion to Los Flores for a fee. Midnight sired Bella Sheba." Randy placed the curved end of his cane on the arm of the chair. "She's his spitting image."

"Dusty said the stallion died."

"The worthless lawyer got drunk and rode Midnight. The horse stepped in a hole, broke his leg, and had to be shot," Mark said with clenched teeth.

What a jerk. "Dusty needs you as his lawyer, Mr. Jacobson."

"Call me Randy, please." He smiled. "I bet my friend, Thaddeus Sinclair, will take the case. He practices in San Bernardino."

"Dad, since I have business to attend to down the hill tomorrow, I can drop you off at Thaddeus' office."

Randy's wrinkled face lit with a smile. "Son, what a splendid idea."

"Is there something I can do?" She had to help.

"Well, missy, winning a trial takes digging for facts. Some might be blatantly apparent, others well hidden. You up for hours of inquiry."

"Sounds like a mystery novel." She'd read her share.

"Exactly. I became hooked on Poe's *Penny Bloods*. The crimes solved have a twist." Randy sighed. "Back to your help, I suggest you see Ken Dickerson. He runs the paper."

"That's a grand idea." Mark rubbed his chin. "Ask to see the archives but be wary what you say around him."

"I will. Reporters tend to bend the truth."

Both men nodded.

"I can't thank you enough. Please check back when you return to town. If I'm not at the newspaper office, you'll find me visiting Dusty." She walked out and headed two shops north.

"Welcome to the Hesperia Gazette. I'm Ken Dickerson." A wiry man with a pasty complexion opened the door. "You're Miss Kellogg. To my dismay, we were not properly introduced at the ball last month."

"Nice to meet you, Mr. Dickerson." She started to offer her hand and dropped it to her side.

"I'd love an interview with you." The reporter reminded her of a mountain lion lurking and ready to attack his prey. "If my sources are correct, you and Dusty recently became betrothed."

"Yes, we're engaged."

The reporter's eyes lit up. "Our readers would love to hear about the engagement."

"Some other time."

"Then why don't you tell me about his arrest."

"He's innocent." She covered her mouth with her hand.

"Care to expound on your opinion?"

"Not at the moment." Ready to redirect his focus, she smiled. "Mr. Dickerson, the reason I'm here is to look at some of your past newspapers."

"May I ask why?"

"I want to learn more about this town's history," she said, proud of her quick reply.

"Anything in particular?"

"Not really." She was the queen of vague.

"Follow me." He led her past a printing press. A young man inked a form, put a paper over it, and turned a three-foot wheel. Rollers dropped the final product into a tray.

Amazing. Machines like this are in museums in her time. A loud thud brought her back to the present. She followed the reporter into an adjoining room off to the side. Bookcases lined the walls. Papers cluttered a long table.

"Folks say Dusty stole the horse to buy his own ranch."

"It's not true." Her temper skyrocketed.

"As a reporter, it's my duty to hear from both sides. Keeps me impartial."

Impartial, my foot. She doubted this guy had an inkling of integrity.

He opened a file cabinet. "You'll find newspapers for the last few years in here. Holler if you need anything."

"You're too kind." She said in her sweetest tone.

"Why thank you, miss." Mr. Dickerson left.

She picked up a folder labeled May 1890, sank in a chair, and sifted through the material.

Hesperia Hotel's Grand Opening a Roaring Success

The article ended up being a fluff piece with little substance.

Slingshot Knocked Cow Down
Moonshine Distillery Discovered by the Old Mill

A clock chimed four times.

The reporter stepped in. "Sorry, Miss Kellogg, but we're closing."

"Already." She hadn't found a single clue.

"Come tomorrow if you'd like."

"I will. Thanks again for being so helpful." With no new information, she struggled to remain optimistic.

She strolled along the covered walkway. The aroma of baked bread and sweet goods drifted from Sally's Bakery. It reminded her of the bakery by her college dorm, although this boxy building had green trim not brown. Peeking inside the tall windows, she saw five or six tables covered with red and white checkered tablecloths. Two cowboys sat farthest from the window.

Wzzzzzzzz. A watering can spiraled in front of her feet.

"What the heck?"

A ping followed. The same can rolled into the middle of the street and settled.

Had somebody shot at her? Cold fear chilled throughout her veins. Her feet stayed rooted in place, frozen.

She waited, trying to figure out where the shooter might be. Maybe the empty lot next to the assayer's office across the street. Was the gunman lurking close to a building? Swallowing, she took quick steps past the optometrist, a few more and paused outside the doctor's office.

Rrr-zzzzzz whizzed past her ear and an object impacted with the lamp post lens in front of the doctor's office. Shards of glass shattered with a piercing-tinkling-crash.

Her hand shook as she curved it above her eyes. The bright sun made it hard to see.

Something thudded in the bench inches below her fingertips, causing her to tremble from the inside out.

Adrenaline surged her on, pushing her legs to sprint along the slatted sidewalk, and rush up the hotel's stairs.

~ * ~

Dusty paced in his tiny cell, feeling like a caged tiger. He stepped over to the window and glanced at the train tracks. Bright sunlight shone on the ground directly below. The light reflected on a shiny copper coin. A penny supposedly gave a person luck. He needed a miracle.

The door flung open.

Out of breath, the short, stout Deputy Ned gasped as he pushed two lanky boys toward the sheriff. Rivets of sweat dripped down his face. "Caught these two mischief makers shooting rocks from their slingshots."

"We was just having a little fun," a blonde boy said.

Dusty recognized Tom Quinn. His mom played the piano at church.

"Doubt your mom will think that." Flynn put down his pipe. "Tell your side, deputy."

The deputy should be frowning with concern, but the man's mouth turned into an upward grin. "There I was, patroling across the street from Walter's and Doc's office. I saw Miss Kellogg acting peculiar—all jumpy like."

"A rock flew through the air and shattered the glass on a lantern near her. I heard these two rascals laughing. Caught this one taking another shot at poor Miss Kellogg." He pointed to a freckly faced kid.

"What is wrong with you?" Dusty rattled the bars.

"I got good aim." Freckle-face stood up tall, like shooting a rock at someone is something to be proud of.

"Let see how your ma and pa feel about replacing the glass from the lantern." The sheriff glared at the boys. They both looked down. "You're just lucky that rock didn't hurt anyone."

"Open this door." Dusty clenched the bars determined to shake them loose, but they wouldn't budge. "I need to see my fiancé." If anything happens to Mia—

"She's fine," the sheriff ushered the two boys into the cell next to him. There bravado seemed to vanish once the door clinked closed.

"I'll stop by the Quinn's place and let them know we're holding their boys in one of the cells. Then, I'll check on Miss Kellogg. See if she wants to press charges."

Dusty had to see for himself she was alright. "She needs me, not some stinking deputy. If I can't go to her, bring her here."

"She's safe at the hotel." The sheriff's tone said his decision was final.

Deputy Plumb puffed up. "I'll take real good care of Miss Kellogg, even escort her to dinner. I'll be more than happy to bring her here in the morning."

Dusty clenched his fists, his head felt like it was about to explode.

"She's been through quite an ordeal already, and I'm sure she'll appreciate the company." Flynn said.

The deputy whistled as he strode out the door.

Dusty glanced over at the other cell.

"That's Dusty Mann. Pa says he's gonna hang for stealing that horse," one of the boys whispered.

"I didn't do it." Dusty glared over at them. He plunked down on his cot, feeling as worthless as a bag of shucks.

Flynn picked up a block of wood, whittled and missed. "Ouch." He used his handkerchief to blot the blood. "I understand your frustrations. If the roles were reversed, I'd want to be with the missus."

"It's not fair. I've lived an honest life. Always did the right thing. I don't belong in jail." Dusty paced the short distance to the window and back to the bars.

"Pray, Dusty. God always gives answers."

Dusty bowed his head and prayed. *God keep Amelia Safe. Find me a way to live and marry her.*

The door slung open. He heard boot steps and looked up. Westin McGraw stomped over to Flynn. "I'd like a word with your prisoner."

"Sure," Flynn said.

This had to be the sign Dusty prayed for.

Westin came close to the bars. "I'd never expected you to steal from me. Since you wouldn't talk earlier, I want answers now. Why'd you do it, Dusty?"

"I'm innocent. Somebody faked the events to get me out of the way."

"Who?"

"Don't know for sure ... might even be your nephew." Dusty should've kept his trap shut.

Westin raised his dark bushy brows. "Reynolds warned me 'bout you. Said you acted arrogant, acted like you owned Bella. And I ignored him until I saw for myself what you did."

Dusty pounded his fists on the wall. "You know I'm no thief. I got framed and aim to prove my innocence."

"Believing your own lies won't save you." Westin turned his back to Dusty. "Sheriff Law, we need to talk."

The two walked to the other side of the room. "When's the trial?"

"Don't know."

"Once Dusty's found guilty, how long will it take to hang him?" Westin's voice lacked empathy.

"He could be innocent. You don't want the wrong man going to his maker." Flynn sounded agitated.

The reality of Dusty's own hanging set in. If convicted, his life would be choked out of him.

"You weren't there." Westin huffed. "I caught him stealing my horse."

"The facts don't add up." Flynn folded his arms and glared. "I think you're wrong."

"You're not paid to think."

"Westin, that's uncalled for."

"Sorry. The fire. And now Bella. With Dusty behind bars, figure things will settle."

"You've arrested the wrong man," Dusty yelled. Why couldn't Westin see reason?

"Facts don't lie." His former boss spat into a spittoon and walked out.

Chapter Fifteen

Mia raced to her hotel room, her heartbeat thumping in her ears. Did the assassin want her dead? Not with the precision he used to hit the watering can and the lamppost lens and the bench inches from her fingertips. A definite warning—this time anyway

Too antsy to lie down, she paced to the window. A knock sounded on her door.

"It's Jenny."

"Come on in." She waited at the edge of her bed.

"You look pale. Did something happen while you were out?" Jenny asked.

"Someone shot at me while I was walking back." The bullets whizzing by were deadly.

"That's hard to believe. Hesperia's always been such a peaceful town." Jenny opened the door, looked down the hall, and called, "Robert, would you have our cook make up my special blend and bring it up to Miss Kellogg's room."

"Yes, ma'am," a voice answered.

Minutes later, Mia was handed a cup. "This should help calm your nerves."

She sipped it. "Yuck. This stuff's bitter."

"It'll help soothe you. Might make you sleepy."

Sleep she could do. Already a bit groggy, she downed the rest.

"See you in the morning." Jenny took the cup. Her voice faded as Mia sank back into the pillow.

She gazed into a full-length mirror. Focusing on her hair, it was now swept up in a loose chignon and topped with a golden tiara to secure her long veil. Where'd the high-necked wedding gown come from? It was spectacular. Pink beads formed small rosettes on the sleeves, lace and silk inlets flared the skirt.

"You're beautiful." Her father stepped behind her wearing a tuxedo and handed her a bouquet of miniature pink roses with baby's breath. "It's not too late to cancel. You sure this is what you want?"

"Yes, Dad," she watched herself say, still trying to figure out exactly where she was as they walked out of a room toward a set of double doors.

The organist played the *Wedding March.*

"Be happy, sweetie." Holding her father's arm, he led her down the church aisle.

The back of Dusty's Stetson silhouetted against the stain glass window. Her cowboy. She must've dreamed his arrest.

She couldn't stop smiling as she grasped her future husband's hand.

He turned. Removed his hat. Long blond hair fell to his shoulders. "Reynolds?"

She floated backward, falling with a hard thump, and woke on the floor. The spiked tea gave her nightmares. Her pulse pounded like the hoofs of Half-Pint galloping.

Based on the light filtering from her window, she'd slept through the night. It's already morning. She had to see Dusty. Hastily, she dressed in a starched-white blouse and a powdered blue flowered skirt and stepped out of her room.

Outside her door, the deputy slouched in a chair.

"Why are you here?"

"Caught two boys with slingshot shooting in your direction." He wore a creepy grin. "Sheriff thought it'd be best if I kept an eye on you. Make sure your safe."

"It wasn't a gun?" Thank goodness.

"No, Miss Kellogg. May I escort you to breakfast?"

"It's not necessary."

"But I insist." He offered his arm.

"Fine." She didn't take it. Downstairs, she picked a table near the side door. The deputy stopped in the foyer and talked with the hotel proprietor, Bob.

A brunette at a kitty-corner table bounced a baby on her lap and said to her friend, "Can't blame Miss Kellogg for standing by her man. Growing up, I had the biggest crush on him."

"Always been rather dashing."

Both women waved at her.

Mia waved back.

Robert served her a platter piled high with flapjacks, four slices of bacon, and an immense portion of scrambled eggs. "It's not right Dusty's in jail. He's no thief."

"Your support means a lot to both of us. He's lucky to have you as a friend."

At one of the side tables, an older man muttered to a man across from him, "Dusty's always been highfalutin. Figures he's better than us 'cause his grandpa once owned a ranch."

"Think he did it?" the other man asked.

"Absolutely. Can't wait to see Dusty hang."

She pushed her plate to the table's center, not about to listen to this type of talk for another second. The deputy continued chatting with Bob, and she slipped out the side door. Nobody paid attention to her as she crossed the street and took the walkway to the jail.

Inside, the sheriff's hat covered his face, and he leaned back in his desk's chair.

Dusty slept on his cot. Patchy whiskers covered his chin, his hollow cheeks meant he hadn't been eating much.

She forced a smile. "Hi, Handsome."

He came to the bars. "Darlin', you okay?"

"Yes."

"You've gotta leave town." Dusty moved like a caged panther. "Somebody shot at you."

"Two boys with a slingshot." She crossed her arms. "I love you and am not going anywhere."

"What's all the commotion? Oh." The sheriff's chair clunked down, "Mornin', Miss Kellogg."

"I'm trying to convince Amelia to go home," Dusty said. "It'd be easier putting a ring in a blasted bull's nose than to get her to listen."

"You're the one who refuses to listen. I'm staying right here." My gosh, he was exasperating.

"Darlin', I'm trying to keep you safe."

Flynn chuckled. "A spirited woman makes life interesting. My little missus can be obstinate."

"I'm not obstinate."

Dusty had the nerve to chuckle.

"It's not funny." But she couldn't help smiling.

He stepped close to the bar. "I'm stuck inside this hellhole when I should be with you. Can't you see, I want you out of harm's way because I love you?"

"I love you, too." She pushed her head between the bars and allowed his mouth to savor hers.

The door slammed against the wall.

The deputy's boots echoed over the wood-planked floor. "I've lost track of Miss Kellogg. She'd been eating breakfast. I stopped to chat with Bob and—"

She marched over to both lawmen and glared. It irked her to be thought of as helpless.

"Darlin', please be reasonable!"

"I am." She folded her arms.

"Darlin', I care 'bout you. So do these people."

"Forget about me. It's way more important to concentrate on clearing your name, Dusty." She took several calming breaths, as the sheriff tipped his hat and walked out the door.

Why did saving him have to be so difficult?

~ * ~

Dusty wished he could talk his headstrong gal into leaving, while the thought of her gonehurt from deep within his soul.

"I've made a map of the ranch." She took out a sketch pad from her bag. "This is the trail along the road. Here's where we entered, and I added the bridge over the river, the ranch house, bunkhouse, stables, and barn."

Dusty examined her work. "Looks like a photograph."

"Thanks. Hmm ... are there any actual pictures, I mean, photographs of the ranch?" Her green eyes brightened.

"Not of the ranch. A few years ago, a man came out and took everyone's photo. It was awful. We had to stay still forever. Hung the pictures in the bunkhouse."

"Think I saw the same photo in a shop's window. Found myself drawn to your handsome face."

"Reckon you needed spectacles."

"Not hardly." She stared at him. "Did Westin have a blueprint for the land?"

"I recall seeing a map of the property. Think it would help?"

"Might, but I doubt it. Describe the area where you found Bella. I know it's in the north section." She flipped to a new page, dipped her pen in ink and sketched, holding up her drawing pad so he could see.

"A bit more to the east where we took a buggy ride." He pointed. "The fence line ends in the corner."

She turned to a new page and sketched what he described, adding details section by section.

"The break in the barbed wire, was it here?"

"Farther north."

She questioned him, tweaking her picture as he spoke. "Did Bella take this path?"

"Yes."

She added strokes, put her book down and arched her back.

"You're quite a gal." A gal who shouldn't be working like a dog to clear him.

Mark and Randy Jacobson strolled in, escorting a silver-haired man. Dusty recognized the lawyer, Thaddeus Sinclair.

"How've you been, Thad?" The deputy stood and shook his hand,

"Besides a little rheumatism can't complain." Thaddeus took off his derby hat. "I'm here to represent Harold Mann. Do you mind telling me his charges?"

"Stole a horse. Flynn knows the rest. You'll have to wait and ask him," the sheriff said with a clipped voice.

"This is Amelia Kellogg, Dusty's intended," Mark said.

"Mark and Randy gave you high praises." Thaddeus straightened his brown suit jacket. "It's nice to put a face with the name."

"It was Randy's idea to hire you," Mia said. Even though he couldn't see her, she smiled in his direction.

"Thad, we'll talk soon." Mark tipped his derby hat and led his father out the door.

Thaddeus picked up Mia's sketch. "Those are remarkable drawings. Visual images often help convince the jury of facts."

"I'm counting on it. If I can find watercolor paints, I'll add color."

Thaddeus came within an inch of Ned. "Please unlock the chamber to allow us a private consultation."

"I'll let you in, Thaddeus, but not Miss Kellogg." The deputy wore an annoying I'm-in-charge scoff.

"Miss Kellogg's input is vital to the case. We can hardly speak confidentially with her on the outside." The lawyer marched to the cell with Mia behind.

"Don't like it. I'll let you inside this once, Miss Kellogg." The deputy unlocked the door.

She scrunched her nose at the urine stench and swatted away several flies swarming around her head.

"It's been too long, Dusty." Thaddeus shook his hand. "Wish we were meeting under better circumstances."

"Me too."

"I'll do everything I can to win this case. Explain your side."

Dusty talked about the fire, riding fence line, finding Bella, and Westin and Reynolds discovering him and the forged bill of sale.

"Have you actually seen the forged documents?"

Anger seethed inside Dusty. "Nope, but I'm outraged. I wonder if I'll recognize the snake's writing."

Thaddeus scribbled notes. "Do you keep your saddle bag in a public place?"

"Yes. Is that good?"

The lawyer's mouth turned up, and his eyes glittered. "I recall a case getting dismissed for the same reason."

"He'll get you out of jail." Mia radiated optimism.

"If you'll excuse me, I'd like to speak with the deputy." The lawyer stepped away.

Dusty wrapped his arms around her. He kissed her, enjoying her sweet lips and sampling her delectable mouth. After their wondrous night together, he craved a lifetime more.

A skinny man in overalls rushed inside the office. "This wire just came for you."

The deputy opened the envelope. "The trial's in three days. Thad, do you know this judge?"

Thaddeus' mouth twitched. "Never went before him, but his nickname is the hanging judge."

She gasped and squeezed Dusty.

"We only have two days to prepare for trial. The jury selection is slated for tomorrow."

Intuition said Dusty's days were numbered.

Chapter Sixteen

June 30, 1890
The Trial.

Rumble. Ka-boom.
Dusty's nerves frazzled like lightning shot right through him. "Thunderstorm's a bad omen," he told Flynn, trying to take the courthouse stairs with some dignity. "Spooks animals and people."

"Won't do no good worrying."

Lightning crackled, singeing the spirit inside Dusty's heart. He stepped into a packed courthouse and stopped. The wall lanterns cast a warm glow. Dressed in their Sunday best, people squeezed into benches like carloads of crammed livestock.

The handcuffs pinched. Seein' as he'd done nothing wrong, he deserved better treatment.

The sheriff prodded him forward. "Keep on walking, son."

Ka-ka-booooom.
Dusty started. The chains on his wrist jangled. A lump of dread clogged his throat. Folks ceased talking, turned, and stared. Lightning shone through the windows and brightened their faces.

"You're innocent," Roy Walters called from the third row.

"The crook'll get strung up soon enough," a cowboy from the Lazy Eight Ranch section countered.

"Quiet down, you two," the sheriff said. "Whatever happens now is up to the court."

Three women wore gigantic bonnets and smiled at him from the second row.

He spotted Mia. Her eyes were puffy, her complexion pale. If only he could comfort her.

She mouthed, "I love you."

Those words had brought him inner happiness. A wave of guilt hit him. *If only I had listened to Mia.*

Randy and Mark waited next to her.

Thaddeus Sinclair motioned for Dusty to come up front. "Be glad you weren't lynched when they caught you. At least now you have a chance."

"That's like telling a hen to jump up on the chopping block." He glanced over his shoulder.

"You'll be out soon," Mia said.

Sunshine filtered through the clouds bringing Dusty rays of hope. "Then we'll get hitched."

Assigned as bailiff, the stout Deputy Plumb called, "All rise. The Honorable Judge Edwin Longfellow presiding."

The judge, not much taller than Mia, found his place at a long table and banged his gavel.

The bailiff brought the jurors in from an adjoining room. They took their places in the juror box on the side. His former neighbor, Clyde, took the head juror's seat. Once he lost the Silver Spur Ranch, he hadn't seen Clyde much over the years, but he should be on his side.

"Keep an open mind, until you have heard all the evidence from both sides. Weigh all options before you decide your verdict," the judge instructed the jurors.

Sounded reasonable. An image crept into Dusty's mind—a lone noose hanging from a tall tree. Not good. Not good at all.

"Mr. Oliver, is the prosecution ready with your opening statement?"

Dark gray clouds replaced the sunlight. Thunder boomed. Dusty flinched as did several of the jurors.

"I am ready, Your Honor." The prosecutor strutted to the jury box. "Gentlemen, I am aware most of you fine citizens have lived in the High Desert for years. You probably recall Dusty as a young, responsible boy who did his chores and respected his elders."

Lightning flashed as the banker, mortician, and barber nodded.

Mr. Oliver wore a pressed black suit and an air of importance. "I am sorry to say the mannered boy you recall has changed. Life's disappointments, the loss of loved ones, and his family farm's bankruptcy has hardened Mr. Mann. His need for money became obsessive."

Dusty clenched his fists, aching to set the prosecution right.

"Mr. Mann is different now. The change may have happened when his grandfather gambled away his stallion, Midnight Sheik.

His gut tightened, and he fought to stay seated. That man had no right to bring up his deceased grandfather's problem.

"The same stallion Mr. Mann believed essential for his thoroughbred breeding program." He smiled at the jurors.

Resentment choked up Dusty's throat.

"As you are aware, Mr. Mann needed money," the prosecution continued. "Once he began courting Miss Kellogg, he became desperate. Asking for her hand made him reckless."

Murmurs erupted from the audience.

"Miss Kellogg conspired with him," somebody yelled.

Someone is attempting to ruin her good name. His hands fisted.

The judge banged his gavel three times. "Quiet in the court."

Dusty glanced back at Mia. She squinted, her face flushed.

"You are intelligent men." Mr. Oliver puffed on his cigar. "We have evidence proving Mr. Mann carelessly left his spur in Bella Sheba's stall when he stole her. Mr. Mann is a thief. A conniving thief who forged a bill of sale."

Gasps came from behind him.

"And Mr. Mann may have set the fire in the morning as a distraction to cover his tracks. He assumed folks would be concerned with the cleanup and not pay attention to their foreman. Once you hear the testimonies and see evidence brought forth, I am confident you shall find beyond a shadow of a doubt, Harold Mann to be guilty. Guilty on Count One ... forging Bella Sheba's bill of sale. Guilty on Count Two ... possession of stolen property."

Not guilty, innocent.

"Thank you, gentlemen, Your Honor." Mr. Oliver gave Dusty a you're-as-good-as-sunk smirk and took his seat.

Dusty wanted to wipe off his smirk, cowboy style. He shifted in his chair. A nagging foreboding settled in the pit of his gut.

As if sensing Dusty might be about to blow, Thaddeus put a restraining hand on his arm. "Don't let the prosecutor's words get to you."

"Is the defense ready, Mr. Sinclair?" the judge asked.

"We are, Your Honor." Thaddeus stood, adjusted his black suit jacket, and approached the jury box. The chunky lawyer looped his thumbs under his suspenders and nodded to the jurors.

"Good morning, gentlemen of the jury. While Mr. Oliver's statement was eloquent, it is seriously flawed. Harold Charles 'Dusty' Mann is respected for his high morals. Even as a young lad, he never stole so much as a piece of penny-candy, much less would he ever attempt to steal a horse. And Dusty was engaged that very morning. Supposedly, he was heading away from the ranch leaving his intended behind. The woman he loved. That doesn't sound like something Dusty would consider. He is the same forthright, honest man you have always known. I tell you, he is innocent."

"No, he's not," somebody in the audience shouted.

"Bailiff, please escort the disruptive gentleman in the fourth row from the courtroom." The judge glowered. "Let this be a warning to the audience. The next person who is out of order will be locked up. Mr. Sinclair, please continue."

"Thank you, Your Honor. The *evidence*, not conjecture or mind reading, will show Dusty Mann is the victim of a scheme. Mr. Mann certainly never stole Bella Sheba. Mr. Mann is innocent."

His lawyer's points were sound. Dusty relaxed.

"Ask yourself, if he wasn't framed, how did Westin McGraw find Mr. Mann so easily? And with the missing horse in hand? Horse theft is a felony offense in this state, and the person who planned this scheme wanted him caught stealing Bella Sheba. Wanted him hanged ... for reasons unknown to us. Having set this deception in motion, the man or men who conspired to fabricate this lie knew exactly where Mr. Mann would be, and thusly informed Mr. McGraw."

Dusty groaned to himself. Mia warned him time and time again to be cautious. He should've listened, should have eloped with her, not finish his chores like a fool.

"After you hear all the evidence against him, you will find whatever is shown or said to be circumstantial. His spur had been deliberately cut off his boot and placed in the stall. The bill of sale had been forged by someone other than Mr. Mann. Listen carefully to the testimonies against Mr. Mann. If you have any reasonable doubt, and you will, you must find Mr. Mann innocent. I believe you fine jurors will make the right decision. You will find Mr. Mann innocent on all counts. Thank you." Thaddeus kept his eyes on the jurors as he took his seat.

"Mr. Oliver, are you ready to call the state's first witness?"

"Yes, Your Honor, I'd like to call Westin McGraw."

Westin appeared haggard; his walk lacked its usual confidence. The bailiff swore him in.

The judge pointed back a few rows to a couple of cowboys. "Gentlemen, take all conversations outside, or you will be considered in contempt of the court."

All noise in the audience ceased.

"Mr. Oliver, you are free to begin."

"Mr. McGraw, on June thirteenth, what time did you notice Bella Sheba missing?"

"Maybe an hour after breakfast. Got delayed. You see, before dawn, Scotty said he spotted Dusty coming out of the stables holding a can of kerosene. Shortly afterward a fire broke out."

"Objection," Thaddeus called, "conjecture is not admissible."

"Sustained," the judge said. "Speculation as to who set the fire is not on the docket."

The words were out. The jurors will suspect Dusty committed arson anyway.

"Mr. McGraw, you were talking about when you found Bella missing?"

"Well, I visited Bella's corral and found it empty. A shiny object glinted in the sun. Discovered a strap attached to a silver spur with the initials *HM engraved*." He pointed to Dusty. "Ain't nobody else owns those spurs but him."

"You certain the spur wasn't dropped last week or even a month ago?"

"Reynolds mentioned the spur hadn't been there the day before." Westin folded his arms and grimaced.

"Hearsay, Your Honor," Thaddeus said.

"Sustained."

Thaddeus dipped his pen in ink and hastily scribbled notes on a pad.

"Well, I have proof. Reynolds and Slick found a pair of boots on Dusty's front porch. One with no spur, the other one intact," Westin continued.

Thaddeus started to rise and sat back down.

The bailiff walked up to each juror showing the found spur, its broken strap, and a pair of boots. One spurless. One with the matching spur intact.

Dusty whispered to his lawyer, "I put a pair of muddy boots outside to clean and polish them. Wore different boots the next day."

Thaddeus jotted down some notes. "Try to stay calm, Dusty."

"How can I? It's obvious someone is out to get me."

The prosecutor pivoted toward the jurors. "Please continue, Mr. McGraw."

"Had this intuition something was wrong. Bella was always in her stall in the morning. Got concerned when I couldn't find my prize colt. Well, I called all the cowboys to help search for Bella. Blackie and Checkerboard were sent to the south end. Scotty and a couple of new hires said they'd start in the middle pasture and moved to the northwest property line. I took Reynolds and Slick with me to the northeast."

"Reynolds or Slick must've led Westin to me," Dusty whispered to Thaddeus.

"Found Dusty near a mile outside the ranch's property leading Bella away. Took a couple gun shots to get him to stop."

Dusty wanted to shout, "Liar."

People whispered behind him. The judge banged his gavel. "Quiet in the court."

"Slick searched Dusty's saddlebag," Westin said. "Found a forged bill of sale."

"Did you sell Bella Sheba to Mr. Mann and write out a bill of sale?" Mr. Oliver asked.

"No, I did not!"

"Let me clarify. Are you saying the signature on the bill of sale is not yours?"

Westin pressed his lips together. "I didn't sign any such paper."

"Can you prove this?" The prosecutor paused. "You must have an official document with your signature?"

"All my important stuff is kept in the safe at my ranch." He scratched his head. "I signed the registry at the Hesperia Hotel. Come to think of it, Dusty stayed there a month ago and would've signed in."

Dusty had met Mia, danced with her, held her in his arms, fell for his gal. Would be hitched if—

The judge turned to the bailiff. "Who are the proprietors of the hotel?"

"Mr. and Mrs. Hayes, Your Honor." The bailiff pointed to Jenny. "Mrs. Hayes is sitting in row two on the left side."

"Mrs. Hayes, you are ordered by the court to collect the hotel registry. How long will it take for you to locate the registry and bring it back to the courthouse?"

"Less than twenty minutes, Your Honor," Jenny said.

"Deputy, would you please escort Mrs. Hayes to the hotel?"

"Yes, Your Honor." The deputy stood and walked Jenny up the aisle and out the door.

The judge banged his gavel. "It's quarter past noon. Since I need extra time to cross-check the signatures, the court will resume at quarter past one. Mr. McGraw, you may step down for the time being. Remember you are under oath and must not discuss the case with anyone. Otherwise, you will be held in contempt of the court and locked up for thirty days." The judge went to his chambers.

Voices filled the courtroom, and people went outside. Dusty turned to Mia.

She scooted to the edge of her seat and put her hand on his shoulder. The strain from his arrest and this trial showed in her eyes. Her usual teasing smile had been replaced with a reassuring one that he could tell had been forced. "You're innocent. This will be over soon."

Thaddeus shuffled through his notes. "Listen to the little lady."

"Always." *Except when it mattered, when I'd had a chance to leave.*

"Thaddeus is quite a lawyer. He'll turn the case around." Randy patted his back.

Dusty tried to will away the dread surging from within.

Chapter Seventeen

The stress of waiting made Mia's heart pound hard and fast. At precisely one-fifteen, the bailiff called for the court to resume.

"I have made my decision regarding the bill of sale." The judge settled his glasses in place. "Closely comparing the signatures in the registry with those written on the bill, I have noted Mr. Westin McGraw signature is not a match. The strokes are far too thick. Mr. McGraw slants his letters to the right. This signature slants to the left. Plus, *M*, the first letter of his last name failed to show extra flourishes. Thus, I conclude his signature has been forged."

The courtroom became as quiet as the stillness before the roll of thunder.

The judge pushed his glasses up on the bridge of his nose. "In regard to Mr. Harold Charles Mann, the lettering on both documents is an identical match in height and spacing. Both signatures angled to the left. The flourished loop before the capital *M* and open *A* proved consistent with the name."

Dusty's shoulders slumped.

Come on, judge. Give my cowboy some good news.

"However, the bill's signature is written as Harold Charles Mann. The name on the registry is Dusty Mann."

She crossed her fingers. *Please create doubt in the jurors' minds.*

"The registry signature used faint pen strokes. The bill of sale was written with bold strokes. The lower case *s* used in Charles and Dusty are not identical. The registry shows a slim pointy *s*. The bill of sale is rounded. Since there are no other signatures available to compare, I cannot prove Mr. Mann forged this document. The bill of sale is hereby dismissed. All jurors must dismiss any testimony or evidence regarding Count One."

She gave a silent, *Yes!* This news could turn the case around. Dusty straightened up at the news.

Again, Westin plodded up to the witness chair.

The prosecutor cleared his throat. "Before we took our recess, you were discussing the sale of Bella."

"Objection." Thaddeus stood. "Count One, the bill of sale, has been dismissed."

"Sustained," the judge called.

The prosecutor pretended to be chagrined. "Sorry, Your Honor."

"Do you recall Mr. Mann spending extra time with Bella?"

"Come to think of it, yes. Quite often, I spotted him with Bella, often giving her an extra apple." Westin groaned. "Hindsight says I should have never trusted Dusty. Thought him to be a hard-working, honest man. Turns out the snake stole from me."

Thaddeus stood again. "Objection, Your Honor!"

"Sustained."

Bullshit! Mia had seen how Dusty worked harder and longer than anybody else on the ranch.

"Ever since his grandfather lost Midnight Sheik in a card game, Dusty's been claiming he'd get the stallion back. Must've torn Dusty up when I paid stud fees for the use of Midnight, even though the man never showed it. Didn't put two-and-two together he wanted the offspring. The man is a natural poker player. Can bluff his way out of a corner."

Does Westin believe the garbage spewing out of his mouth?

"Objection. Speculation," Thaddeus called.

"Mr. McDraw, please refrain from stating your own opinion." The judge glared at Westin.

"Yes, Your Honor."

"Mr. McGraw, you were talking about the stud fees you paid for Midnight Thief," the prosecutor stated.

"Paid for the stallion's services twice, the last time nearly a year ago. Not long after I returned Midnight to his owner, the stallion broke his leg and had to be shot. Bella was born shortly after. Seein' as Midnight sired Bella, my nephew, Reynolds mentioned Dusty acted like he owned her."

"Objection," Thaddeus called. "The witness is feeding the jurors false conjecture."

"Sustained. The witness is to State only the facts, or I will hold him in contempt." The judge did not smile.

Would Thaddeus' skills be enough to get Dusty cleared? Her stomach balled tightly.

The judge motioned to Thaddeus. "Mr. Sinclair, you may cross-examine the witness."

"Thank you, Your Honor. "Thaddeus smiled at the jurors as he stood. "Mr. McGraw, how many years have you known Dusty?"

"Most of his life."

"Has he ever done anything dishonest ... like steal, lie, or cheat?"

"No, but that doesn't mean—"

Thaddeus cut him off. "Dusty had access to your office. Do you own a safe?"

"Yes, sir."

"How does the safe open?" Mr. Oliver backed up two steps.

"It uses a key. I keep the master. Dusty has the spare. If I'm out of town, he has the authority to pay the staff."

"How long have you owned your safe?"

"Maybe two years. Never figured I needed one, but the missus insisted." Westin glanced at the gallery and smiled in the direction of his wife.

"Has Dusty ever opened your safe?"

"Plenty of times." His right eye ticked and he looked up to the left.

Mia spotted the signs of lying.

"Ever find anything else missing, say like money or coins?"

He better not say, 'yes.'

"Nope. Dusty is well aware I count the money daily." Westin had *another eye twitch.*

"You accuse Dusty of stealing. Wouldn't stealing money from your safe be a whole heck of a lot easier than stealing a horse?"

"Objection," the prosecutor said. "Mr. Sinclair is leading the witness."

"Sustained."

The bailiff produced Mia's sketches. "Please show us the exact location where you found Dusty."

"Here," Westin pointed to the top right corner. "A mile outside the ranch's property line. I don't get it. If Dusty planned to bring the horse back like he said, why did I find him heading east, riding away from the Los Flores Ranch?"

"Are you certain Dusty was riding away when you came to him?"

"Yes. He headed east."

"So Dusty rode to the east. Did he have his horse walk, trot or gallop?" Thaddeus tilted his head.

"I'm ... pretty sure ... yes ... the horse trotted."

"When I'm riding, stationary things appear to be moving. Was Dusty's mount actually stopped? Remember, you're under oath."

"No. Dusty was riding away. I saw him with my own eyes." McGraw paused and glanced down.

"Is it true that Dusty announced his engagement to Miss Kellogg that very morning?"

"Yes, he said so at breakfast."

"Did he seem happy about marrying Miss Kellogg?"

"Yes, he did." Westin didn't smile, actually grimaced.

"You mentioned that Dusty was heading north away from the Los Flores Ranch boundaries?" Thaddeus tilted his head and glanced at the jurors. "It doesn't make sense. Why would Dusty leave his future wife, Miss Kellogg behind?"

"Objection," the prosecutor said. "Mr. Sinclair is using speculation."

"Sustained."

"I have no further questions." Thaddeus nodded.

Checkerboard testified next. He thought Dusty to be a fair boss. When he explained how Dusty moved Bella to an open stall behind his cabin to keep an eye on her from his bedroom window, the testimony hurt more than it helped.

As Reynolds testified, his brows knitted together, and he sent a daggered glare at Dusty.

Mia had spurned the spiteful man. She figured Reynolds wouldn't mind seeing her hang alongside her cowboy.

"Dusty said he'd do just about anything to get money." Reynolds wore the same smug smirk he'd used when he tried to kiss her.

She couldn't stand the hateful, lying son of a bitch.

"Could you be more specific when the incident occurred?" Mr. Oliver asked.

"The morning before he stole Bella." Reynolds sneered in Dusty's direction.

"Your Honor." Thaddeus jumped up. "The witness is inferring guilt without evidence."

"Sustained."

The jurors never once looked in Dusty's direction. The town's clock tower chimed three times. The testimony dragged on for almost six hours.

The owner of the saddle shop came to the witness chair.

"Please state your full name and occupation," Thaddeus said.

"Michael Winston, but people call me Cinch. I own Cinch's Saddlery. Make custom saddles, belts, and boots."

"Would you consider yourself an expert on leather?"

Cinch sat taller. "I'd say so. Been doing my job for nearly thirty years."

"Your Honor, could the bailiff please bring the spur and boots forth for Mr. Winston to examine?" Thaddeus asked.

"Bailiff, show Mr. Winston the said evidence."

Mia glanced at the jurors. Every eye stayed on the saddler.

"In your professional opinion, has the detached spur strap been cut?"

Cinch held the cut spur strap-up to the light, turned it to the right, then to the left. "It's cut alright. Might've been a knife." Cinch brought the strap an inch from his eyes. "Might've been clipped by barbed wire."

She cringed. Cinch's sure fire testimony went up like a puff of smoke. She refused to give up, sure at least one juror believed in Dusty's innocence.

Thaddeus stood. "Your Honor, I request a recess to confer with my client."

The judge banged his gavel. "The court will reconvene at precisely four."

People chatted. Most went outside. Dusty stayed seated next to Thaddeus.

"May I sit next to Dusty?" She needed to be closer to him.

"I'm sorry, Miss Amelia." Thaddeus shook his head. "You must remain behind the portioned wall for the audience. If you move up here, the judge will find you in contempt."

"It's okay, "Dusty said.

"We had not planned for you to take the stand, Dusty, but I believe it is necessary now," Thaddeus said.

217

"It'll be a mistake." Dusty's lips slanted together. "Like digging my own grave."

"The object is to convince the jurors of reasonable doubt."

"Is this your only option?"

"Yes."

"What do you think?" Dusty asked Mia.

His testimony seemed to be a good choice. "You should go on the stand," she said while doubt filled her mind. His please-don't-make-me resolve softened as he gazed into her eyes.

"All right, I'll do it."

Dusty was sworn in. After two weeks in jail, he'd become thin, his eyes dull, until they met hers. A glimmer of his old self shone. His lopsided grin might not be full on, but it caused her heart to patter.

"Please state your full name," Thaddeus said.

"Harold Charles Mann. Folks call me Dusty," he said with a slight drawl.

"Do you remember where you found Bella Sheba on the morning of your arrest?" Thaddeus asked.

"On the other side of the downed fence, the fence somebody intentionally cut."

"Objection," the prosecutor shouted. "Not in evidence."

"Sustained."

"Show us on this map where you discovered Bella." Thaddeus placed Mia's map pinned on a wooden easel and handed Dusty a long pointing stick so the jurors could see.

Dusty pointed to the northeast section outside the Los Flores boundary. "Found it odd for Bella to be so far from her stall. True to her firebrand character, she didn't come when I called. Figured we were playing chase 'cause she kicked up her heels and cantered off."

"Did you chase her far?"

"Near a mile. Finally lassoed the filly, but she took to bucking. I snatched an apple out of my pocket, ready to dismount and calm her."

Thaddeus rubbed his elbow, the signal for Dusty to look at the jurors. "You said you were ready to dismount. Did you get off your horse?"

"No time. Heard riders. Thought they might be rustlers and remained cautious. I spied Westin's mount. Then Slick and Reynolds horses. Waved 'em over. Expected the men to be grinnin' like a gambler with a royal flush seeing Bella was safe. Instead, Slick and Reynolds pointed the barrels of their guns at my head."

Several in the audience gasped.

"Any idea how Westin and his men found you?" Thaddeus tilted his head and glanced at the jurors.

"Wouldn't be hard. Westin was distressed about the fire in the morning. At breakfast, he asked me to be extra careful checking the fence. Seein' as I was framed later the same day, I assume the fire had also been intentional. Someone used the fire as a ruse to keep everyone distracted from his intent of stealing Bella."

"Objection. Speculation on the part of the witness," Mr. Oliver called.

"Sustained. Mr. Mann, please refrain from voicing your assumptions. They are not evidence."

"On June thirteenth, you checked the fence line." Thaddeus continued. "Can you state the approximate time you began?"

"Eight, eight-thirty."

"Is Westin the only person who knew where you'd be?"

"Heck no. Everyone at breakfast heard me and Miss Amelia were engaged, heard me asked for the day off to take my intended to town right away to get hitched." Dusty's smile tore at her heart. "Westin insisted I secure the ranch first."

"Do you ever change up your route?" his lawyer asked.

"Never. Been riding the same course for the past four years. Always start in the southeast end below the barn, continue east, turn north, and loop west around the property."

Dusty answered this perfectly. She crossed her fingers his testimony worked.

"Do you have routines for other days?"

"Sometimes, ☐specially during brandings and roundups." Dusty eased back in his seat. "Rest of the year, we all pitch in, mucking out stalls, coercing cattle to higher pastures, birthing calves and foals, breaking horses, baling hay."

"Is June thirteenth the day you found Bella on the outside of the ranch property?"

"Yes, sir." Dusty swallowed hard.

He could use a sip of water. It bugged her that none was offered.

"And is it your opinion someone planted Bella Sheba outside the downed wire?"

"Yes. I'm innocent. I've been framed," Dusty's voice cracked.

"Objection," Mr. Oliver shouted. "The attorney is leading the witness."

"Sustained," the judge said. "The defendant needs to stick to the facts."

"Did you steal Bella Sheba?" Thaddeus glanced at the jury.

"No. Somebody contrived the scene in order to make me look guilty. Wish I knew for certain who would try to frame me, but I have my suspicions."

"Objection, the witness is using conjecture." Mr. Oliver glowered, and his cheeks turned ruddy.

"Sustained."

"He's guilty," a man yelled.

The sound of the judge's gavel pounded through the room, four or five times. "Order! Order in the court! Bailiff, apprehend the dark-haired man with the beard in the last row and lock him up for thirty days."

"Did you set the fire?" Thaddeus asked.

"No, I didn't. I would never do such a thing."

"Where do you store your saddle?" His lawyer's voice kept strong.

"My saddle's on a sawhorse in the stable next to those of the other cowboys."

"Do you keep your saddle out in the open?" Thaddeus raised his hands above his head for emphasis. "Where anybody could cut your cinch or possibly slip a bill of sale into your saddle bag?"

"Yep. Must be how the document got stashed in the pocket. I certainly never wrote it."

"Objection, the bill of sale in Count One has been dismissed," Mr. Oliver shouted.

"Sustained. Refrain from mentioning Count One."

"At breakfast that morning, did you make an announcement?"

"Sure did. I told everyone me and Miss Kellogg were getting hitched." He looked right at her and smiled.

"Were you happy about your engagement?"

"Heck, yes. She's the best thing that's ever happened to me."

"According to Mr. McDraw, you were leaving the ranch and your intended behind."

"That's a lie. I had just caught Bella Sheba outside the fence and was about to bring her back to the ranch." Dusty clenched his hands so tightly they were turning white.

"Were your boots missing a spur when you were brought to town?"

"No, sir. The boots I'm wearing have both spurs."

"Thank you Dusty. I have no more questions." Thaddeus went to his seat.

She prayed at least one juror believed Dusty was innocent.

Mr. Oliver stepped with cocksure strides for his cross-examination. "Mr. Mann, would you like to own your own ranch?"

"Yes. But—"

"Have you been unhappy since you lost the Silver Spur?"

"Objection, speculation." Thaddeus stood.

"Mr. Oliver, is there a reason for this question?" the judge asked.

"Yes. Your Honor." The prosecutor grinned at the jurors. "Mr. Mann, am I correct in assuming that you've been dissatisfied working as a foreman? Thus, you stole Bella Sheba for money to buy your own spread?"

"It's a lie." Outraged, Dusty stood. His lawyer motioned for him to sit. Dusty exhaled and sat back down.

Anger shot through Mia.

"Objection, the prosecutor is attempting to lead the defendant," Thaddeus' fists were clenched, his calm composure showed agitation.

"Sustained. The jurors must disregard the last words."

She hated Mr. Oliver.

"Mr. Mann, you said you didn't set the fire. Do you have any witnesses who could prove you weren't there?"

Dusty stared at the prosecutor.

"Mr. Mann, please answer the question."

"Yes."

"Please name the witness."

"I can't."

"You're under oath. Who was the witness?"

"I can't in good conscience say the name." Dusty wouldn't even look at her.

The prosecutor smiled at the jurors. "Were you and Miss Kellogg conspiring to steal the horse?"

"Objection. Leading the witness."

"Sustained." The judge banged his gavel.

"I have no more questions." The prosecutor looked at her. He must've known Dusty would never say anything to damage her reputation. If she spoke up, the jury would assume she'd been in cahoots with him.

"You may give your closing statement, Mr. Oliver."

"Gentlemen, Mr. Harold Mann chose to be a horse thief. You have heard testimony proving how Mr. Mann had become malcontent. He despised his foreman's job, believing he should be the ranch's owner. His spur and strap were found in Bella Sheba's stall, proof Mr. Mann had easy access to the horse. His recent engagement put further burden on Mr. Mann, and he became desperate. Mr. McGraw caught the horse thief, Dusty Mann, leading Bella Sheba off the ranch's property and heading east. Mr. Mann stole Bella Sheba. Guilty as charged on Count Two."

Liar! Mia fought to stay quiet.

"There is no doubt, my friends. Mr. Mann is guilty of possession of stolen property, Bella Sheba."

She thought about Dusty's newspaper article in the future. Had she been sent to the past to save him? If so, why didn't she find evidence in his favor? Her stomach cinched even tighter than a corset.

Thaddeus shuffled to the jurors and faced them. "Gentlemen. You all know the real Dusty Mann, an honest, hardworking cowboy. A man who found an expensive horse owned by Mr. McGraw in a place she should not be. He planned to keep her safe until he had completed his rounds and could return her to the stables, and get back to his fiancé, Miss Kellogg."

Her heart felt as heavy as a wagon wheel. She expected to see one or two outraged jurors nodding, not their blank expressions.

"Dusty Mann is innocent. Dusty Mann is the pawn in a fraudulent machination, a vicious scheme to make him look guilty." Thaddeus paused and leaned on the juror box railing. "Let's look once again at the evidence. His Friday routine made him an easy target for malicious intent. Anyone could have snipped off a spur from his boots left on his front porch. Anyone could have set him up and moved Bella to a spot where Dusty would find her."

Go, Thaddeus.

"Dusty Mann did not set the fire, but the fire provided a diversion, allowing the assailant to move Belle Sheeba off the ranch undetected. The same assailant snipped the fence and waited for Dusty without any notice. The assailant left Bella in the perfect location at the precise time. Otherwise, Mr. McGraw would not have located Bella Sheba with Dusty." Thaddeus cleared his throat and looked straight into the eyes of the jurors. "Gentlemen, the only logical conclusion is that, for reasons we do not know, Dusty Mann was framed. Dusty is a victim. I ask you to find Dusty Mann NOT Guilty. He did not commit a crime. Set him free. Dusty Mann is innocent."

The lawyer gave a great argument. Would it work? Mia thought about the alternative, Dusty hanged. The idea made it hard for her to swallow, much less breathe.

The judge gave the jurors' instructions. "It is your duty to weigh the evidence, decide the disputed questions of fact, apply the instructions of law to your findings, and render your verdict. Remember that the defendant is presumed innocent. If the prosecution has proven without a reasonable doubt that Harold Mann is guilty, then each person on the jury may vote guilty. If any juror has reasonable doubt, it is his duty to speak out and express his opinion."

Mia wondered if the jurors understood the judge's legal jargon. They shuffled into a side room, and the door slammed.

As Mia sat behind Dusty, worry threaded inside her soul.

"Dusty, I'm quite confident you'll be free today." Thaddeus' lips turned up at the corner a smidgen. "Even if they don't all say you're innocent, I believe there will be enough doubt to cause a hung jury."

"That'd be okay." Dusty gazed at Mia over the partitioned half-wall. He stretched his fingers to take her hand in his.

"Soon, you'll be free to marry Miss Amelia." Randy tapped his cane.

"That's all I've been thinking about." Dusty's words made her heart still.

"Me too." She said a silent prayer.

Chapter Eighteen

Forty-five minutes later, the jurors marched to their seats. None looked happy.

Dusty swallowed back the disquiet in his throat.

The bailiff stood, his belly hung over his belt. "All rise for the Honorable Judge Edwin Longfellow.

The judge sneezed, pulled out a handkerchief and blew his nose with the cloth. "Mr. Hayes, have the jurors reached a verdict?"

"Yes, Your Honor."

Dusty held his breath. *Please say innocent. Please say innocent.*

We the jury, find the defendant, Harold Mann, GUILTY on Count Two, the theft of Bella Sheba."

"This can't be happening," Mia cried.

"Dusty had it coming," a man shouted.

"No, he didn't. He's been framed," another person yelled.

The judge banged his gavel. "Order, I demand order, or the court will be cleared."

Instant silence did not ease the lump wedged inside Dusty's lungs. He should've listened to Mia, should've run while he had a chance.

"There will be a ten-minute recess while I render my sentence."

Based on the location of the sun, he figured it to be close to five. He'd sat on the hard-wooden bench for seven hours, but it felt like seven days. Idleness never set well, and he'd done practically nothing for two weeks. He ached for fresh air.

Tears flowed down Mia's cheeks.

"Darlin', I'll probably get only a couple years in prison." Dusty tried to reassure her, while he knew the hanging judge never gave prison sentences—only death sentences.

"I'll wait for you."

He kissed her hand. "If you didn't, I'd understand."

She closed her eyes. "It's not fair. I failed you, Dusty."

"Can't change fate." He weaved his fingers with hers. "Meeting you is the best thing to ever happened to me."

"I love you." She kissed his knuckles.

The judge came back.

Dusty stood.

The judge's dark eyes held no compassion. "Mr. Harold Charles Mann is hereby sentenced on July 4, 1890, at precisely twelve o'clock noon to hang by the neck until he is dead."

Did the judge just sentence him to hang? It couldn't be true.

"Noooooo!" Mia's scream echoed.

Somebody applauded. Others in the room shouted or cried.

He turned and listened to voices.

"He deserves to die."

"Dusty's been railroaded."

"He's a crook."

"Never liked the guy."

"He's a no-good horse thief."

Mark's face turned bright red. "This is wrong. You're innocent."

"This sentence is outrageous," Thaddeus said. "We should have won, Dusty. The jury convicted you on mostly hearsay. Hindsight tells me I should have added Randy and Mark as character witnesses. The judge may have been more lenient. I will file for a mistrial."

"Don't bother." Dusty glanced at Mia. His poor gal withered. "Darlin', please don't cry."

~ * ~

Why had Mia been sent to 1890 if she couldn't save Dusty? Tears dripped down her face. Her lungs must've collapsed because she couldn't breathe.

The courthouse cleared out at least fifteen minutes ago, leaving behind only Dusty, the sheriff, and her.

Dusty stretched his fingertips to his shirt pocket; his cuffs stopped him inches short. "I want to take care of you and can't even hand you a handkerchief. Darlin', I'm sorry you were mixed up in all this."

She pulled out the hanky herself and dried her tears. "I wouldn't be anywhere else."

"Dusty, it's time to head back," Flynn said in a flat tone.

Mia remained at his right as they went down the stairs. Flynn walked behind.

"The jury's wrong," a young freckle-faced teen in overalls yelled.

"Couldn't agree more." Poor Dusty. His chuckle held a crackle of defeat.

God, she was upset. She'd lost faith in the jurors. She'd lost faith in society. Hell, she'd lost faith in her destiny.

"You're shaking." Dusty slowed, moved behind her and ushered her forward. After all he'd been through, he worried about her. His concern made her love him all the more.

"Hold on there, partner." Flynn gripped Dusty's shoulders and pulled him back from her. "You're as jumpy as an old bullfrog. Not thinking about bolting, are you?"

"I'm trying to keep Amelia from harm.

The sheriff eased up on his hold. "It's my job keeping the peace and safeguarding the folks in this town."

Mark and Randy waited near one of the hitching posts and waved.

"Darlin', you're worn ragged. Have the Jacobson's take you to the hotel. See me after you've rested."

"Good try, but you're stuck with me, cowboy." She loved him far too much to abandon him.

~ * ~

Flynn unlocked the jailhouse door. Dusty tried to rub his handcuffed wrist together. His right hand slipped out. Interesting.

Mia's eyes widened. She remained silent as he squeezed his fingers together and put the cuff back in place.

Flynn pushed open the door. Mia entered first, followed by Dusty.

"I'm right sorry you're not being released," the lawman said.

"So am I."

She wrapped her arms around Dusty's neck. He brought his lips to hers and kissed her. The sheriff cleared his throat.

"I love you," Dusty whispered. Led to his cell, his handcuffs were removed, the door slammed sounding confinement. Dammit. He didn't belong in this rat's haven. He didn't steal Bella.

Her slender fingers curved around the bars. "Dusty, it's not fair."

Pretending to be strong, her eyes echoed his own sorrow. "Don't be sad."

"How could the jury not see you're innocent?"

"It's done." He squeezed her hand. "You can't stay here and watch me hang."

"I won't leave you."

"This is wrong. I know you're innocent," a voice outside his jail cell window called in.

Dusty looked out. "Thanks, Robert. Glad you're on my side."

"Always, my friend." The man left.

The verdict hit Dusty. Sweat formed above his brow. *I'm gonna hang. I don't want to die.*

Randy Jacobson stood in the doorway. "You'll get an appeal."

Mark helped his dad over toward his cell. "Dusty, you were wronged."

"It isn't fair." Mia tried to mask her devastation with a false smile, but he saw through her attempt. Poor gal tried to warn him, worked tirelessly to get his name cleared.

"I'm trying to talk Mia into leaving town, but she's not buying it," Dusty said to Mark. "I'll hang in two days and don't want her to see it."

"He's right you know." Mark leaned against the sheriff's desk. "Why don't you take the train to Barstow? Noticed one's heading north early tomorrow."

"Excellent plan," the sheriff said. "My aunt booked a seat. You could keep her company."

"I won't abandon Dusty."

"It's only for a couple of days." Dusty pleaded for her sake. The words made his soul empty.

"Why won't you listen to me?" Her glare seemed almost as dangerous as a live bullet. "I'm not leaving you."

"Miss Amelia, we're worried about you. This town is filling up for the Fourth. Keeping you out of harm's way will be hard. You don't want Dusty worrying?" The sheriff spoke with a fatherly tone. A tone that broke up fights and restored peace.

She sighed, her hands dropped to her side, a sign of consideration.

"It's been a long day." Mark's deep voice interrupted. "I'm taking Dad home, but I can return in a few hours and escort Miss Amelia to the hotel."

She took a proud, steadfast stance. "No thanks. I'll stay here tonight."

"Sorry," the sheriff said, "but it's against the rules to have visitors after ten."

She rolled her eyes. More than aggravated, she was livid.

"My shift ends at nine, and I'll bring you to the hotel," Flynn talked like everything was already settled.

"Good call," Mark turned to her. "I'll secure a seat for you on the train tomorrow, just in case, and leave your ticket with Jenny."

"That's not necessary." Why wouldn't anyone listen to her?

"Maybe not, but it will be done," Mark said and left with his father.

"You're all being ridiculous."

"Darlin', I don't want to fight with you. Come over closer." Dusty kissed her from between the bars. "I'll always remember what you did for me. You'll take the train tomorrow, right?" He loved her far too much for her to stay, even though sending her away caused his heart to crack like a broken egg shell.

"I doubt it."

"I love your determination."

The front door opened with a clunk against the wall. Myra Wisenheimer, the mayor's wife, held her nose in the air, followed by Sandy McGraw. Dusty didn't appreciate Myra's glower directed at Mia. Myra, the town's busybody, stirred up trouble with constant scuttlebutt. The old biddy placed her hands on her over-sized hips. "You have to keep Miss Amelia away from that criminal."

"Miss Kellogg has a mind of her own and can do as she pleases." The sheriff said in an official tone.

"Her reputation will be sullied. She'll soon become a thief like him." Myra sneered at him.

"Myra, you've got to be joshing?" Flynn widened his stance.

"I wouldn't pun about such a serious matter." She replied in an unpleasant, churlish voice.

"I suppose not."

"Dusty's no criminal, he's my innocent fiancé. Someone framed him. Set him up to be the fall guy for something he would never do." Mia's hand went to her left hip.

"You're misguided if you believe that." Myra pointed a gnarled finger at her. "He's a thief."

"You were a good teacher." Sandy turned to Mia and spoke softly. "Forget this nonsense with Dusty, and I'll find someone to take you back to the ranch."

"I'm not leaving Dusty." Mia held her ground.

Dusty loved watching her in action. She would not let these old biddies get the better of her.

"I hate to tell you this Sandy, but that woman failed to follow the proper conduct of a teacher," Myra said in an I-know-a-secret tone. "Late one night, Dusty was seen leaving Miss Kellogg's room."

"Did you witness this yourself?" Flynn let out an exasperated huff.

The old biddy lifted her chin. "No. But Gertrude's boy, Scott, works out on the ranch. Gertrude said Scott saw Miss Kellogg kissing Dusty goodbye on her front porch, wearing only her nightgown, acting like a saloon harlot." Myra reminded him of a howling jackal. "The town could have a double hanging—Dusty and Miss Kellogg are two of a kind."

"I'm appalled at your behavior, Myra." Flynn paused, waiting for a second or two. "What you've mentioned is hearsay. Hearsay is not admissible in court nor accepted here."

"She's a sinner, I tell you. No decent unmarried Christian woman would be seen with a man without a chaperone." Myra harrumphed.

Dusty couldn't stand haughty people like her.

"Myra, you've gone too far." Sandy snapped.

"Either Miss Kellogg leaves town today, or, I swear you'll be sorry." Myra had the gall to say out loud. "Don't forget my husband runs Hesperia."

"Myra, is that a threat?"Flynn asked.

"No." She picked up her skirt. "But you haven't heard the last of me." She stomped out of the office.

After defending Dusty countless times in the past two weeks, now Mia was forced to defend herself. She stepped over to Dusty and threaded her arm through the bar and took his hand.

"You were amazing," he whispered.

"Thanks," her tone lacked conviction.

Sandy came over to the bars. "I forgive you," she said to Dusty.

"Forgive me?" Dusty shouted. "What the hell are you forgiving me for?"

"Stealing Bella."

Dusty groaned. "I was framed. You and Westin are too dumb to figure it out."

Sandy's eyes flashed ire. "You, sir, are both a moron and an oaf?"

"Dusty's innocent," Mia spoke icily. "When the truth comes out, and it will, you'll live knowing the wrong man died! But it's not too late to stop this nonsense."

Death. The word hit him hard.

"Amelia, you are a naïve little soul." Sandy wagged her finger at her. "Dusty stole Bella. You're fooling yourself if you think otherwise."

Mia folded her arms. "And you'll go insane once you realize you allowed an innocent man to hang."

"Good day Sheriff Law." Sandy strutted out the door.

"Sandy's trying to make herself feel better," Mia said quietly.

"I have to admit her indignant attitude got my goat." Dusty shook his head.

Flynn put down his whittling and stood next to Mia. "You two have been through hell. I rarely break the rules, but in your case, I'll bend them a bit. Give you time together."

"You're the nicest man," she reached up and kissed him on the cheek.

"It's the least I can do," the sheriff blustered.

Anxious as a horse awaiting a bucket of oats, Dusty rushed to the door and heard the lock click open.

Mia deserved much better than a short moment alone in a rundown jail cell. She should leave this hellish nightmare, run and never look back. Still, she roped her arms around his neck. "It seems like forever since we were together."

"Sure does." He bent his head down, cupped her face in his palms and kissed her thoroughly. He finally met his match. "Why don't we sit a spell?" He kept his hand on her waist, directed her over to his cot, and they sat side by side.

"It's not right, I fall in love and—" She leaned against his chest.

"Let's enjoy right now." His lips brushed hers.

The sheriff made a hum-hum sound.

Jenny walked in carrying two plates of food and gave one to Flynn. She turned to Dusty. "I'm sick about the verdict."

"Thanks, that means a lot," Dusty said to her.

"Bob's so upset, he's lying down."

Flynn unlocked the door.

Jenny advanced inside and put a platter on a side table with tears in her eyes. "Believe me, I'm not the only one in town praying for a miracle."

Miracles didn't happen to people like him. Depression hit Dusty.

Jenny swiped at her wet cheek with her hand. "I'd better head back to the hotel."

Mia tried to hide her despair, but her mouth quivered.

"You're all that matters to me. Nobody ever cared about me like you do—with your whole heart."

"I love you, Dusty."

He tenderly caressed her mouth, finding comfort holding her close, craving her warmth and solace.

The door flung open. "Howdy, Flynn." The deputy clomped into the room.

"Nine o'clock already?" The sheriff placed his carving on the desk.

The deputy picked up the object. "Good likeness of a stallion." His eyes drifted over to the cell. "What the hell is Miss Amelia doing with that convict? You arrest her, too?"

"Honestly Ned." He gave an exasperated sigh. "They're engaged. Least I could do was let them say goodbye."

The deputy cocked his head. "Well, it ain't right."

Flynn unlocked the cell. "Sorry, Miss Amelia. It's time to escort you to the hotel."

Dusty held onto her. "Come on Flynn. Give us a few more minutes."

"I suppose."

"I'm in charge now." The deputy puffed out his chest, a self-important idiot wearing a badge.

"Not till I'm officially off."

Dusty kissed her as if his lungs starved for oxygen. He pulled away and felt a restless emptiness only she could fill. "I'm blessed you came into my life."

"I'm the lucky one." Water misted her eyes.

"I'll be at the hotel early, say five-thirty." The sheriff guided her out and to the entrance door. "That'll give you time with Dusty before the train departs."

"I'm not taking the train," she snapped.

Dusty grinned at her spunkiness.

~ * ~

The cell door snapped shut with a hollow clank of finality. In less than forty-eight hours, a rope would snap his neck. He massaged his dry throat and wiped his clammy palms on his pants. The words his grandfather said when Dusty was a little boy hit him. *If you're gonna fret, you might as well keep busy and muck out a couple of stalls.*

No stalls, no barn, no stables, no horses, no cattle to chase.

Sulking in his cell wouldn't chase away the inevitable. Mia and his sister each deserved a letter. He started with his sister. Why hadn't he written to her more frequently? Why hadn't he ever said, "I love you, sis?" Why hadn't he attempted to visit his sister in the last year? The four-hour ride to her father's ranch wasn't far.

"Deputy, could you bring me several sheets of paper, ink, a pen, and throw in an envelope or two?"

The lawman brought inside his cell a wobbly table and the requested items.

Dusty grabbed paper. A dreadful hurt settled deep inside his soul.

Dear Josie,
By the time you receive this letter, I will already be dead, hanged for stealing Westin's horse, Bella Sheba. The truth is I didn't do it but was framed.
You deserve happiness. Enjoy your life. Find yourself a good man to marry.
I love you, sis.
Your favorite brother,
Dusty

That was hard. Mia's would be even more difficult because she deserved a letter from his heart. Dusty used his forefinger and traced the garnet on his belt buckle. He caught a fuzzy image of Mia reclining on her bed. It disappeared.

He traced the stone once more.

Nothing.

Did the gemstones connect him to her? Rubbing the stones, he saw a fleeting image of her blonde hair.

He loved her enough to let her go. Unfathomable pain wrenched in his gut. He preferred to be gored by a bull or thrown from a bronco or bit by a rattler than be in this stinky chamber. Melancholy sunk in, the kind where a man aches from inside out.

He pulled up a rickety chair to the writing table. Surely, she'd return to her own time. In case she was stuck here, he'd write.

Darling,

I will never forget how you barreled into me like a skittish colt.

Her green eyes had him hooked from the get-go.

I fell for you instantly. You tenaciously rode Half-Pint with plenty of complaints. I love your spirit.
I love the way you smile, love kissing you, love how you give fully of yourself. Your kisses will warm me throughout eternity. My love for you will never die. It will stay in my heart forever.
Don't mourn for me. Move on with your life and find love again. You deserve to be happy whether you remain in the past or move on to the future.

She had to let him go.

Your loving cowboy,
Dusty

Never one for tears, a few slipped out as he sucked in his sorrow. It wasn't fair. He'd found his destiny with a spirited, independent woman. They should grow old together. He folded the letter, put it in an envelope and tucked it into his pants pocket.

He dropped his head on the table and sobbed.

Chapter Nineteen

July 2, 1890

Mia couldn't sleep. The grandfather clock chimed four times. Four a.m.—an ungodly hour to be up. Flynn wouldn't be here for over an hour. Might as well go see Dusty now.

She went to the table by the window and turned up the lamp. Quickly getting dressed, she needed to see Dusty before—sadness blurred her eyes. There must be some way to save the love of her life. Since it was dark outside, she held the hotel lantern in one hand and her bag in the other and made her way along the walkway next to the train tracks. The night created blurred, surreal shadows.

A board creaked behind her.

"Is someone there?" She spun around and scanned the scattered benches. Was there a person pressed against the building?

An hour ahead of schedule, a bell clanged the train's arrival.

The locomotive pulled into the station like a dark monster. The chuffing created rhythmic temporal lobe throbbing. Her fingers pressed to her temple and willed away the headache.

241

White steam billowed out of the smokestack forming a misted cloud that floated along the ground. The brakes scraped and screeched. A shot of steam blasted from a pipe and caused her skirt to flutter. The noisy pistons continued chattering.

She glanced around the area and scooted by the passenger car.

"Amelia," she heard Dusty yell from his cell window.

Her garnet ring felt warm against her skin. She ignored it and kept walking.

The band became hot. She twisted and turned it, but it still wouldn't budge. Another fifty steps and she'd reach the jailhouse door.

"You shouldn't be out there alone," Dusty's voice sounded frantic.

The temperature of her band rose, burning into her finger. She had to get it off. Pulling and tugging, she finally yanked it over her knuckle and clasped the ring in her left hand. The momentum caused her to fall toward the train.

The area around her spun, making her dizzy.

~ * ~

The jailhouse clock dinged four times. Stale suffocating air forced Dusty toward the glassless window. Through welded iron bars, a full moon shone brightly, irradiating the iron railroad tracks, boarded walkway, and scattered benches.

Vreeeee. A whistle broadcasted the train's arrival.

Light footsteps clicked along the wooden pathway next to the tracks. A muddled silhouette of a woman appeared.

"Amelia?" he shouted.

The locomotive's engine chugged into the station, drowning his voice. A gush of steam blasted out several feet and hit her ankles. She jumped and pivoted to face the car.

"You shouldn't be out there alone. Where's your escort?" he screamed, but she didn't answer.

Murky shadows melded with the corner of the building. A cloudy fog cloaked the bottom inches of the station's platform, making the scene seem like an illusion. Was he hallucinating? "Amelia!" he called.

A woman alone before dusk. Not the safest thing she'd ever done. He wasn't taking any chances and screamed, "Deputy, check on Amelia. I saw her outside."

The man snored.

"Amelia," Dusty shouted so loudly his lungs hurt.

She stopped and appeared to be fiddling with something.

"Shut up back there," the deputy grumbled. "I'm trying to sleep."

Dusty couldn't keep quiet. He kicked the side of the cot and hollered, "Amelia's in trouble!" His gut said the deputy needed to check on her.

"Knock off that racket." A tortoise would walk to the cell faster than the deputy

Dusty stayed rooted at the window, praying the strength of his adrenaline would knock the bars out. "You have to help Amelia!" Out there by herself, anything could happen.

"I get it. You're gonna try to escape. Could've come up with a better story."

"It's the truth." Troubled about her welfare, Dusty rattled the window bars.

"You think I'm that stupid?" the deputy yelled. "I'll step out that door and get clobbered over the head by one of your friends. I'm not doing that."

"Let me out of here." Dusty's fingers clutched the cold metal. He willed the bar to bend, shatter, melt to allow him to get outside. "Help, please, anyone." His voice sounded loud, furious, foreign.

"Quit your caterwauling." The deputy's tone didn't have an inkling of sympathy.

He watched Mia as she fell toward the locomotive and vanished. Like she slipped through a distorted reality. She was gone as was the locomotive. Was this how time travel worked? He had no idea.

He hoped she was safely back in her time. With his last shred of energy drained, Dusty flopped onto his cot face down. He failed to save the ranch, failed to support his sister, failed to keep his mother safe, and without Mia—he had no reason to live.

~ * ~

"What's wrong with Mia? She's dead-white," a foggy-familiar voice said.

Birdie?

Fingers pressed against her forehead. "She's like an ice-cube."

"Auntie Mickie?"

"Sweetie, are you okay?"

"Huh?" Mia squint-opened her eyes to a brilliant, blinding light. "Where's Dusty?

"Dusty? The guy from that photo?" Her cousin arched a brow. "You're so bewitched by that cowboy you're dreaming about him."

"Oh, no." She'd tried to save Dusty. Tears filled her eyes.

"Cuz, what's going on?"

"Nothing." She pictured Dusty's sparkling eyes, his half-cocked dimpled smile, his sensuous mouth.

She scanned her surroundings. Flecks of gold accentuated the red carpet. The seats were made with maroon-colored velvet. Birdie wore her pink gown and silly feathered hat. Auntie Mickie still had on her long skirt and high-collared white blouse.

A three-year-old girl in a periwinkle bonnet and dress ran over and latched onto Mia's leg.

"Zoey, come here." The girl looked up at Mia, noticed she clung to the wrong leg and ran back to her mother. "Sorry, I must've dozed."

"It's okay."

She glanced down at her gown. What happened to the simple cotton dress she wore this morning? She shouldn't be wearing the same dress she'd had on a month ago. It shouldn't be spotless and freshly pressed, the ornate white lace collar unmarred. How could she be riding on the same train at the exact moment she'd left—a month ago? Her senses swirled. The last she remembered, she took off her ring at the depot in 1890.

Her cousin pulled a water bottle from her bag and unscrewed the cap. "Bet you're dehydrated. Drink this."

A sip of liquid soothed her thirst. It did nothing for her inner turmoil. "Thanks, I'm better," she lied.

"Sweetie, you're still awfully pale. Anything else I can get you?"

Dusty, please. "Excedrin, if you have it." She gazed out the window. Cars sped beside the train. Several turned off toward the Calico sign.

"You're still going to the ball tonight, right?" Birdie tilted her head.

"I'm not feeling well. Think I'll get off at the next town."

"But we've been planning this night for months. Come on. It'll be fun."

Partying. The last thing she desired. "With the way my head's pounding, I'd be a drag. Plus, I feel nauseous. Think the train gave me motion sickness."

"Next stop, Barstoooooooow, Caaaliforniaaaaaa," the conductor called.

"I'm getting off."

"Please stay. What works to keep from getting sick, Auntie?"

"Ginger ale. Sometimes peppermint."

"Too late. Hand me a trash can." She put her hand over her mouth.

"Here you go?" Auntie Mickie pushed her a metal container. Mia emptied the contents of her stomach.

"You poor dear," her aunt pushed a strand of hair behind Mia's ear.

"I'm a little better."

"My brother's working not far from here. You know he'll do anything to get out of mucking out stalls."

Dusty used the same term for cleaning out horse manure. My, how she missed him.

Birdie whipped out her phone. "Hey. Think you can pick up Mia in Barstow? Great." She turned to her. "He's on his way."

"I'll stay with you." Auntie Mickie stood.

"Then who'll tweet the event?" She'd rather be alone.

"I'll do it," her aunt's friend said.

The train slowed.

Mia embraced Birdie, grabbed her bag, and rushed to the door, hoping to ditch Auntie Mickie. No such luck. Her aunt remained by her side as she scurried down the steps and ambled to the depot's front entrance. "Are you okay?"

"I'm fine, just a little tired." She was far from fine. Without Dusty, the desert seemed as vast and lonely and bleak as her future.

~ * ~

The next morning, a grandfather clock chimed seven times. Mia opened her eyes to pink polka dot sheets. Where was she?

Her grandparent's spare bedroom. They were on a world cruise and had asked her to housesit.

Logic suggested she had dreamed of living in the past, but she'd never dreamed in color. Everything had been real and vivid. She recalled Dusty's gray eyes, his tanned complexion, the jagged scar on his chin. Her mind couldn't conjure up a charming, contrary cowboy like Dusty. Still, she tried to rationalize her time in the past. Dreams didn't last for weeks nor were they coherent. No, this hadn't been a dream.

And she knew in her heart she wasn't going crazy.

She grabbed her bag, pulled out her boxy phone, and plugged it in. Mom's picture showed. Great. Might as well get this talk over with. She pressed the call back button.

"Heard you're not well."

It seemed like months since she talked to her. "I'm okay."

"You sound weak. I'm coming over."

"Not necessary." She wasn't ready for her mother's coddling.

"If you had a husband—"

Dusty had been her fiancé in eighteen-ninety. She willed away her tears. If she started crying, she'd never stop. "Mom, I need to go. Call you later." She sucked in her sorrow.

Why had she time traveled? She needed answers. Hmm ... she'd call Uncle Al since he's into parallel universes.

It took three rings for him to pick up.

"Can we talk?" she asked.

"Sure. What's up?"

"I have some physics questions I'd like to discuss in person."

"My favorite topic. I'm busy this morning but can swing by around four-thirty on my way back from the gym."

"Perfect." She went into the living room, picked up her iPad, sat on the couch, and searched the internet for Dusty's death records. Archived records for San Bernardino County stopped at nineteen-fifteen. She clicked on a genealogy website, typed in his information, tapped the search button and prayed he hadn't hanged. The report came up.

Harold Charles Mann. A.k.a. Dusty. Born: July 9, 1862. Died: July 4, 1890. Cause of Death: Hanged.

Her cowboy hadn't escaped the noose. She flopped face first on the couch pillow and cried and cried and cried.

Tiger meowed, hungry as usual. Her head ached as she fed the cat.

She should drive down to the shop where she saw the article. She called. The answering machine said they'd were closed on Mondays. Old documents and newspapers are digitized. Nothing came up about the hanging in *Hesperia Weekly Gazette*.

She'd try the college library.

"High Desert Library," a pleasant-sounding woman answered. "This is Ruth speaking."

"I'm looking for an article in eighteen-ninety about a Hesperia man who hanged." Her eyes welled. The only man she'd ever loved didn't deserve to be screwed over.

"Articles that old are stored on microfilm. Would you like me to pull the canister and put it on hold for you?"

"Yes, please. You're a saint."

She changed into jeans and a T-shirt and headed out. She arrived at the library around eleven. Half-a-dozen people worked on computers. She rushed to the counter. "I'm here for the microfilm from eighteen-ninety."

"You must be Mia," a gray-haired woman wearing square glasses sai.

"That's me."

"Is the man who hanged your ancestor?"

"I don't believe so." *Hanged*. The word reverberated through her mind.

"The machine's in a room toward the back. Let me show you how it works." The clerk holding a canister led her to a room with what could pass for an old computer monitor.

"It's been awhile since I've used one of these."

249

"I'll load this for you. Use the knob at the bottom to flip forward and backward on the reader and scan the pages. The San Bernardino Sun comes up first." The clerk picked up the canister. "If you want copies, you'll need to insert a credit card into this slot."

"I can't thank you enough." Mia sat and searched. She started with January eighteen-ninety. Holding a knob, she slowly scanned the pages until she came to June thirtieth, July first, second, third.

She stopped at the headline.

Local Town to Celebrate in Big Ways

She glanced at the word Hesperia. Inserting her credit card, she printed several pages to read later. Besides advertisements, the newspaper wrote about celebrations in San Bernardino and Colton.

She forwarded the microfilm to June in the Hesperia paper. *Hesperia Hotel Ball* showed near the bottom of the first edition for June. Might as well print those pages and peruse them later. She skimmed the rest of the month without seeing anything substantial. Then she saw it.

Hesperia Horse Thief Hanged

The same article from the antique shop.

All of a sudden, the room sweltered like someone turned up the heater. She breathed in and out fast. Her body shook. Her peripheral vision narrowed, becoming fuzzy, fading out as she tumbled to the floor.

She woke to rough carpeting digging into her cheek. Opening her eyes, she found herself next to a chair.

Disoriented, she gulped in oxygen, about ten breaths, and slowly sat up. The sight of the microfilm reader brought her mind back to reality.

The clock on the wall showed half past two, and the library closed at three. A bit dizzy, she went back to the machine. Not bothering to read the content, she continued to print pages and kept going. When she got home later, she'd see what it said.

Chapter Twenty

Three syncopated knocks sounded on her door.

"It's open," Mia called.

Uncle Al wore cargo shorts, a dark Nike t-shirt, and sandals. Not precisely college professor clothing, but typical for him.

She rushed into his outstretched arms. "Glad you could make it. I have questions about time travel."

He dropped his hold and stepped back smiling. "What do you want to know?"

"How does time travel work?" she blurted out.

"Since I've never transported anywhere myself, I can't say for sure what happens, but I've heard some pretty bizarre stories. There's a 1940's photograph where a guy in sunglasses and a hoodie is shown at the opening of the South Fork Bridge in British Columbia. And moments before a Charlie Chaplin premiere, a movie clip featured a woman talking on her cell phone outside the once named Grauman's Theatre. Then there's a claim that a model appears on a freeway and disappears. Also, some guy claims to have been transported back to Gettysburg." His voice sped up, excited. "Still, these images may be hoaxes."

She used to think claims like this were ludicrous, but not anymore.

"Why do you ask?"

"Because I went back in time to 1890."

He eyed her and let out a snorting laugh. "You've always had a great sense of humor."

"Uncle Al, I'm not joking. Honest." She had to get him to take her seriously. "Let's sit in the living room. It'll be easier to talk."

"Talking I can do." He took the right side of the leather couch and leaned his elbow on the sofa's arm. "Since you think you went back to the nineteenth century—why don't you tell me the details?"

"Sure." She eased into the empty cushion on the left. "It started last month when Birdie and I visited an antique shop."

"I thought you two visited right before your trip with Mickie."

"We did."

"I hate to break it to you, but it was two days ago," he corrected.

"Not for me. I was in the past for a month."

"Weird, but I'll go with it."

"More than weird, crazy." She tucked her legs beneath her and sat on her feet, something she'd done since she was a little girl to appear taller. "Anyway, a photograph in the storefront window intrigued me. I bought this garnet ring there and put it in my purse." She glanced at her hand. Where was it? I think I slipped it in my bag."

"Garnet. Interesting choice."

She rushed into her room and brought out her leather bag. "The owner claimed the gemstones had special properties. It's supposed to fire up the heart for love. At the time, I assumed it was a ploy to sell the ring. Because I liked it, I bought it anyway."

She pulled out her sketchbook and flipped through several pages. "This is Dusty." Her eyes misted as she stared at the likeness of the man who held her heart.

"You're drawing shows passion, but I thought you weren't into cowboys anymore."

"That's what I kept telling myself, and then I met Dusty." She pictured his lazy smile right before he kissed her. "I love him, Uncle Al. He asked me to marry him."

"You do realize he died a century ago."

She turned to the next page, the one where Dusty rode his stallion. "Technically, yes."

"Tell me more about the shop."

"Oh, right. In an old scrapbook at the front register, I spotted an etching of Dusty Mann and read he'd been hanged in Hesperia. His death bothered me."

"One of my high school teachers had us debate whether we thought he was innocent or guilty." Her uncle shook his head. "Which side do you think I picked?"

"Innocent."

"If I recall correctly, there's an article that proves his innocence, but I could be wrong. Anyway, how'd you travel back in time?"

"The train reached the Cajon Pass when Birdie asked for gum. I pulled out a pack of Juicy Fruit and found the box with the ring. When I slipped it on my finger, the band felt hot, really hot, and I tried to take it off. The room spun, and I closed my eyes. The train stopped. I looked around; things were different."

"What do you mean?"

"Strangers sat in Birdie and Auntie Mickie's seats on the train. I didn't recognize anyone else around me either."

"Wow. You must've freaked."

"I started to, but then this guy blew nasty cigar smoke in my face. I needed air."

"Sounds like you. Did you see the hotel and head over for a drink?"

"In a roundabout way." The beastly horse caused her to shiver. "I'll tell you the story another day. Well, I literally ran into Dusty inside the hotel lobby." Memories flooded her mind. Memories of sitting across from him, dancing, making love. Memories. She couldn't sit still. "I'm getting ice tea. Want one?"

"Better make it Long Island."

"Can't. Don't have any liquor. Planned to buy wine but never got to it." She padded into the kitchen, the tiles cold on her bare feet, put two plastic glasses on the counter, and poured the tea. "Sugar?"

"Straight."

She spooned one, two, three heaping teaspoons into her own glass, stuck in a swizzle stick and brought the drinks to the couch.

"Here you go." She set her glass on the coffee table. "I was there through Dusty's trial. The evidence didn't seem strong, yet they found him guilty." Anger flared inside her recalling the injustice.

"Jurors can be unpredictable." He put his arm around her shoulder and hugged her. "You tried to warn him, but he still hung. Don't tell me you watched him die?" Her uncle took her hand and held it.

"I end up in the present, the day before the hanging was scheduled." She sighed. "I still don't get how I time traveled."

"I have a few of my own speculations."

"Of course, you do, Mr. Astrophysicist." Growing up, her dad and other uncles discussed football, while her Uncle Al quizzed her on the periodic table.

"You know my degree's in psychology, and I'm not an expert. More of a dabbler." He never did care for compliments. "My buddies and I have blogged for months about Hawking's Projection Conjecture."

She put up her hand. "Whoa, you've lost me."

"It is the idea that time and space are unalterable, that time travel is impossible. One of the guys, an eccentric astrophysicist from JPL, disagrees. He argues how space and time were not static realities. With the right push, time itself could be altered." Her uncle rubbed his chin. "Time jumps—both forward and backward."

"Did he say how?"

"Space curvatures. He conjectures space could fold in on itself." Uncle Al picked up a napkin and folded it in half. "Where the two pieces come together, where they touch, they can be bridged."

She took the napkin and slowly unfolded it. "So Dusty's time and ours—that's where the fold touches?"

"If it were simple the other passengers on your train would've come with you. There has to be a connector to both times—one opens the door between them." He rested his chin in the palm of one hand. "I haven't quite figured that out. People take trains all the time. We're missing something."

"I think it has to do with my garnet ring." Although she had no idea why.

"How did you know the gemstones were garnets?"

"Because of the deep red color. Dusty's stone on his belt buckle was the same color as mine. If his gemstone had been ruby, not garnet, his family's ranch would've been saved. Dusty never would've hanged." She wiped away tears with her finger.

"Garnets are said to have mystical properties. Native Americans use gems and crystals to aid in their dream quests. And vortexes? I felt their circular energy flow in Sedona."

"You know, inside the train, when I placed the ring on my finger, the room turned psychedelic and started spinning."

"The dimension shifted." He took out his iPhone and scrolled. "The string theory. Think of a model of DNA, but instead of our bodies, superstrings are larger, more complicated structures that deal with forces of the universe. Twist them one way and the strings become a proton—a different way, they become electrons or photons of light or gravitons. The mysterious particles of force create dimensions of space, time, or undiscovered energies with upflow and inflow patterns of electrical pulses."

"It kinda makes sense." She thought about how her ring sparkled in the light. Wait, it should be in her purse. She took out her hairbrush, wallet, romance novel, and felt along the bottom. "Here." She handed the band to him. "Could the garnets be a catalyst?"

"Possibly. It might connect directly with specific events."

"When I was in the past and stood near the train tracks and twisted my ring, I saw this time for a brief moment." She recalled Dusty nudging her to continue walking.

"I believe friction caused by turning the ring may have opened a portal and showed you a glimpse of our time."

"I'm pretty sure I saw a portal when I ended up back in the future. I mean, it seemed like I fell into a void." She threaded her hands together. "Did the combination of the garnet and the train's momentum enable me to time travel?"

"It's a brilliant analogy." He hugged her. "The catalyst of motion combined with the gemstone's friction created a vortex or wormhole in time."

Maybe she could do it again. She slipped on the ring. "Uncle Al, please help me figure out a way to go back and save Dusty."

"From what I've read, going back to a precise date is nearly impossible to replicate." He picked up a sheet of paper from a box on the coffee table. "*Hesperia Gazette, 1890.* Where'd you get this?"

"At the college today. Why don't you hand me a stack and take some pages for yourself? I'm hoping to validate my experience. Maybe find some clues to who framed Dusty."

She scanned the headlines for June 3, 1890

United States Census Begins Today. 175 Enumerators Hired.

San Bernardino County Scheduled to Collect Census Data This Week.

Neither headlines appeared helpful.

Hesperia Hotel Ball

"Uncle Al, listen to this.

Elegance and Plenty of Entertainment at the
Hesperia Hotel Ball
Judge Halleck's band played lively waltzes, polkas,
square, and round dances. Hogs and steer were
barbequed outside in the fire pits. Homemade peach
pies, apple fritters, triple-layered chocolate cakes, and
sugar cookies sweetened the night.
The well-attended soiree entertained folks like K.H.
Ferguson from New York City. Other visitors included
Miss Ruth and Miss Helen Walters, Roy and Edna
Walter's granddaughters, and the newly hired Los
Flores Ranch School Teacher, Miss Amelia Kellogg.

"I was there." The news didn't make her happy—it
made her long to be in Dusty's arms.
"Unbelievable. This clears up all my doubts about
your experience." His surprised expression mixed with
awe.
"You've always been on my side. Must be why you're
my favorite uncle."
"I'm not finding much in the second week of June.
There's an article about problems in the Oklahoma
Territory. Ads for buggies, saddles, cough medicine.
Hogs for sale at Clearview Farm." He put the pages face
down on the table and took more.
"Keep searching. There has to be something."
Her uncle thumbed through pages. "Did anything
unusual happen when you were in the past?"
"I left the newspaper office and was shot at."

Her uncle bunched up his hands.

"By a slingshot, but at the time I thought it was gunfire," she said with a smirk.

"You can be such a pain."

Reality hit her like an unexpected earthquake. "If I had died in 1890, would I have been on a missing person's list in the future?"

"You might." He shrugged. "Tell me a little more about your adventure."

"Dusty's conviction devastated me. After a long restless night, I fell asleep around three a.m. An hour later—a chiming clock woke me. I figured I might as well go see Dusty and rushed over to the jail to see him."

"I hope you got dressed first."

"You're crazy." She giggled and slapped his arm.

"And proud of it." Uncle Al looked over his glasses at her. "Tell me about how you came back here."

"My ring became really hot like it had before I traveled to 1890. This time I yanked and twisted and finally got the thing off. When I did, I fell toward the train, probably into a portal. My vision blurred, and I found myself inside the same passenger car from a month earlier. It was as if nothing changed—as if I'd remained in the present the whole time."

"That's quite a story. I certainly wouldn't admit what you said to anyone else."

"I won't. I don't want men in black suits and dark sunglasses whisking me away to a remote location and interrogating me." She shuddered.

"I'm upsetting you." He hugged her.

"The whole ordeal is upsetting."

"After Dusty's arrest, he became so thin. Lost his easy nature, his easy smile." Her poor cowboy. A wave of ice passed through her veins.

Her uncle dropped his head into his hands. "I'm so sorry."

She dabbed at the droplets leaking like a dam about to crack. "Can you believe I became a teacher at the Los Flores Ranch?"

"Can't picture you a school marm. High-collared blouse, glasses, your hair in a tight bun."

"Actually, I did well." She stepped into the kitchen to top off her tea and talked over the counter. "You've always told me to be myself. I liked teaching kids to draw."

"But you're terrified of horses?"

"Dusty helped me deal with my fears. He taught me to ride."

"He sounds like quite a man."

"The best." She willed her heart to quit aching.

"You know, you've always been strong. I remember you as a toddler, determined to get to the cookie jar on the kitchen counter. You pulled a chair up to the ledge. Discovering it hadn't been tall enough, you struggled to lift a phone book onto the seat, and boosted one leg on the counter."

"And fell flat on my face."

"Nope. Got caught by your mother. You never flinched, just batted your eyes and asked her for a chocolate chip cookie." The corners of his mouth tipped up into a smile.

"You made that up." Her eyes scanned another copied page.

"Nope." He held up two fingers together Boy Scout style. "Any idea who framed Dusty?"

"It's hard to say. Might be Reynolds, the owner's nephew. Never liked the guy. He cornered me outside my room, tried to—"

Uncle Al's jaw tensed. "Did he hurt you?"

"Chill. I was about to say, *kiss me*. Reynolds was close to this cowboy named Slick. They may have worked together." She thought about the odd friendship.

"Usually owners and ranch hands keep their distance."

"As the wife's nephew, Reynolds held no direct blood ties to Westin McGraw, but he acted entitled. The cook said Reynolds got into trouble and was sent to the ranch. Slick agreed to teach him how to put in a full work day—*cowboy him up*. Must've been difficult. Reynolds was not interested in becoming a cowboy. Slick kept on him. In the process, they became friends."

Her uncle scanned another page.

"In mysteries, it's usually the nice guy who's guilty," her uncle joked.

"Or the person who seems harmless. That would be Cookie, but she adored Dusty."

He picked up another copied page from the box and stopped. "You won't like this."

"I can take it."

"Keep in mind it's written in the past." He inhaled and exhaled.

"Convicted Horse Thief's Fiancé, Amelia Kellogg, Skips Out of Town."

She forced herself to listen.

"The day before the hanging, Miss Kellogg left town. According to Myra Wisenheimer, 'Miss Kellogg pretended to be a sweet schoolteacher, while she craved fancy clothing and expensive jewelry. She was in cahoots with Dusty. Wouldn't surprise me if she pushed him into stealing the racehorse.'"

"That's horse manure." Her agitation caused her to shriek.

"Horse manure?" Her uncle's hearty chuckle dissipated some of her anger. "That visit to the past really changed you."

"It has. Still, Myra's such a—"

"Busybody?"

"No, bitch." She snatched the page from him.

Her uncle looked over her shoulder at the headline. "Myra won a first-place ribbon for her pie."

"I can see her superior-smile." Scanning to a side column, she saw Dusty's sketch.

Local Foreman Hanged at Noon

"What's wrong?"

"Dusty was hanged." His death record on the internet seemed surreal, but seeing the printed words slammed her heart with a double blow, and she cried. Sobbing didn't erase the word *hanged*. Sobbing made her head hurt. Sobbing turned her eyelids into abrasive sandpaper rubbing against her corneas.

"I'm sorry—so sorry."

"So am I." Her temporal lobes pounded.

Her uncle brought her aspirin and a cold cloth from the kitchen.

"Relax and close your eyes. I'll keep scanning." The sound of papers rattled. "Listen to this from July seventh:

While Folks Enjoyed the Hesperia Festivities—
Cattle Were Rustled at Los Flores Ranch

"Cattle rustling had been mentioned. Who did it?" Whoever did better have suffered.

"I don't know yet." Her uncle laughed. "Let me read."

"Go on then."

Charles "Checkerboard" Flannigan stated that after he saw his friend, Dusty "Harold" Mann, hanged, he headed back to the ranch via the Los Flores Ranch's central gate. He spotted a haze of dirt just east of the property line. Initially, he assumed it was nothing more than a dust devil.

Leaving his horse in an outdoor stall, he walked toward the stables. Flannigan reports that he heard laughter coming from the tack room, so he leaned against the wall and listened. It was then that he recognized Thomas "Slick" Washington who told Kenneth "Blackie" Black that he should be the foreman now that Mann got what he deserved for snooping.

"Those jerks set Dusty up."

"Apparently." Her uncle gave he a sympathetic smile.

Black responded, says that with Mann no longer alive, they could quit worrying about him figuring out what they were doing and turnin them in. Black congratulated Washington for his part in getting the ranch owner's nephew riled up about Mann's relationship with the new teacher, Mia Kellogg. It is Flannigan's theory that Washington planted the notion of Mann trying to steal a horse, and Reynolds bought right into it.

"Dusty lost his life because of them!" She stood and kicked the couch. "I'd shoot them myself if I saw either one of them."

"Calm down." Her uncle pinched his lips together. "They died a long time ago."

"It's the principle of the thing. Please keep reading."

Flannigan stated that he heard Black say they needed to hide the money before folks arrived back at the ranch.

Trevor stopped.

"What about the rustling?"

"Don't know. The story's cut off." He grabbed the empty box top. "You make any more copies?"

"Ran out of time. At least this clears Dusty's name. I hope Blackie and Slick died a slow agonizing death."

"I'm with you, Mia. Guess we'll have to wait another day to find out." Uncle Al shook his head. "Criminals like Slick and Blackie assume they'll never get caught."

She closed her eyes. "It isn't fair. Dusty died because of those two."

Her uncle wrapped her into his arms. "I'm sorry, Mia."

She couldn't help sobbing. He held her for the longest time.

"You really loved Dusty." He pulled away and grabbed a box of tissues.

"I did." She wiped her face.

"Wish I could do something to make the pain go away." He rubbed his chin. "You know, I'm dropping off a batch of Mickie's peanut butter cookies at Los Flores tomorrow morning. I could bring you along—if you're up to it."

"Absolutely." It might be difficult, but she had to see the place again. "Just get me back in time for my parents' Fourth of July party?" Not that she wanted to party, but her presence was expected.

Chapter Twenty-one

The next morning, a howling dog outside broke the quiet. A man slept next to her—sun bleached hair, a faded tan complexion, and a day's growth of stubble shaded his strong chin. "Dusty?"

He propped on his elbow and perused her body. "Mornin', darlin'." Inching closer, he rubbed his coarse whiskers against her cheek, and gave a quiet ... purr.

She opened her eyes. Her cat's iridescent green eyes glowed and taunted her.

"Darn it, Tiger. You ruined my dream." She grabbed the cat, hugging him tighter than usual, and the feline wriggled out of her grasp.

She changed into a yellow sundress and checked her texts. Her mother reminded her to be at the party by five. Her cousin, Birdie, invited her to her parent's beach house next weekend. A client asked to reschedule a future meeting.

Uncle Al's truck pulled up and honked. She hopped inside. "Think we'll find anything significant at the ranch?"

"Not likely. The place's pretty run-down." He pulled onto Arrowhead Road. "I stayed up late googling wormholes, space curvatures and dimensions. It's July fourth here, and you said you were in the past for a month. Did you leave two days before the hanging?"

"Yes."

"Your train pulled out of Rialto on July second, and you arrived at the Hesperia Hotel on June second, right?"

"June first."

"A thirty-day gap." His truck drifted toward the road's shoulder.

"Uncle Al! Watch where you're going!"

He jerked the wheel and corrected his mistake.

"So theoretically, if I left today, I'd arrive in the past on June third. Dusty didn't get arrested until June thirteenth. That'd give me twelve days to get Dusty out of there. You've gotta help me go back."

"As I said yesterday, the event's most likely a one-time thing."

Like an empty balloon, her lungs deflated.

The truck slowed on the ranch's washboard road pitted with potholes. Dirt patches, deer grass, and tumbleweeds covered the pasture. Fallen posts and broken barbed wire intertwined with fences.

Country music on the radio blocked out birds twittering, cattle mooing, insects chirping. Preferring natural noise—more proof she had changed. "You should've seen this place. The south pasture must've grazed at least a thousand cattle." Less than two dozen cattle and horses remained.

The truck veered to the west. "If you keep going north, you'll come to the path where Dusty taught me to drive a wagon."

"Got you to drive a wagon? Sounds like quite a guy."

"He was."

The truck crossed the riverbank, the same riverbank where she'd picnicked with Dusty. She pictured his strong hands spreading out a blanket. She chastised her mind not to go there. Of course, her brain rebuffed. "The Mojave had been at least twice this width."

"Progress some would say, but in my opinion, the local planners did the high desert a disservice building Silverwood Dam. My dad told me stories about the quaint town of Cedar Springs. Now it resides at the bottom of the lake."

"Dusty pointed out Cedar Springs from high on a hill. Said he'd take me there sometime." Her eyes watered, and she blinked to fight away waterworks.

"Some idiot at the state decided they needed a man-made reservoir. Wonder how he profited?" Her uncle pulled into the horseshoe-shaped drive. The stables were now painted beige, not red. The barn remained red with peeling paint. He parked the truck in the dirt driveway next to a modest-sized house. The house had been built over the family cabins she'd strolled by with Dusty.

A husky, middle-aged man approached them. Her uncle grabbed a container from behind the seat and handed it to the man.

"Always look forward to your wife's cookies."

"Gives me an excuse to come out here, Jack." Her uncle introduced his old friend, the ranch foreman.

He had a warm smile. "Your uncle tells me you're interested in the history of this place. Said you'd like to learn about Dusty Mann."

"Absolutely." Hearing his name made her long to see him.

"I grew up on this ranch. Used to sit around the campfire with my dad and listen to cowboys talk. Recall hearing an old timer, Slim. Said his father worked with Dusty. Said a good cowboy should have never hanged."

She tensed. "What was his grandfather's name?"

Her uncle put his arm around her.

"Sounded like a board game. Dominoes, Yahtzee, Chess."

"Checkerboard?"

"Could be. Don't rightly reckon for sure."

She knew it had to be the kindly man, Checkerboard.

"Can we walk as we talk?" her uncle asked.

"Forgot it's the Fourth. Holidays used to be such fun out here. Big barbeque, music." Jack led them across the center courtyard.

"You should come to my parent's party," she offered.

"Your uncle already tried twisting my arm. I'd rather enjoy a peaceful night here."

Huge trees created a cool canopy above the original cast-iron bell. She recalled its clang announcing dinner.

The old wagon wheel bench remained. She had shared the bench with Dusty at least ten times. The foreman led them inside the massive structure.

"This stable was built in eighteen-seventy. Brought logs in from Wrightwood and Big Bear. Heard there was a fire in the late 1800's, but it didn't damage the structure."

The morning of the fire, she'd made love with Dusty.

Jack slid open one of the double doors. Except for the stalls being painted green, the inside hadn't changed much.

It didn't have the manure stench and was virtually silent.

"You should've seen this ranch after Allysheba won the Kentucky Derby in eighty-seven. Thoroughbreds boarded in our newest stable. Horses and cattle filled the pastures. Between the workers and visitors, I often found it hard to breathe."

She peeked into the first stall and expected to see Rock Sand, the newborn foal, not emptiness.

Her uncle and the foreman continued talking. She couldn't comprehend, couldn't listen, could barely function. Crates had been piled in the stall where she had an impromptu picnic with Dusty. She stopped, focused on the massive wood-beamed ceilings, and refused to cry.

The men had wandered outside. She caught up by sprinting.

Jack unlocked the bunkhouse. "Nobody's lived here for at least five years."

In the two-story building, ugly yellowed paint and plaster covered the walls. A blue rectangle remained where someone painted around a now non-existent picture. The poster of a naked girl had a tear at the bottom. Belt buckles and rusty horseshoes hung on the wall by nails. A battered couch dipped in the middle with stuffing coming out of the cushions. A chunky old TV sat in front of the fireplace. In the cobwebbed corner, an empty carton of Budweiser remained on a round table with mismatched chairs. She envisioned cowboys playing poker there.

"Ready to see the cabin where Dusty lived?"

"Y-yes," her voice stumbled.

The gray paint peeled along the exterior with hints of umber-brown undertone from its original color. Jack pried the door open. He pulled up the blinds, allowing light to emit through dirty glass. "Lots of folks have lived in this house."

Stained orange carpeting replaced the original rough wood flooring. A boxy, white oven-range replaced the pot-bellied stove. A stainless-steel double-sink replaced the stand with a pitcher. A chipped laminate kitchen table took the space of the wooden one where she talked with Dusty.

"Been some weird changes over the years," Jack chuckled. "At least they got the bedroom right." She followed him into a remodeled bedroom. It had a walk-in closet. The elaborate bathroom showcased a marble shower. It was as if Dusty never left an imprint.

"Feel free to explore the ranch. I'd better get back to work."

"Thanks, Jack." Uncle Al shook his hand.

She picked up a poker and pushed ashes around the fireplace. A spider crawled up the bricks into a crevice. She used to hate spiders, but now its presence didn't faze her.

Her uncle grabbed a dented tin cup off the mantle and spun it by the handle, picked up a bronze horse statue, a box of matches. He ran his fingers along the bricks on the right side. "I saw this in a mystery movie. The cops found the killer's gun under a loose brick."

She touched the left side near the bottom. "This brick feels funny."

Uncle Al used his pocketknife to pry it out and gave her a matchbox car.

"I was hoping for something important."

"It's a 69 Camaro. If you don't want it—," he held out his hand.

"Here," she passed the toy over. "Let's check out the schoolhouse."

They wandered into the yard. No pigtails flying where the teeter-totter used to reside. No children swinging in the willow tree, now a billion times taller. No white picket fencing, plenty of weeds. The outside of the building needed a fresh coat of whitewash. The stairs were rickety, the door locked. She peeked inside.

"See anything?" Her uncle stood behind her.

"Nothing but boxes and crap. I wonder if they used the old desks for firewood."

He shrugged. "Probably."

"I'd like to see if we can get into my old bedroom." They walked around the corner and up the stairs. The door was locked. No drapes covered the window. She spotted a twin bed. This is where she and Dusty made love. He'd promised to marry her, make her Mrs. Dusty Mann.

"I brought you here too soon." Uncle Al wrapped his arms around her. His action didn't take away the pain but gave her a little comfort.

"It's okay." She wasn't okay.

"Wanna look around a little more?"

"Of course." The dry wash remained constant and unchanged. She remembered the buggy ride with Dusty alongside the same wash. Memories of Dusty were everywhere. She swallowed hard and willed her mind to take over where her heart failed.

Her uncle pulled out his pocket watch. "It's already two. We'd better go."

Her mind was numb during the trip back to her home. She closed her eyes and woke when Uncle Al's cell phone buzzed.

"Gotta drop Mickie's brother off at the train station."
He pulled into her driveway. "See you tonight at the
party."

"Thanks for bringing me along today." She trudged
into the empty house alone. Without Dusty, she'd never
be complete.

~ * ~

Mia pushed aside red-white-and-blue crepe paper
and opened the gate's latch into her parent's backyard.
"Stars and Stripes Forever" blared from outdoor
speakers. She spotted her older sister, Nancy,
smoothing out a tablecloth.

"'Bout time you showed up." Her sister hugged her.
"Cute dress."

She glanced down at her sundress, unsophisticated
compared to the jade gown she'd worn to the ball.

"You're quiet, must be upset 'cause Mom invited
Craig."

"Craig?" Her high school sweetheart. Not someone
she cared to see.

"She didn't tell you?" Nancy bent down to pick up a
star decoration; her low-cut slinky dress accentuated
her curvy figure.

"Nope." She rolled her eyes. "You're welcome to
him."

"That's okay. If I wanted a jerk, I'd have stayed with
my ex." Her sister had a rough divorce, but she looked
happy now.

Mia scanned the backyard. People seemed different,
stood in clusters, cliques. She and her sister skipped the
food line forming under the eaves, pulled water bottles

out of a red cooler, and found seats under an umbrella-shaded table. Their teenage twin brothers ran by, each carrying a bucket of water balloons.

Nancy laughed. "I don't even want to know what they're up to."

"Neither do I." It took stamina to keep up with those two. "Ugg. There's Craig now."

Her mom waved from a few yards away. Craig stood next to her. With his shirt tucked into his jeans, his slight gut showed. Dusty had a firm-muscular stomach, incredible biceps and triceps. Recalling his fantastic body, a warm and tingly sensation quivered inside. She used her hand to fan her face.

"You can't possibly want Craig back?" Nancy's tone held a no-you-wouldn't snap.

"Of course not, but that won't stop Mom's determination to see us reconnect."

"You never told her he cheated?"

"Never." Six years ago, he'd been her first lover. Less than a week later, she caught him at the movies kissing Melissa Turner. She once despised Craig. The mention of his name made her livid, but not anymore. "I'm glad I didn't. I would hate to ruin Mom's friendship with his mother."

Nancy took her elbow. "Come on, might as well get on with the torture."

She took leaded steps closer. Craig tipped his pristine white Stetson and leered at her with shifty brown eyes, nothing like Dusty's smoky gray.

"Hello, babe." Craig's scratchy voice lacked Dusty's sexy drawl.

Her mother pushed her closer to him. "I'm sure you two have lots of catching up to do."

"But—"

"Nancy, I need your help in the kitchen?"

Her sister mouthed, *sorry.*

Mia glanced at Craig. How could she have loved him? Well, she'd chalk it up to being young and giving her heart to someone undeserving.

The band warmed up under the gazebo. A trumpet blared. A bow glided across a fiddle. The saxophone player fingered the scales.

"You're even prettier than you were in high school." Craig brought her hand to his lips and kissed it. No sparks. No attraction. Plenty of repulsion. "You wanna dance?" He winked.

"No thanks." The last thing she wanted was to be in this idiot's arms.

"Come on, they're playing our song."

"You mean 'Your Cheating Heart.'" She laughed.

"I was a jerk then. Babe, I've changed, honest." He gave her a dopey grin, the grin she once thought cute. Now the grin made him look like an overgrown boy. A brunette twirled on the dancefloor; her short skirt swirled and flared. His eyes drifted to the woman as he said to Mia, "I've missed you." His tone sounded non-committal and practiced.

She couldn't help laughing.

"It's the God's truth, I've been thinking about you—a lot. Your mom already said you're single." He chuckled like a squealing warthog. "Aw, babe. Admit it; we were good together. Give us another chance."

"No way."

"It's obvious you still like me." He winked.

"I don't." Did he actually believe she'd swoon over him?

"I'll give you a chance to miss me and be back after I grab a beer. Want one?"

She shook her head. No surprise, he moved in the direction of the shapely brunette.

"Stupid jerk," she muttered.

"What'd I do?" Her father stood next to her, wearing jeans, a plaid western shirt, and a George Clooney grin.

She smiled at the father she adored. "Nothing, Dad."

He took her in his warm and secure arms. "Is Craig bothering you?

"I can handle him."

"I know." Her father's compliment lifted her spirits. "May I have the next dance?"

"Of course."

The singer crooned, "It Had to Be You." She tried not to listen to the lyrics, tried not to think about Dusty, tried to concentrate on the one-two-three rhythm.

"Glad you moved back. Could use a little help with the twins."

"Can't believe you said that, Dad."

"Just trying to loosen you up. Something's bothering you, and I doubt it has anything to do with Craig." His *father radar* must be kicking in. He could always tell when something was wrong. He twirled her under his arm. "You can tell me anything."

If only that were the case. "It's the move. Too many changes."

"I'm here if you need me."

"You're the best."

He pulled her closer. "You'll always be my little girl."

She fought off waterworks threatening to spill. The band took a break. She held her father's arm and strolled across the grass toward the house.

"Uh-oh. One of the twins is helping himself to the keg." Her dad's expression turned serious.

She let go of his arm. "Thanks for the dance."

"Anytime." He sprinted like a man half his age after one of her brothers.

She pulled the slider open and headed inside where it was cool. Men surrounded a seventy-inch flat screen, mesmerized by a stock car race.

"Mia, here's a spot for you." An old friend patted the couch cushion next to him.

"Not tonight." She craved quiet and solitude, a difficult task with the house in full party mode. Noise echoed to the top of the vaulted ceilings.

To her right, the stylish kitchen's dark cabinets and stainless-steel appliances were excessively modern. A microwave beeped. Water from the fancy faucet splashed on the counter. The atmosphere fictional as if she were a visitor observing from the outside.

"Hey." An elderly neighbor sat on a bar stool next to her husband. "Tell us about your in-tra-net business."

The last thing she cared to discuss. "You don't want me to bore you with that tonight. Another time." She forced a polite smile.

A six-foot granite bar separated the kitchen from the next area. Inside the family room, a group of teens crowded around a boy and girl competing in a Wii dance-off. The music's loud off-sync beat hurt her ears.

She walked down the hall and peeked into the dining room. Craig had his back to her, lip-locking a brunette on his lap. Typical Craig behavior. *I've changed. Not.* She held back a snort. At least she wouldn't have to deal with him anymore tonight.

The monotonous music caused her head to boom-thud-boom to the drumbeat. It became hard to breathe. She missed the friendly folks and simplicity of life in the past century.

She had to get away from this inane, cheerful party madness.

Opting for the formal living room, she went past the tile entryway and found the area empty. She'd rest here for a few minutes, then she'd slip away to her car and leave the party craziness. She sunk into the loveseat, removed her pinching sandals, rubbed her sore feet, and sighed.

The doorbell rang.

"It's open," she shouted.

Auntie Mickie pranced inside wearing a knee-length dress and pink cowgirl boots.

Uncle Al placed his arm on his wife's shoulder, dressed cowboy style—jeans, a white button-down shirt with embroidered yokes, and a black Stetson. He grinned like a cat in a creamery, the kind of grin that spoke of mischief. "Come on." He motioned to someone behind him.

Chapter Twenty-two

It was the Fourth of July, and Dusty was alive. Fate saved him from hanging and somehow managed to land him in the future. He'd never take another day for granted. He plucked at the collar on his tight-fitting loaner shirt, glancing at the grand mansion. Mia's parents were wealthy, while he didn't have a penny to his name. What if her parents forbid him to court her? Well, he'd fight for her.

"Come on." Al motioned for him to enter.

He felt as skittish as a newborn colt. He was about to be reunited with the woman he'd truly loved. Using cowboy courage, he trudged forward.

And then he saw her. Perched on a two-seater couch, flashing her shapely bare calves. Dusty's eyes traveled to her face. Her light hair fell past her shoulders. Her emerald eyes glanced up at him. Dang, she was prettier than morning greeted by a sunrise.

He removed his hat, expecting to see recognition and joy. "Hello, darlin'," he said quietly.

"D-Dusty," her voice rasped, and she blinked.

"I'm right here." He crouched in front of her and held her clammy hand.

"You can't be here. You're dead." Her eyes became wide. Her color drained.

His surprise appearance had been too much. Panic wrung his gut inside out as he squeezed in next to her.

Mia tilted her head and stared at Dusty with a fragile uncertainty. "You're not really here. I must be seeing things. Hallucinating."

"Nope. It's me." He brushed a strand of her hair behind her ear.

Her uncle moved to the sofa's arm. "You okay?"

"I'm excellent." Mia leaned her head against Dusty's chest. "I can't believe you're here. You're really here."

"Knew you'd be thrilled." Her uncle wore a goofy grin.

"How'd you find him?" She asked, threading her fingers through Dusty's.

"I dropped my brother-in-law off at the train station and spotted your cowboy alone on a bench. I couldn't believe it. Your drawings were spot on."

"I remember those drawings." Dusty stared into her beautiful green eyes

"Al told me everything. It's quite a romantic tale." Mickie smiled.

"Since you're all right, we're gonna head outside. Give you some time to talk." Her uncle turned to Dusty. "I'm counting on you taking care of her."

"I'll never leave her side." He meant it.

"Feel the same way about Mickie." Love shone in Al's eyes.

"Thanks again for the hospitality." Dusty waved at her uncle.

The couple walked off—leaving him alone with Mia— sort of, considering the noise meandering from the other rooms. He peeked over the back of the sofa.

Dozens of folks crowded the hallway. Most of them teens.

"I've missed your devilish grin." She smiled full of sexiness and promise. This woman taught him to love, taught him to trust, taught him to believe in what seemed inconceivable.

Her fingertips traced along his jaw. "How'd you get here? I don't understand."

"Let's just say the grim reaper had a weaker grip." He cupped her face, keeping his eyes connected with hers. "God, I've missed you. Inside the jail cell, the only way I stayed sane was remembering your kisses."

She curled a lock around his finger and let it go.

"You know you play with your hair when you're unsure."

"I do?"

"Yes." He laughed. "I've missed how your eyes sparkle whenever you look at me. I never thought I'd see you again." He used his thumb to outline her bottom lip.

"Me either."

"Being here feels right." Slanting his mouth over hers, he kissed her slow and leisurely. "Your lips still taste like honey."

"And you're as charming as ever. How'd you get away?" Her quiet tone called him back to her. "I read your obituary. You—"

"Hanged."

She flinched.

"Relax, darlin'. As you can see, I'm very much alive." He kissed her forehead.

She ran her fingers along his arm as if testing to see if he was real.

"Reckon we tricked fate." He gazed into her eyes, eyes he'd never tire of seeing. "Seems preposterous that this morning the sheriff handcuffed me and brought me outside the jail. The notion pounded me like a nail being hammered into my own coffin. I'd die for something I hadn't done."

Her breath hitched.

He pressed his lips softly to her cheek. "If it helps any, the string of curse words I said would peel the hide off a Holstein."

She giggled and got up off the couch.

His lungs emptied. "Where you going?"

Her bottom dropped into his lap, and she looped her right arm around his shoulder. "That's much better."

He swallowed several times and stared at her pink painted toenails. He liked them. He liked her tiny feet. As much as he liked her on his lap, they were sitting in her parent's living room. "Darlin', this doesn't feel right." He moved her off and placed her next to him.

She leaned over and pressed her lips to his. "I love your old-fashioned values."

He couldn't resist giving her a long, heated kiss. He savored her lips and kissed her with a searing passion. The kiss left him breathless. If he looked at her lips or her eyes or her face, he'd kiss her again, so he focused on the fancy mahogany front door.

"You were talking about the sheriff bringing you outside."

"Was I?" It took him a few seconds to register what she said. "Well, the handcuffs rubbed against my wrists. I went from frightened to furious. I knew I didn't deserve to die." He'd never forget his bitter trepidation. "I walked along the train's platform. Each step I took brought me closer to the noose. Once I reached the stairs, I knew it'd be two blocks to White's Hanging Tree."

She gasped.

He squeezed her hand. "My belt buckle felt warm. With my hands in front of me, I rubbed it. The stone seemed to glow and felt like it'd burned through my pants to my skin."

"Like my ring."

"You mentioned the heat when you came to the past. I rubbed the stone again and noticed a locomotive stopped on the tracks next to the walkway. The whistle blew. The wheels started rolling. I slipped my wrist out of the metal cuffs."

"Like you did after your trial." Her fingertips trailed along the red streaks on his wrist. Her simple touch jolted his love and desire.

"You can doctor me all you want—later."

"I will."

He pressed his mouth to hers, confident he'd never get enough of her kisses. "Back to my lack of cuffs. You had said you thought a window of time opened to bring you here. I hoped that window would appear and bring me to you."

"You saw me leave through a portal?"

"I saw you vanish. I prayed you went to the future. I pushed people aside, jumped onto the nearest car and gripped the railing.

'What are you doing,' the sheriff shouted.

My hands shook as I climbed to the top step and looked down. My eyes met Flynn's for a brief second, and he looked confused."

"Can't blame him," she giggled.

"I landed inside the train and dropped into a bench by the door, amazed I'd escaped the noose. The stone on my belt became unbearably hot. Again, I tried to unfasten the buckle, but it was stuck. I remember yanking as my fingertips brushed the smooth garnet. Then my vision fogged."

"My ring burned. When I came to the past, I twisted and turned the band. Colors danced before my eyes." She sat up straighter.

"The inside got as cold as a winter's night."

"That's air-conditioning—the machine acts as an ice box." Love shone in her eyes.

"I've missed you." He leaned over and kissed her cheek. "When I opened my eyes, at the end of the bench, a man wore a bright flowered-shirt, short pants, and board-like sandals. Strange music floated from the air. I heard a voice saying the next stop, Victorville—not Victor."

"It must've seemed crazy."

"It was unbelievable. I was alive. Never knew such utter bliss, I mean, besides meeting you."

"You're too much." She kissed his cheek.

"Where was I?"

"Getting off at Victorville."

"Well, the train stopped. Lost, confused, and worried about where I'd landed, two men pushed past me in a hurry. The back of one of their shirts had *Beer Drinkers Make Better Lovers*. It made me laugh."

"See you haven't lost your humor."

He teased her lips until they parted, and their tongues tangled.

She pulled away panting. "You're a fantastic kisser."

"You sure you want to hear the rest. I could finish later." He longed to sweep her away from here but had no idea where he'd take her.

"Go on. Once we go to my place, we won't be doing much talking."

"Your place. You don't live with your parents?"

"Nope."

Desire jolted throughout his body. Tonight, he'd have her all to himself. He sucked in a deep breath and stared at the floor. "Reckon I'd better talk fast. I followed the crowd. Heard roaring louder than the Calico Silver Mill running full force, but different. Breathed in a stench like a blacksmith's fumes forging metal. Thought maybe I'd gone to hell. Decided to keep going anyway. Figured I'd recognized the Comstock Saloon across the street and headed that way."

"My fearless cowboy."

"Not fearless, plenty driven. I sat on a bench to decide what to do next. A man stared at me. His eyes all round and buggy."

"Was it Uncle Al?" Laugh lines crinkled the corners of her eyes.

"He said he recognized me from a sketch you showed him. Said you told him about traveling through time. Said you were miserable without me. Said I stunk like rotten eggs and needed a shower." Dusty chuckled. "Suppose time in jail can ruin a man's scent."

"Your clothes are a bit tight, but sexy." She squeezed his bicep. "Uncle Al was with me right before he headed for the station. Why didn't he call?"

"Al tried. You didn't answer."

She shook her head. "Turned my phone off because my mom kept texting me about this party."

"We're together now."

"What do you think of the future?"

He hesitated, waiting for the right words. "To be honest, some of the newfangled machines make me as nervous as a long-tailed cat under a rocking chair."

"I've missed your humor," she leaned into him.

"There are so many new inventions to cipher. Al brought me into his kitchen, opened a silver box, took out a carton with a picture of stew, and put it in a small boxy thing. He told me the mike-wave heats up food."

"With your appetite, the micro-wave may become your new best friend." Her low and seductive tone had his lower extremities responding.

He could use a cold dip in the river. Water reminded him of taking a shower. "I must've been in the shower for an hour. Found the see-through door strange. Al gave me these clean clothes." He tugged at the knit-collared shirt. "Can't understand why he threw my old clothing into the trash. Seems a shame to waste a perfectly good pair of britches."

"I'll take you shopping at the mall tomorrow." She eyed him from top to bottom.

Was she embarrassed by how he dressed? "What's a mall?"

"It's a place with lots of shops. You're gonna love fast food."

"Fast food? The mike-wave was quick." He combed his fingers through his hair.

"Reckon I've got plenty of learnin' to do." He didn't fit here and pulled his arm from her shoulder.

"You helped me, even taught me how to ride a horse. Let me help you. It will be an adjustment, one we'll face together." She took his hand. "It'll all work out."

287

His feisty gal made him believe in himself. "You came along determined to save my life—and you did. I didn't hang because you were honest with me, willing to share what sounded impossible."

"I sure had a hard time convincing you I was from the future."

"I can be a little hardheaded."

"One of the many reasons I love you." She kissed his cheek.

"I love you, darlin'. Loved you ever since you barreled into me at the hotel." He went down on one knee and took her hand. "Don't have a job or a ring for your finger, but I've learned to live life and not take a minute for granted. I'll figure out a way to support you. I promise. Marry me, darlin'?"

"Yes." She hugged him. "I love you."

The three words caused his heart to expand in his chest. He expressed all his love in a soul-shattering kiss.

Loud booms sounded, and he flinched. "What's that?"

"Fireworks. Let's go outside? It's time to introduce you to my parents."

His stomach twisted like barbed wire was inside. "I'm not ready. Look at how I'm dressed."

"You're perfect. My folks will love you—like I do."

"Reckon I can handle anything with you at my side." Holding hands, they strolled out the front door.

A streak of light floated where stars lit the sky. Fireworks exploded into shooting streams of red, white, and blue. Another rocket set off. Yellow, pink, and green streamers rained down. Dusty tightened his grip around her waist, bent his head and whispered, "I still can't believe a pretty little thing like you went back in time and did everything in your power to save this cowboy. And because of you, I'm holding you in my arms."

She leaned back and wiggled her bottom against him. "Cowboy, you saved me by showing me what is real love."

The End

If you enjoyed TIME TO SAVE A COWBOY, you might want to read COWBOY'S CUPID from my Love's Magic Series.

A Forbidden Love

When Cupid's arrow accidentally strikes the wrong cowboy, she's supposed to fix her mistake—not fall for the alluring mortal.

Cami Calypso receives her first assignment just in time for the Valentine season. As a newbie Cupid Archer, her life is perfect until her arrow accidentally strikes the wrong man. She has sixty days to secure a job as his housekeeper on a ranch and find the cowboy his soul mate—not keep him for herself.

Rhett Holloway needs a housekeeper and cook.
He doesn't need an adorable blonde to distract him.
He doesn't need her to fix his love life.
But here she is, and he finds her irresistible.

Read an excerpt from COWBOY'S CUPID.

Rhett had a strange feeling in his gut during dinner. Cami kept checking her watch. He'd asked what bothered her, but she said everything was fine.

After a long day, he helped her clean up the dinner dishes, and they walked to her apartment. Her stance was rigid, her body tense. She didn't shift toward him as he strode with his arm around her shoulder.

"What's wrong?"

"I need to tell you something." She shrugged but wouldn't look at him.

They'd only known each other close to two months, but his heart was all in. He unlocked the apartment door. Seated at the edge of the couch, Cami put a distance between them and avoided eye contact.

"Go ahead." He stood by the kitchen table and waited for a response.

"We were never meant to be together," she said, still not looking his way.

His chest tightened. She was breaking up with him.

"I've got a secret. When I show you, I hope you'll still love me."

"Whatever you've done in the past doesn't matter. We'll get through it." He'd made his share of mistakes.

She extracted a glass vial from her pocket. It sparkled and shimmered. "It's not what I've done, it's what I am."

"What are you?" He didn't even see a flicker of a smile.

Her lips tightened into a grimace. "Please listen carefully to what I say."

"All right. Spill." He tapped the side of his pants.

She licked her lips and took a deep breath. "I told you I was a Cupid when you took me to the archery range."

"Okay."

She folded her arms. "I live in Zeus' Kingdom up in the clouds."

His teeth ground, as he sat next to her and said sarcastically, "Of course you do."

"You've seen my archery skills. Even said I was talented." She lifted her chin and blew out a breath. "I am a Cupid, a real live Cupid."

"That's crazy." Maybe she was crazy. His primal instinct told him to leave, but he couldn't move.

"My occupation is an archer." Tears pooled in her eyes. "I'm telling you the truth."

"If you're leaving me, say so, and quit making up this lame story."

"I don't want to go anywhere." She twirled a curl around her finger.

"You don't? And here I thought you were breaking up with me."

"If only things were different. I've got to return home." She looked at her watch.

"So, you are leaving me? Why?" He was confused.

"I don't want to. I'm happy here." Her body slumped, her chin dropped. "My whole life I've dreamed of being good enough."

"But you are good enough." She was the best thing to ever happen to him. "You're perfect for me."

"Don't make me cry, please let me finish." Her eyes softened. "I've dreamed of visiting Earth and infusing humans with arrows of love. When I got my first earthly assignment, I hit the wrong man, namely you."

Those blue eyes. "You shot me with your arrow of love?"

"It was a mistake. My assignment ducked, and I hit you instead. I was sent to rectify my mishap and set you up with your soulmate. We were never supposed to fall in love."

"You love me." His spirits soared.

"Yes."

"'Bout time you admitted it." He moved closer, but she backed up, out of his reach.

"Will you accept the real me?"

"What do you mean? The real Cami's right in front of me."

"Watch." Rocking back and forth on her heels, her cheeks flushed to a rosier red.

His eyes riveted to her hands.

She unscrewed the glass vial and poured out a glittery substance. Iridescent pink dust swirled and surrounded her. Her body shrunk to the size of a doll, dressed in a shimmering gown. Iridescent wings formed at her shoulders. She flew up midway between the floor and the ceiling.

"Holy shit!" He stared, not frightened, confused.

"I'm a C-Cupid." Her words came out broken.

He froze, became immobile. "This can't be happening."

"I love you, always will." She hovered close to him, and he felt her lips kiss his cheek.

"It's unreal."

"Tell me about it." Her eyes were wide. Wary.

"You really are a Cupid?"

"Yes. Do you still love me?"

He didn't know what to think. "It's too much." He turned his back to her, put his head in his hands.

His girlfriend—a ruler-sized pixie. It couldn't be true.

Except he'd seen her.

REBEL'S CUPID
Released March 31, 2019

A Cupid's Family Secret

Driven by curiosity, Cupid Belle Brooks is determined to find her banished aunt, even if it means breaking rules, sneaking off to the world below, and into the tavern owned by a captivating, aggravating mortal biker.

Lucky O'Sullivan accepts his bachelor status.
He doesn't need the gorgeous redhead who snuck into the bar's stockroom.
He doesn't need to assist her in discovering what her mysterious key unlocks.

But Belle asks for his assistance, and his desire fires up.
Until she says she loves him.

Dear Readers,

Thank you for reading TIME TO SAVE A COWBOY.

I hope you enjoyed my story as much as I enjoyed writing it. Won't you please consider leaving a review? Even just a few works would help others decide if the book is right for them. Best regards and thank you in advance.

Niki J. Mitchell

I look forward to hearing from my readers.

Visit me at https://nikimitchell.weebly.com/

Follow me on FaceBook at author Niki J. Mitchell

Twitter Niki Mitchell@NikiMitchell7

Instagram NikiJMitchellAuthor

About the Author

Niki Mitchell writes children's books along with paranormal, fantasy, and historical time-travel romance. She was born in Chicago, Illinois, and moved to Whittier, California in first grade. With a houseful of books and a local library located a few short blocks, her love of reading began at a young age.

Married for over thirty years and a romantic at heart, she enjoys writing about strong female characters in unusual settings. When she isn't playing with her cats, she enjoys reading, taking walks, water aerobics, photography, and traveling.